BEYOND *ecstasy*

KIT ROCHA

BEYOND ECSTASY

Edited by Sasha Knight
Cover Artwork by Bree Bridges

ISBN-13: 978-1984348548
ISBN-10: 198434854X

To Jay & Tracy,

who keep the lights on at the Broken Circle
while we're plotting revolution.

1

Hawk couldn't decide which would drive him crazy first—the shadows or the light.

The shadows, that was the easy answer. The sectors had been dark for a month now, driven back to the earliest days after the Flares. Back home in Six, things wouldn't be so bad. The farms had always survived off wind and solar energy, and as powerful as Eden was, they couldn't still the air or blot out the sun. But sectors like Four relied on whatever electricity they could borrow, beg, or steal from Eden's grid. Blackouts had always been an infrequent annoyance.

Now they were a constant reality—and Sector Four was unraveling under the strain.

That was why Hawk was out for his fourth night in a row, patrolling the market square with Jasper. He could *feel* people watching them from behind closed

ing walls. Watching and waiting. Calculating their chances of getting away with whatever trouble they'd been planning to start. Out of fear or desperation, or just to relieve the unrelenting tension.

But all those stares couldn't raise the hair on the back of his neck the way glancing over his shoulder toward the city did.

The darkness was awful, but the light posed the real danger. Hell, it was going to make them crazy. Eden's damn glowing walls, sparking with the power they'd stolen from the sectors. Precious electricity twisted into a weapon and a warning and brazen, bragging psychological warfare.

During the day, you could almost ignore it. But when the sun dipped below the western hills, all anyone could see was Eden's walls lighting up the night in a silent reminder that everything had changed.

"Nothing," Jas growled. "I hate the waiting."

I hate the waiting. Words that summed up life in the sectors now, on every fucking level. "It's only a matter of time."

"The intel is good." Jasper pulled a cigarette from his pocket, but he didn't light it. "Two shops and someone's house have been hit on this block in the last week."

The intel might be good, but crime wasn't simple anymore. Some people were stealing out of greed and need, but more and more had been starting shit just to start it. The wave of petty crime had dropped after the O'Kanes bumped up fight night to twice a week—an approved outlet for violence with a chance to make some money was math even an idiot could do—but the *feeling* was back, seething from the shadows, growing day by day.

If something didn't happen soon, every damn

Jas rubbed the spot between his eyes with the heel of his hand. "Let's take a walk."

Hawk nodded in agreement and fell into step next to Jas as he turned toward the city. Even this far away, an ache was already forming behind his eyes. He knew how many blocks they could walk before the ache blossomed into pain, and how many more before nausea joined the party.

No one could live this close to the wall anymore. Some of the shopkeepers who'd kept homes above their shops had been driven back after the first two weeks. A few stubbornly stayed—pale and drawn and increasingly sick from the constant exposure.

Hawk couldn't understand *how*. When they cleared the last row of buildings, he could feel the damn thing in his bones, thrumming, *humming*. It took all his self-control not to turn the fuck around and run for it.

But he couldn't. Not until he and Jas had completed their most grisly task of the night.

The open space closest to the curving walls was strewn with abandoned carts and trash no one had bothered to pick up. No shadows lurked here—just eerie, unnatural illumination that made Hawk's eyeballs itch and washed everything out into silver and blue.

Especially the dark form standing at the wall, his hands wrapped around a line of wire.

"Fuck," Jasper muttered. "*Motherfucker*."

Suicide-by-Eden. The newest threat facing the sectors, and the most hopeless.

Jas was pushing through the carts, looking for something they could use to knock the body loose. They'd pry this poor bastard off the wall the way they'd done the ones before, but they couldn't hide what was

9

would be a little worse than today.

People were giving up. Old-timers who'd lived through the first terrible years after the Flares, who couldn't face doing it again. Their children, who'd grown up with the horror stories, with nightmares that only intensified in the telling.

The worst were the kids. Teenagers, really—adults by the rules that guided the sectors but still fucking *children* in the way that mattered. Too young to understand mortality and too fucking scared to fight, because they'd already spent all of their short lives fighting. If they had to drag another kid off the wall—

Jas came back with a board, and Hawk reached for it. "I'll do it."

He hesitated only for a moment before handing over the plank of wood. "Careful, man."

Hawk didn't relish getting closer, but Jas couldn't afford to take the risk at all. Too much rested on his shoulders—and Hawk sure as fuck wasn't going back to the compound to face Noelle after letting her boyfriend fry himself. "I got it."

He approached carefully, setting each foot down firmly to eliminate any chance of tripping. By the time he was within swinging distance, his teeth were vibrating. The low buzz filled his ears, and maybe that was a blessing.

There was nothing pretty about trying to knock a corpse off the wires that had electrocuted him.

The first swing didn't budge the man. And it was a man—or had been. His clothes were as singed as his skin, burned black by the heat generated by the high current coursing through him. The sickly scent of roasted flesh invaded Hawk's nostrils, and he held his breath as he swung again. Harder.

man's grip on the wires, and he tumbled to the cracked pavement in a heap.

Jasper closed his eyes with a low, pained noise, then dropped to a crouch beside the prone body. "Burial detail?" he asked hoarsely. "Who's on it tonight?"

"Flash and the new kid. Tank." Hawk joined him. "Do you recognize him?"

"No." Jas looked up. "Seems like that would make it easier, doesn't it?"

Nothing could make this easy. This moment—the horror of it, the fucking useless *waste* of it—it would always hurt. And it should.

But at least they didn't have to go back to the compound and break the news to the dead guy's friends. Not like last week, when they'd trudged home to face Tatiana. The woman they'd peeled off the wall that night had brought Tatiana lunch from her food cart every day for damn near five years.

Hawk might still end the evening drunk, but he wouldn't be covered in someone else's tears this time. Practically a banner fucking night—his most morbid thought yet. "I hope it never gets easy. I don't want to think about what that would mean."

"Truth." Jas turned his head away from the wisps of smoke rising from the corpse and stood up. "I worry about the effect this has on people."

Hawk had spent enough time with Jas now to read between the lines. The man would never betray a weakness in the king and queen of Sector Four, but shit. You'd have to be a monster not to feel it, and while Dallas and Lex's reputations could be plenty monstrous, Hawk knew they were both very, very human.

And, friend or not, Jas had to break this news to them every damn time.

better. No way to fix it. All he could do was toss the board aside and grab a ragged tarp from one of the carts to cover the body. "I'll find Tank and Flash. Get it taken care of."

"No, I'll handle it." Jas punched him lightly on the shoulder. "You've been working hard. Have some fun tonight."

Hawk huffed. "Fucking hypocrite."

"Hey, it's my load to bear, not yours."

Easy words, but they were the reason Hawk had come to this sector. The reason he'd joined the O'Kanes, and the reason he had come to embrace them. For Jas, they weren't only words. He meant them. The O'Kanes didn't just believe in the pleasure that came with power. They believed in the responsibility, too.

For that, Hawk would follow them into hell. Maybe literally.

He squeezed Jas's shoulder. "You sure? I got nowhere to be." No one waiting for him, either.

"Hell yeah." Jasper jerked his head in the direction of the O'Kane compound. "Go. Crack open a bottle. We're all gonna need it tonight."

Hawk should have protested again, but an order was an order, and his churning gut and aching head were motivation enough. Dignity kept him out of a flat run, but he still made it through the market in record time, not slowing down until he reached the first row of tall apartment buildings and their reassuring shadows.

The darkness definitely wasn't the enemy.

Neither was the silence. Noises teased at the edge of his senses—a slammed door, the scuffle of footsteps. Voices carried on the wind, too far away to reach him as more than a whisper. Hawk kept his hand close to his gun and pretended he wasn't half-hoping someone

12

It was two more nights until he'd have a chance at climbing into the cage. Two more nights of twisted-up tension and anger and frustration with no damn outlet, because the only outlet he wanted—

No. No, he wouldn't think of her like this, not while he smelled of death and dreamt of violence. He needed to purge the darkness first.

He needed a fucking drink.

That was what he told himself, anyway, when he swung right and headed for the entrance to the Broken Circle instead of the back gate that led to the living quarters.

Zan was guarding the door. He took one look at Hawk and cursed viciously. "Another one?"

So much for his poker face. "Yeah. Jas didn't recognize him, but…"

Zan's scowl deepened, then disappeared behind his hands as he scrubbed them over his face. "You headed inside?"

"I need a drink. Has it been crazy?"

"Different kind than usual." Zan's glower returned full force. "Not real busy, but we're having to keep four on the floor so the little shits'll stay in line."

Maybe he'd get his fight after all. Hawk slapped Zan on the shoulder. "I'll keep an eye on things."

"Swing by the kitchen," Zan advised as he pushed open the door.

Hawk stepped inside. The music washed over him, the throbbing of the bass vibrating in his bones in a different way than the electric pain of the wall. It dragged his gaze to the stage even though he'd promised himself he wouldn't look—

He didn't know if he was disappointed or relieved to see Trix up there, midway through her most popular

13

ments were the O'Kane reputation distilled into a dance as potent as their whiskey.

The crowd was going wild. Cheering and hollering, leaning forward in anticipation that built with every teasing twist of her body. Hawk hesitated—not watching her, but the room itself. Bouncers bracketed the stage, a burly reminder not to get any ideas about appreciating the show up close and personal.

Trix would be fine. If Hawk had had any doubts, he would have stayed. Not just because he owed it to Finn to look after his woman, but out of fondness for Trix herself.

Most of the time, he coped with the O'Kane women by treating them the way he would his sisters. With Trix, that came easy. She'd been to his home, had met his family. She was bound to Hawk's oldest friend among the O'Kanes, the first one he'd called *brother* and meant it.

Affection would have prompted him to stay if she needed protection. And affection was the reason he booked it to the kitchen. This night was fucked up enough without watching a sister take her clothes off.

The kitchen was bright compared to the front room, light gleaming off steel counters and appliances. Somewhere beneath their feet, the finest collection of generators in the sectors were humming away, providing an oasis from the silent darkness of the rest of the sectors. Hawk suspected they could cancel the shows altogether and people would still show up, as much for the light and the sound as the liquor.

But the kitchen was quieter, the cheers and music muffled. Rachel sat on a stool at the high counter, a sharp knife in one hand and half a lemon in the other. "Hawk." She gestured to him. "Have a seat."

and eyed the lemon. She was just a few months pregnant, barely even showing yet, but the baby was definitely making its presence felt. "Queasy again?"

"Mmm." She dropped another slice of lemon into the glass of water in front of her and lifted it. "This is the only thing that helps right now."

No wonder Zan had sent him to the kitchen. Growing up on the farms in Six meant spending your life surrounded by women in various stages of pregnancy. But in a sector like Four, pregnant women were mysterious, dangerous creatures who suffered from inexplicable symptoms that sent the men—and women—around them into a panic.

Hawk honestly didn't know how Amira had gotten through it without stabbing them all.

He edged the cutting board away from Rachel and picked up the knife. "You use ginger in your beer, don't you?"

"In some of them. Why?"

"You should try that." He gestured to the glass with the knife. "You can brew it into a tea. It helped my stepmothers and sisters."

Rachel smiled and laid her head on his shoulder. "Thanks, Hawk."

Poor girl. Hawk kissed the top of her hair. "I'll show Cruz how to make it when he gets back in."

"I think he'd like that." She looked up. "Bad night?"

"Not the worst. Not the best, either." He offered her a crooked smile. "We hiding any of the good stuff back here?"

She reached under the cabinet nearest her and pulled out a bottle half-full of rich, amber liquor. "Not the best," she said, turning his words around on him. "But not the worst, either."

out a triple, then raised it to her in silent salute. She clinked her glass of water against his, and they both took a sip. "Shit, not the best is still better than we had on the farm."

"One of the perks of being an O'Kane."

There were many, and only one of them had factored into Hawk's determination to join. He'd been on a mission, with Dallas O'Kane square in his sights. Dallas hadn't even been the general of a newly formed rebellion back then, just a sector leader with a barbaric reputation that clashed with his history of being calculated, clever, and dangerous as fuck.

Hawk had recognized power. It took intelligence and forethought to cultivate an image that made the O'Kanes' enemies consistently underestimate them, even in the face of overwhelming evidence to the contrary. The drinking and fucking and partying were perks, but they were also part of the act—painting themselves as sinners fighting just hard enough to indulge their lusts in luxury.

Rachel was watching him. "Everyone thinks this is what it's about—all the booze you can drink, and all the hell you can raise. That, or the sex. But there's something to be said for comfort, you know? For not having to be alone with your thoughts after a hard day."

He swirled the liquor around his glass and tried to find the words. That was what she wanted—for him to unburden himself, to fall into the easy rhythm of chatter and sharing that seemed to come naturally to everyone else.

He could talk about ginger tea. About his sisters' new farm, or cars, or the business of keeping the sector running. Facts and knowledge, clean and simple. Small talk. But Rachel wanted *more*.

16

woman about the corpse he'd just pried off the walls, walls that surrounded a city that might attack them at any second? Tell her about the smell of it, so stark and pungent that even the lemon and whiskey couldn't overcome it?

Tell her about the fear in their guts every time they faced another suicide, wondering if this time they'd turn the body over and find what was left of a familiar face?

He snorted and took another sip. "Some thoughts are too damn bleak to share."

"And some are too bleak to keep to yourself." The lights overhead flickered, and her fingers tightened on her glass. "We're in a stressful spot here, Hawk. It's bad enough even if you do let yourself deal with it. But if you lock it away..."

"I know." He rubbed the edge of his glass. "It's dark out there, Rachel. And we all thought we were good at that, living in the dark. But this isn't the same."

She brushed his hand, a light touch that lasted for only a moment. "Just remember that you don't have to be alone, okay?"

"I'm not alone." The truth wrapped around a lie, because there were so many ways to be lonely, and Rachel could say it wasn't about booze and sex, but it wasn't that simple. Not when you were an O'Kane.

Rachel sighed. "You don't do subtle, do you?"

No, he didn't. Especially not the way these O'Kane women did, issuing invitations and propositions with their smiles and their soft touches—not that he thought Rachel was coming on to him. But there'd been another poured drink, another soft touch—

Don't think about her. Not now.

Because telling yourself not to think about

drink, reached for the bottle, and tried to prove Rachel wrong. "Jeni's not dancing tonight?"

Surprise and a little rueful amusement flashed in Rachel's eyes. "She's upstairs, working on something new."

Hawk turned the knowledge over as he splashed more liquor into his glass. Jeni, upstairs. Alone, maybe, working on a new dance. Sweat glistening on her skin, her breath coming short and fast, her body loose and supple.

Practice meant *Jeni*. Not the wigs and costumes and makeup that turned her into any of a dozen characters she used to work the stage or the bar, but the woman he glimpsed in quiet moments.

Beautiful. Fearless. Sad.

He could go upstairs. Bring the bottle with him, smile at her. He knew shit-all about romance and women, but he knew now how good fucking could be. Fast and hot enough to burn through all the tension tying him up, better than a thousand fight nights.

And then it would be over. Jeni would leave, because that was how the O'Kanes worked. Friendly. Casual. Easy.

Until someone else smiled at Jeni at the next party, and Hawk was overwhelmed by the unacceptable urge to punch their damn teeth in.

O'Kanes definitely didn't do jealousy.

Rachel was still watching him, her rueful amusement melting into a smile. So he headed her off. "Don't get any ideas. I got a couple dozen sisters, Rachel. I know that look."

"I have no idea what you're talking about," she denied. "I was just saying that a little company never hurts. *And*," she added, talking over his half-hearted

hundreds of ways to reach out to someone, and that's just truth."

"I know," he grumbled. And because he *did* have a couple dozen sisters, he knew he had to do one thing—change the damn subject. "That's why I'm in here, drinking with you."

Her smile turned into a grin, and she lifted her glass of water again. "To friends."

"To friends," he echoed, knocking their glasses together. Tonight, he would avoid Jeni and track down Cruz instead. Every discomfort Rachel suffered put the poor bastard on high alert, and Hawk could sympathize with his feeling of helplessness.

Brewing ginger tea might not seem like the best use of an elite soldier's time, but feeling like he'd helped would soothe Cruz, which would soothe Rachel and Ace. Not a bad exchange for a little cup of tea.

And maybe with Ace in a good mood, Hawk could ask him a few questions. Casual. Easy. Just two O'Kanes, making small talk about life and fucking and all the ways they intersected in Sector Four.

If he could figure out the right damn questions, someone might give him the answers that ended with Jeni in his bed for more than one night.

2

Strained, closed-door meetings around tables spread with maps and tablets were a lot more common now in Four.

To be fair, they'd probably been happening all along, only Jeni had never been invited to them. But now, with the city locked down and the sectors dark, she didn't have the luxury of avoiding them.

No one did.

Jared stood at one end of the table, his arms crossed over his chest. "I don't like not knowing what's going on in there."

"No one likes it," Dallas replied, squinting at one of the maps. "Noah? Any progress?"

The hacker drove his fingers through his hair, leaving it standing up wildly as he slumped back in his chair. "Depends on your definition of progress. The

heightened monitoring. Can I get in? Sure. How much can I do before they catch me?" He shrugged. "That's the question."

"One we can't afford to test." Lex braced both hands on the edge of the table. "There are people in there who could answer questions, feed us intel—" Her gaze flickered to Jeni. "Hell, folks we'd like to check up on."

Jeni bit her lip. It was sweet of Lex to care, but there were more important people to worry about. Rachel's family, Bren and Cruz's old buddy, Coop. Even the most casual O'Kane contacts were more important at this point than Jeni's mother.

At this point, she wasn't even sure her mother would recognize her.

Lili leaned forward, her gaze unusually intent. "I think something has happened to Markovic."

Jared pinched the bridge of his nose. "Just because he went quiet on us doesn't mean he's in trouble. If he's smart—which he is—he's keeping his head down."

"I know it sounds naïve, but I have a feeling..." Lili shook her head. "He wouldn't have condoned what happened in Two, and I don't know if he's a good enough liar to pretend otherwise."

Jeni knew Dallas better than most. She could see the truth in his eyes—he *did* think Lili was being naïve. But he still turned to Noah. "Can you find out?"

"Sure," Noah replied easily. "They scan those bar codes all over the city. If his hasn't popped up recently, it'd be a pretty good sign something happened. But can I do that without getting caught?" He shrugged again. "Couldn't say."

"Another thing we can't afford," Lex whispered. "Even if he is in trouble, we can't help Markovic. And

curiosity."

"Give me another couple weeks." Noah patted Lili's shoulder. "I'm working on a way to set up anonymous, untraceable communication between Eden and the sectors. We'll finally be able to talk to Coop, and Bren says he has eyes and ears everywhere."

"Good idea. In the meantime..." Lex flipped another map over, covering the city schematic with a larger view of both the city and the sectors. "Their food stores won't last forever. Even if we assume the city leaders took everything they could for themselves, it won't hold out for long. When the important people get hungry, they'll come out."

Mia spoke up for the first time, leaning forward to prop her elbows on the table. "There isn't much food left in Seven. It's mostly just the wind farms now." Her small, sudden smile was downright vicious. "Which Ford and I control."

Dallas tapped his finger on the table. "Someone make a note for later, see if we can figure out how to spread that power around. Turning the lights back on might not be much of a tactical victory, but it'd sure as hell be a psychological one."

Jyoti stood next to Lex and traced her finger along the edge of the map. "The communes and illegal farms are out of Eden's reach. I have yet to come to agreements with all of them, but even the ones holding back are glad to have the sectors standing between them and the city as a buffer. They understand the situation. If Eden shows up, it will be to take everything they have with no hope of payment."

Because this was war. Marching armies had taken what they needed for eons, leaving devastation in their wake. If Dallas could manage to protect the communes,

communes, they'd have to go through the sectors first. And if it was food they were after, there was only one place for them to go—right through Sector Six.

Right through Hawk's home.

He was standing on the other side of the table, staring down at the map. At the boundary of Six, just beside Lex's left hand, and his expression made Jeni's chest hurt. Not because he seemed stricken or shocked, but because he didn't. His features were fixed, careful not to betray the slightest hint of his thoughts.

But she already knew he worried about his family every single day, and this was why. He'd seen this coming long before Ace had laid ink around his wrists, before he'd even set foot on the O'Kane compound.

Hawk looked up, his gaze clashing with hers. His expression was controlled, but his eyes—

Hot frustration. *Anger.*

Lex spoke. "Hawk?"

He glowered at the map. "Defense is a nightmare. We're all too spread out. The only advantage we have is that the city can't risk destroying the crops—it would defeat the purpose of coming at us."

Lex's voice gentled. "Someone should make sure they know the situation. You can head out in a couple of days."

It wasn't a question. He nodded shortly.

"Whatever they need, let us know," she told him firmly. "I mean it. They're not alone."

Hawk hesitated. "Can they have more land at the edge of Four? A few more of my sisters have been thinking about leaving."

"As much as you need," Dallas said. "Hell, if they need another barn or two, pull a few of the new recruits out there and set them to building. I'm getting used to

As if he couldn't get anything he wanted, even at a time like this. But concealing generosity under a veneer of selfishness was practically Dallas's trademark, and Jeni hid a smile as the people gathered around the table began to disband. Some left the room, and others grouped together, talking quietly.

She lingered until Dallas looked her way, then squared her shoulders. "What can I do?"

He tilted his head. "Noelle said she downloaded everything Eden's archives had on herbal medicine. You looked it over yet?"

She'd pored over the texts and pictures until her head ached and her vision blurred. The most important things she committed to memory, of course, but she had to be familiar enough with the rest to know where to go next with her research. "I read through it."

He tapped her temple gently. "And how much of it do you have up here now? Most of it?"

"Enough to handle that project we talked about."

"Good girl." He smiled and stroked his fingers through her hair before leaning back. "Put together a list for Hawk before he leaves. Everything we need to get started. They're probably growing a lot of this shit over there already."

She kissed Dallas's cheek before he could turn away. "Thank you for helping him."

He winked. "I'm not. I just like bacon."

"Right." Jeni winked back and headed for the door.

Lex caught up with her halfway. "Can you do me a favor, honey? Cover Trix's dance tonight? It's killing, and I hate to take it out of the rotation, but I think you're the only one who's learned the steps."

"Yeah, sure." She had more reading to finish, but she could work on it backstage, between numbers. "Trix

"Twisted ankle. Nothing's busted, but she has to take it easy for a few days. No dancing." Lex shook her head. "So, of course, Finn is carrying her everywhere."

"Of course." It was adorable how the O'Kane men managed to face down bullets and bloody fights like they were no big deal, but they all melted for their women.

"Thanks, Jeni."

"I got it." It felt good to stay busy. On some level, it meant she was useful, not just decorative.

Hawk was standing on the other side of the room, talking to Jasper and watching her, his eyes unreadable. Their gazes held while she thought about what it would take to make him smile or laugh, even cross the room to speak to her. Hell, she even had a good reason to talk to him this time. But she just stared back, and he finally broke the contact, returning his attention to Jas.

It figured. She was good at working people—it was her most vital, marketable job skill—but when it came to Hawk, she was hopeless.

One thing Jeni had noticed—Hawk's vices of the flesh were very particular.

He drank whiskey, straight up—though if you poured him one on the rocks, he wouldn't decline. He hardly ever dressed in anything but T-shirts and jeans worn so soft they clung to him like a lover. He liked manning the rooftop grill with Finn, but his favorite thing ever was when Lili baked. He'd grab slices of bread still hot from the oven, slather them with fresh butter, and eat them on the spot—and the sounds he made, low in the back of his throat, were enough to

And, twice a week, he stripped off his T-shirt, climbed into the cage, and beat the holy living hell out of someone.

By the time fight night rolled around, he was so tense he was practically vibrating, wound so tight that a lesser man would have already exploded. But if there was one thing Hawk valued, it was his control. His precious control.

Jeni dug her fingernails into the leather arm of the couch and watched as he entered the cage ahead of his opponent, a bulky blond she'd never seen before. The man rounded the perimeter of the cage, flexing and grunting for the crowd, while Hawk waited with the patience of a saint.

"Is that *another* new guy?" Nessa dropped onto the couch beside Jeni with a sigh. "Lex, you're gonna need to add a third night a week at this rate. Bren's been breaking up fights over who gets to go next."

"I know." Her gaze was fixed on the would-be fighters clustered around the cage door.

Trix paused with her beer bottle halfway to her lips. "We could always lock them all in the courtyard and let them at it."

"Brawl night." Nessa wrinkled her nose. "You know, I should be into the wide-scale violence, but it's not the same."

No, it wasn't. Then again, nothing could compare to that first swing, not when Hawk was the one throwing it. He didn't lunge for his opponent so much as he just stepped up into his space, as if he belonged there.

As if *it* belonged to *him*.

The blond hulk took the hit well, though when he circled around, his lip was bleeding. "This one's going to take a while," Jeni mused aloud, to no one in particular.

"Come on, you see it." Jeni spared her a glance, though it would have taken something even more seductive than Lex's dark eyes to keep her attention away from the cage. It would have taken a miracle. "Hawk's been waiting for this. He'll make it last."

"He's been patrolling with Jas." Noelle perched on the arm of the couch. "It's rough on both of them."

Of course it was. The same desperation that lured prospective fighters through the doors in droves saturated the sectors. For some, waiting for Eden to make their next move was unbearable. Others had just thrown in the towel, straight up—no hope, and no faith.

Most of them had no reason to believe that anyone could pull them through this mess—*this war*, she corrected herself silently. Jeni knew better. Dallas himself might insist otherwise if you put him on the spot, but the man didn't know how to fail.

She reached for her drink and tried not to wince as Hawk landed another solid blow on his opponent.

Lex arched an eyebrow. "Going soft on us, honey?"

Normally, violence didn't bother her, especially the way it played out during fight nights. The matches were clean, fair, and everyone who climbed behind the cage bars knew exactly what they were getting into. It was a thousand times better than what most people ever got.

But something about Hawk made it seem...tragic. He spent so much of his time *creating*—repairing, growing, or building things—that watching him throw himself headlong into this kind of wanton destruction felt wrong. There were better ways to embrace the sweet edge of pain, nobler ways. Ones that weren't so at odds with who he was outside of the cage.

Lex was still looking at her, so Jeni shrugged. "He

opinion."

Nessa snorted and nudged Jeni with her elbow. "Only one way that's gonna happen. Ready to put your booty where your mouth is?"

"Nessa," Noelle chided.

"What? He follows her around like a puppy." Nessa grinned. "Tell him to roll over, I bet he'll let you pet him all night long."

How many people looked at them and saw that—a woman with a panting man in the palm of her hand? Certainly anyone who thought Hawk was the type to *roll over*. In reality, he'd be the one turning *her* over his knee and—

"I've already tried," she told Nessa, "but the man's a rock."

Noelle stroked Jeni's hair before squeezing her shoulder lightly. "He's focused. I don't think he makes casual decisions. Everything's a mission for him."

It was that focus that made him irresistible. No matter what he was doing, he was *there*, in the moment, and it was so damn easy to picture other things. For Jeni to close her eyes, block out the sight and sounds of the escalating fight, and imagine all that determination turned toward her.

Too easy.

A collective shout from the crowd opened her eyes just in time. Hawk had his opponent up against the bars, unleashing a flurry of punches that left the man sagging and then sliding to the floor. And just like that, the fight was over, ended by a tiny, delicious slip in Hawk's iron self-control.

If she followed him now...

A shiver slid up Jeni's spine, and she looked down at the melting ice in her glass. It wasn't fair to push

through his veins. He would come to her when he was ready.

Unless he didn't. And he was leaving soon, heading to Six on O'Kane business.

She grabbed one of the open bottles from the table as she rose. "You ladies have a good time tonight."

Nessa let out a whoop of unfettered encouragement. "Go get him, Jeni."

Lex was more reserved, limiting herself to a wink and a slow salute with her drink. But she didn't have to speak for Jeni to read the caution in her eyes—*watch yourself*.

It was a good idea. A man who was down to fuck and ready to go would have already taken her up on one of her invitations, which meant there was something holding Hawk back. Whether he was just new to the O'Kane lifestyle or had something deeper going on, it would serve her well to remember his reserve.

Then she pushed through the back door of the warehouse, out into the courtyard, and all of that vanished. Without the exterior lights that normally burned, there was only the moonlight washing over his skin. Her breath caught in her chest, and she couldn't pretend that she hadn't been waiting for this moment. That she hadn't chosen to wear her favorite little black dress tonight on purpose, or decided to go bare beneath it, or strapped on the heeled sandals that made her legs look eight miles long.

All for this moment.

He turned to look at her, his tattoos cutting intriguing shadows across his chest and shoulders and down his arms. She'd watched the artwork take form, week after week, month after month—Ace's clever storytelling, his eye for beauty. The ink flowed with

He was massive. Unshakable, like a tree with roots that went deep. Except for his eyes.

His eyes were *hungry*.

Her knees went weak, so she leaned against the door and held up the bottle.

He flexed his fingers as he took a step forward. It seemed like forever before he reached for the bottle, but that made it feel *purposeful* when his fingers slipped over hers, rough and warm and caressing. He tugged the bottle away and lifted it to his lips.

His throat worked as he swallowed, and she couldn't resist. She leaned in and touched her tongue to his skin. Hawk groaned and slid his fingers into her hair. She froze, certain for one endless moment that he'd pull her away.

But he didn't. He held her there, her mouth to his neck, so she licked a slow line up from the base of his throat to the spot just under his jaw.

His fingers clenched, sending tingles along her scalp and down her spine. His chest heaved. Then he moved, and a thousand different sensations flooded her. The cool metal of the door against her back. The breeze on her skin. The hot, solid wall of his chest pressed tightly to hers.

There were a hundred seductive things she could say. In the end, she only managed his name. "Hawk..."

The bottle slipped from his fingers and clinked against the pavement. It rolled away, spilling priceless whiskey as it went, but Hawk ignored it. His hands were already moving, sliding down her body, skimming her hips—

He curled his fingers under her ass and hauled her up. Her skirt rode up her legs as she wrapped them around Hawk's body. His jeans scraped her inner

His pants and his self-control. And the latter broke on another groan as he caught her mouth in a bruising, starving kiss.

His lips were lush, firm, and warm against hers, but it was his tongue that undid her. She'd expected a halting exploration, maybe even with a hint of shyness, but this was something else entirely. He licked his way into her mouth, stroking her tongue with a skill that matched his passion, and everything else vanished. All that was left in her entire world was Hawk, kissing her with whiskey on his lips.

His skin was hot under her hands, hard and soft all at once. His muscles tensed at her touch, turning the vague, empty ache that had plagued her for weeks into a deeper throb of need. It pulsed hotter when she slid her hand down over his stomach to his belt—

Hawk caught her wrist and broke the kiss. "Not yet. Not like this."

They were words, and she knew they made sense, but not in that order, and not right now. She inhaled to clear her head, but all it did was fill her with Hawk's scent, and she almost moaned. "What?"

"We have to do this right." He eased her hand away and tipped her head back so she had to meet his eyes. "I need to get you a collar."

The words fell into the space between them, heavy and loud. They were still echoing through her like ripples in a pond when she found her voice. "A collar."

"That's how O'Kanes do this, right? That's how they say they want...this."

He was staring down at her with such earnest gravity that a laugh bubbled up. She swallowed it and shook her head. "We do what we want, sweetheart. If we want to fuck, we fuck."

32

want."

Oh Jesus, not another one. Not *him.* "No." Jeni pushed at his chest until he put her down, and she avoided looking at him as she straightened her skirt. "You—you what? Want to take care of me? Save me from my life?"

Hawk blinked, clearly startled. Then his eyes narrowed, and his intensity melted from hunger to danger. "Do you need saving from something?"

"Hell, no. Absolutely fucking not."

He studied her in silence for another painfully awkward moment. "I don't understand, then."

The last thing she wanted to do was hurt him, so she took another deep breath and chose her words carefully. "We've barely spoken, Hawk. I know that we're attracted to one another, but what you're talking about—a collar? That's different."

"Because it's serious," he said finally, not so much questioning as confirming. "It's a commitment."

Not just a commitment, but the most serious one an O'Kane could make short of ink. "Yeah," she said gently. "And you can't commit to someone you don't know. It's a disaster waiting to happen."

"I understand." He took a step back, then another. "I asked for too much."

He'd asked for something unfathomable. Unimaginable. "Why?"

His brow furrowed. "Why did I ask for it?"

He said it as though the answer was obvious, and the question unnecessary. "Yes. Why?"

"Because it's bad enough not having you. If I touch you..." He looked away, casting his expression in shadow. "Not having you is bad. Not getting to keep you would be worse."

33

know bothered her more—that he'd felt this way and she hadn't had a clue, or that he thought he had to collar her to keep her from moving on after one night.

Both were equally heartbreaking.

She moved closer to him again, stopping just out of reach. "What would a collar mean to you?"

"That you trust me," he replied softly. "That you choose me. That you're mine."

The words slid over her like a slow caress, and she shivered. "You don't need a collar for that."

"Yes, I do." He looked back at her, his gaze shrouded. Dark. "Because not wanting one—that means something, too."

It wasn't the way O'Kanes did things, no matter what Hawk thought. She couldn't think of a single collar that had been bestowed except as a prelude to ink. But it *was* a statement, that much was undeniable, and it didn't have to be permanent the way the marks were. If it didn't work, if Hawk grew tired of her—

They could still walk away, no harm, no foul.

"I'll think about it," she told him finally. "I have to—I have to think."

"I understand." He reached out, his fingers hovering just above her cheek. "I'll wait, Jeni. You're worth it, however long it takes."

Part of her wanted to lean into his touch, so she leaned back instead. "I'm going back inside. I'll see you tomorrow?"

"Of course."

Jeni turned and grasped the door handle, fully ready to head back into the warehouse in search of a distraction. Then she caught sight of her reflection in the high, shatterproof window. She barely recognized the woman staring back at her from wide, glazed eyes.

with none of her usual calm composure.

How long had it been since someone had torn her apart with a single kiss?

She let go of the handle and headed up the exterior stairs that led to the living quarters instead. The night was young, but there was no way she could go back to the warehouse like everything was normal, no big deal, when her world had just been turned on its side.

She'd do all that thinking she promised Hawk instead. Christ knew sleeping wasn't an option, not after that kiss. Not after those *words*, words that still wrapped around her, the ones that meant he wanted her, needed her, *saw* her—

A collar was a promise. It would be so easy to sink into it, to trust that Hawk had done enough thinking for both of them and everything would turn out okay. But she'd sworn to herself she wouldn't do it again, just let herself fall and hope like hell things didn't end in heartbreak.

So she'd think. And somehow she'd figure out what to do.

3

Farming was in Hawk's blood. Before the guns and fighting, even before the cars, his earliest memories were of helping his mother in the kitchen garden. He couldn't have been very old; by nine or ten, most boys were out with the men, working the crops they cultivated for Eden. But no one escaped chores in Sector Six, not once they were old enough to gather eggs or pull weeds.

Working the garden in Sector Four was different. Jyoti's rooftop garden had spread across the sector and into Three, part of Dallas's long-range plan to secure against food shortages. Each garden was unique, its design driven by one overriding concern.

Space.

Back home, the kitchen garden sprawled across an area twice the size of the O'Kane compound. Here,

precedence over beauty, but the collective creativity of the O'Kanes had paid off.

The roof of the living barracks was alive with greenery. Raised beds, vertical beds, trellises—even a clever contraption Trix and Finn had assembled from burlap sewn with dozens of snug little pockets for lettuce to grow.

Usually, stepping out into the garden brought Hawk a measure of peace. The setting might be strange, but the work remained the same. Plants needed tending, needed water, or fertilizer. Needed thinning. He could do the work drunk. He could do it half-asleep. Hell, he could do it half-dead.

But he couldn't do it this morning. Not after a restless night with Jeni's taste on his lips and her voice in his dreams.

We've barely spoken, Hawk.

All that damn time worrying about Sector Four's rules and customs, wondering how to make his intentions clear, and he'd skipped the most important step. He'd spent months watching Jeni, cataloging her moods, her ever-changing costumes, and the different ways she smiled. He knew her. Maybe not enough, not nearly as well as he wanted to.

But he knew her better than she knew him. Which meant he'd fucked up. *Bad.*

"I think you're drowning that one."

Hawk jerked the hose away from the raised bed he'd been watering. Jeni yelped and jumped back, but water still splashed her sandals and her legs—

He'd seen her legs before. Hell, he'd seen *all* of her before—her dances at the Broken Circle left little to the imagination. But last night those legs had been wrapped around him. He'd felt their lithe strength, had

38

He could have let go of her hips, trusted her to hold herself against him as he satisfied his overwhelming need to bury both hands deep in her hair, to see just how hard he had to tighten his fists before she moaned for him.

Fucking *hell*.

He released the lever on the hose, and the spray of water cut off abruptly. Hawk forced his gaze to her eyes, even as the heat flooding his face told him he was blushing. Forty fucking years old, and he was *blushing*. "Hi."

"Good morning." Jeni bent over to swipe water from her skin. The wide neck of her loose, flowing blouse slipped off one shoulder, and she hauled it back into place as she straightened once again. "Lili needs some lettuce. For lunch."

He nodded and stepped out of her way. "There's plenty of it to go around."

"I know." She picked up one of the baskets they used for harvesting and held it in front of her like a shield, both hands clutching the woven edge. "So. How was your night?"

It was awkward as hell, but her anxiety triggered something inside him, a need to soothe that overcame his lingering embarrassment. He gave her a little space, moving to the next raised bed to resume watering. "Not bad. I went to see if I could get back in the cage, but I ended up breaking up fights over who got the next round."

"Oh." She set the basket at her feet and began to pull lettuce leaves. "Lex mentioned that they may have to move to a lottery system to pick the fights. Seems like an awful lot of trouble, though."

It sure as fuck clashed with the freewheeling,

so popular. The mood was shifting week by week, turning grimmer, harsher. People flooded in like moths clustering around the only light in the darkness, desperate and scared and eager to fight to prove they were neither.

"A lottery might work," Hawk said, but he couldn't find any conviction. The only thing that might work was another night. More chances for everyone to work off their frustration. It would solve their problems for a week, maybe two, until the pressure built again.

They'd run out of days of the week before they ran out of trouble.

"Right." Jeni fell silent, keeping her attention focused on the hanging planter in front of her.

The awkwardness swelled. Hawk cursed his clumsiness and wished, not for the first time, for a hint of Ace's easy charm or Mad's forthright charisma. They'd be over there already, holding the basket for her, making her smile. Ace would be flirting outrageously, saying shit so obscene it should get his stubble slapped off his face but somehow just made women laugh.

The only things Hawk could talk about were cars, guns, and farming.

He finished watering the second bed and set the hose aside. The silence grew and twisted, unnatural and miserable. And it was his fault, for moving too fast, for putting her in this position. For kissing her, when he knew—he *knew*—that he'd want more, demand more, and that she wasn't ready.

This was his problem to fix.

He picked up the basket and held it so she wouldn't have to bend. "It's okay, you know. I don't expect an answer today. I know it'll take longer than one night."

"That isn't—" Jeni sighed and faced him. "I feel

40

was happening. I'm scrambling to catch up."

"I know." He opened his mouth to tell her she had all the time she needed, but the words wouldn't come. Because Eden loomed to their left, the walls more innocuous in the early-morning light but still sparking a violent reminder.

No one had all the time they needed anymore.

"We could all be dead tomorrow," she said softly, echoing his thoughts. "If you felt this way, why didn't you say something sooner?"

Because she'd belonged to Dallas and Lex. And then she hadn't, and he'd been faced with the possibility of having her.

The possibility of *losing* her.

He rubbed his thumb over the edge of the basket. It was coarse, familiar. So were the scents of fresh lettuce, of damp earth. The buzz of insects attracted to the blooms that turned this roof into a scrap of wilderness in the middle of concrete. Not really like home, but still enough to stir memories. "Things are different in Six. Sex, marriage..."

She looked at him expectantly.

How could he explain the tangle of brutal practicality that formed the bedrock of Sector Six? "There's no courtship. No romance. When you're old enough, the head wife checks the genealogies and finds you a husband or wife from a nearby farm. Or if they want fresh blood, they get some poor girl from the communes who comes to your wedding night in tears."

"Hawk." She touched his arm just beneath his sleeve. "I'm sorry."

Skin contact was dangerous. Heat flooded him, stirring the memory of her thighs beneath his palms, her lips parted under his. "Things are different now. On

son of a bitch, but Shipp took him down. And Shipp's crew... Well, some of my sisters and stepmothers found men they could marry *and* love. But they still take things slow there."

"I don't have a problem with that." Her fingers moved, gently brushing over his skin, and she smiled. "But I do need to know something's happening."

"Got it." His voice sounded low and harsh even to his own ears, and he clutched the basket tighter as a reminder not to reach for her. "We'll just have to get to know each other, right?"

"Mmm, when you get back. Which reminds me..." She dropped her hand and dug through her pocket before pulling out a folded piece of paper. "For you. Dallas wanted me to send along a list of things, just in case you knew where to find them."

He shifted the basket to one hand and unfolded the paper. A cursory glance revealed the pattern. "Medicinal plants?"

She nodded. "Just in case. We're stockpiling gel and meds, but if we lose Five, they'll go fast. We need a backup plan."

Most of the stuff on the list would be easy to find. Some he knew his family had growing in their garden already—real medication was still expensive, even if your farm headquartered a crew of smugglers. And there was still time to plant more. Plenty of other farms might be willing to contribute in exchange for a few bottles of precious O'Kane whiskey.

But the list was more than practicalities. It was an opportunity. "Maybe you should come with me."

Her denial was immediate. "No, you're going to see your family. I'd be intruding."

"Jeni." He liked the way her gaze locked on his

live there. A handful of my stepmothers, dozens of siblings, more nieces and nephews than I can keep track of, and probably about seven new in-laws since the last time I visited. And Shipp's crew on top of it. If you're scared to face that sort of chaos, I wouldn't blame you. But you won't be intruding."

"And your mother," she retorted. "Your *mother* lives there, Hawk."

She said it like it mattered more than all the rest, and maybe it should. But his mother had been barely old enough to have children when she'd given birth to him. She'd always been more of an overprotective big sister than a parent, and even that had mellowed once he'd come back to the farm with Shipp.

Alya would *notice*. She wasn't stupid. But he couldn't believe she'd give Jeni a hard time. "She's fine. She'll love you. Ask Trix."

"That's not the same."

"Fair enough." He cupped Jeni's cheek, savoring the silk of her skin under his fingertips. "Trust me, just this far. Maybe if you see where I come from, you'll know whether or not you can trust me all the way."

She closed her eyes as a fine shiver ran through her. "All right. Show me where you come from, Hawk."

He could have her now, right here amongst the plants and the dirt. Up against the greenhouse or over one of the tables or standing right where they were, with her legs around him, using all that dancer's strength to ride him—

He could have her, but it wouldn't be what it could be, what he'd seen between Jasper and Noelle—the firm hand and soft sighs and quiet trembling. The absolute trust that made everything deeper and darker but also perfect.

since the first, furtive time. Secret, forbidden affairs fueled passion, sure. And then they broke hearts and ruined lives.

Hawk moved his thumb to Jeni's lower lip. He could still feel the curve of it pressed against his mouth, still remember how she'd tasted. When her lips parted beneath his touch, a thousand shameful possibilities roared up inside him. Things he would have been ashamed to want before he met the O'Kanes.

If he was honest with himself, things he was still ashamed to want.

"I'll arrange it," he whispered, as if lowering his voice could hide the roughness. He had to get away from her before his control slipped again. This time, it wouldn't end with kissing. He'd have her on her knees, her soft, pretty lips around his cock. Sucking him off, even if the whole damn gang lined up to watch.

Fuck, *especially* if they lined up to watch.

"Thank you." The words kissed his thumb, but before he could give in to the urge to edge the tip between her lips, she took the basket and walked away.

His jeans were too snug. His entire fucking body was coiled tighter than it had been last night before his fight. They'd be out in Six for a few days. A week, at most.

A week to prove she could trust him. And then they'd find out how deep into his shame-laced fantasies she wanted to go.

4

The farms at the outer edge of Sector Six were beautiful, like something out of a kids' storybook. The gently rolling hills had been cleared of scrub and planted in lush green plots, some with crops and others with grass for grazing animals. Cabins and barns dotted the landscape, and people milled around them, carrying out their midmorning chores.

This was Hawk's home, a quiet, peaceful world so far removed from the city that it might as well be on another planet.

They passed a fenced-off gravel road that wound toward a large farmhouse perched on a hill, and Hawk nodded toward it. "That's Anderson's farm. They're our closest neighbors. Three of my stepmothers are Andersons."

She blinked. "So some of your brothers and sisters

"Sounds more fucked up than it is. I told you, the head wife keeps records on everyone's bloodlines." He snorted. "Probably next to the ones they keep on the cows and horses. We're all good, hardy stock. Bred to be tough."

Jeni barely managed not to wrinkle her nose in disgust. "No romance. You weren't kidding."

"They don't have time for romance. It's a hard life. You work until you can't take another step, or you have babies until it kills you."

It cast the lush green land in a whole new light—a sickly pallor that raised goose bumps on Jeni's arms. "That's terrible."

"It's the reality. Eden's tithes are so high..." He exhaled roughly. "Shipp saved us from that. The smuggling runs make enough money to buy us some breathing room. But the only real hope is for Dallas to pull off this revolution."

It was easy to think of the fight against Eden in strict, direct terms now—if they didn't defeat the city, they'd all be crushed, or worse. But it had started because of the city slowly encroaching on the livelihood of the surrounding sectors. They always wanted more—more food, more energy, more of the resources sector-dwellers gave their time, effort, and sometimes blood to procure or produce.

"Dallas will win," she told Hawk confidently. "There's no other option I'm willing to consider."

"If anyone can pull it off, it's him." Hawk shifted gears as they started up a curving hill. "Get ready. When we reach the top, you'll be able to see the farm."

What lay in the valley before them looked like the rest of the area, but with one difference that proved the truth of Hawk's words—smuggling had been very, very

barn back beyond the main house, there were pieces of fairly modern equipment that Jeni hadn't seen at the other farms.

Her jittery nerves had calmed a bit, soothed by the rough but velvet cadence of Hawk's voice. They returned now with a vengeance as people turned to watch their approach.

"Steady," he murmured, resting one hand on her leg. His palm was massive, large enough to engulf her knee, and his touch burned even through her clothes. "You're an O'Kane, honey. You eat backwoods farmers for breakfast."

He was teasing her, and she couldn't resist throwing it right back at him. "Just the ones I really like."

His fingers tightened, and his voice lowered. "You gonna eat me for breakfast, Jeni?"

Even with the windows down, there was no *air* in the car. "Wouldn't dream of it," she rasped. "I mean, you've got plans for me, right?"

"Oh yeah." He steered with one hand, guiding them down the hill as his thumb teased suggestive circles on the outside of her knee. "You have no idea."

Maybe this was what he'd been waiting for, what he needed. To get her on familiar territory, someplace where he was comfortable enough to open up in spite of the differences between them.

She would have asked, but the front door of the main house opened, and a tall woman stepped out. Jeni had spent most of her life around powerful women, and there was no mistaking this one's posture or the air of command that surrounded her.

Everything here was hers.

Hawk coasted to a stop and parked the car. Then he was out the door before Jeni could say a word,

He held out his hand to help her. She took it automatically, but all thoughts of letting go again vanished the moment his fingers wrapped around hers. It was one point of contact, chaste by anyone's standards, but something about the way he looked down at her as she climbed from the car...

Her skin heated, and everything else disappeared. They were alone in the world, wreathed in a tension so palpable that it connected them as surely as their clasped hands.

Then he smiled and tugged her toward the farmhouse. "Come meet Alya."

The words broke through the sensual haze, and she willed herself not to blush as they turned toward the porch. The woman standing there had hints of Hawk in her features. They had the same hazel eyes, the same nose, a certain similarity in the tilts of their chins.

Alya's gaze locked on their entwined fingers. When she looked up, she studied Jeni appraisingly, curiosity warring with something darker. It wasn't judgment— Jeni was too familiar with that, would have recognized it in a heartbeat—but Hawk's mother definitely wasn't particularly happy to see her.

That changed in an instant when she turned to Hawk. Her gaze warmed, and her mouth curved into a smile as she leaned one hip against the porch railing. "You better have a trunk full of that fine Sector Four whiskey, or Big John'll toss you halfway back to O'Kane territory."

"Big John's getting old," Hawk replied with a grin. He tugged Jeni up the steps before releasing her to wrap his mother in a hug. "He couldn't toss me past the end of the driveway these days."

son fiercely, then released him and returned her attention to Jeni. "And who's this?"

"This is Jeni." Hawk settled his hand at the small of Jeni's back, warm and encouraging. "Jeni, meet my mother, Alya."

She held out her hand, willing her fingers not to tremble. "Hi."

Alya's grip was as warm and firm as Lex's. "Nice to meet you, Jeni. Welcome to my farm."

"Thank you. It's beautiful."

"It has its moments." Alya turned for the door. "Why don't you two come inside? We have leftovers from breakfast, and you can get Jeni settled in."

"I was going to show her around first—"

"Hawk." Alya cut him off firmly. "I know you have manners in there somewhere. Your girl could use a bite to eat and a little time to catch her breath. Shipp'll be back from a run tonight, and that means a rally. Let her rest up."

Alya disappeared into the farmhouse, and Hawk exhaled on a laugh. "You should have been there the first time she and Lex met."

It wasn't hard to imagine. "Badass lady standoff of epic proportions?"

"I wasn't sure if they were going to love or kill each other." Hawk smiled. "Dallas had no doubts. He says Alya's the reason I'm the only new recruit who's never pissed Lex off."

"Makes sense." So much about him still didn't, but at least he was comfortable here, relaxed in ways she'd only glimpsed back in Four, and even then only in the rooftop gardens he'd helped cultivate.

Maybe he was right. Maybe everything she needed to know about him could be traced back to Six, to the peace that hummed beneath the noises of a working farm. If people were products of their environments, then Hawk *was* Sector Six.

And she only had a few days to learn everything she could.

If Sector Six had a version of fight night, it was a rally.

It had been fifteen years since the first one. Fifteen years since he'd rolled back onto the farm, young and angry and determined to rescue his mother, one way or another.

Shipp had been the knight in shining armor that day. Though he was only five years Hawk's senior, Shipp had seemed decades older in maturity and poise. He was like Dallas—a person with the inner strength and charisma that it took to draw men looking for someone to believe in, along with the steel will required to get the job done.

Fifteen years ago, that had meant preventing Hawk from committing patricide.

At first, Hawk had resented Shipp for thwarting his revenge. It had taken years for him to understand that the only reward he could have claimed for killing his own father would have been a lifetime of looking himself in the mirror, too aware of the blood on his hands.

Shipp had understood. And he'd taken on that burden, just like he'd taken on the burden of protecting the bruised, terrified victims of Hawk's father's legacy. That first rally could have been a disaster waiting to happen—a crew of outlaw smugglers and a farm full of women and children still reeling from their unexpected

Instead, they'd found common ground. Drinking, dancing, and driving. Laughter and food, and celebrating the heady feeling of being so far from Eden, you could almost forget they were there at all.

Tonight, people seemed to want to forget. The cars were gathered in the field, headlights illuminating the darkness as engines purred and music blared. Jeni was down there in a cluster of Hawk's sisters, still nervous but *smiling*, and so gorgeous he wanted to sweep her up and lure her into the shadows.

The couples sneaking away were headed to rendezvous plenty tame by O'Kane standards—but there was a charm to kissing in the darkness, frustration burning until the need for *more* was unbearable. Tension could be delicious when you knew it didn't have to last forever.

But Eden was out there. And he had to talk business before indulging himself. "It's getting bad, Shipp."

"Yeah?" Shipp lit a cigarette, the lighter and the tip both flaring in the darkness. "You're going to have to be more specific."

"Everyone thought they'd have made a move by now." Hawk shoved his hands deep into his jacket pockets and tried not to stare back toward the city. It shouldn't have been visible at all from the farm, but the new lights charging the walls created an ominous glow to the east. "Hunger's going to drive them out. And you know what that means."

"Course I do. I know how wars work, Hawk." Shipp gazed out at the revelers in the clearing, cast in harsh relief by the headlights. "Food's always the thing. Either an army will need it, or they'll want to make damn sure their enemies can't use it." He arched an eyebrow. "We should probably be glad your new boss

No one in Sector Four had said it—at least where Hawk could hear—but he saw it in their eyes. He saw it in the way they refused to look at him every time Jyoti delivered an update on the state of the farms and communes—food the sectors had access to that stood beyond Eden's reach.

Dallas didn't need Sector Six to win the war, and he couldn't afford to let Eden get their hands on it. "There's land on the edge of Four, Shipp. The girls are doing great with their farm. Round everyone up and get the hell out of here before anything happens."

Shipp snorted. "You know better. Your mama's not leaving this place while there are still two boards to rub together."

He knew. For twenty-five years, this place had been hell on earth for Alya—but for the last fifteen it had been *hers*, the land she'd reclaimed inch by inch, stone by stone. She and Shipp had built it into a secret haven for lost wanderers and runaway children.

She wouldn't give it up any more than Dallas would abandon the Broken Circle. "She may not have a choice."

"If it comes to that, I'll pick her up and carry her myself," Shipp agreed. "But it has to be down to that—no other choice. You understand."

"I understand." He squeezed Shipp's shoulder. "Laurie and Tanya mentioned wanting to move over to Four. Dallas said I can put some of the new recruits to work building another couple barns and an addition on the house. Anyone else who wants to come, we'll have room. And you know I'll take care of them."

"Yeah, you will." The corner of Shipp's mouth tilted up. "You're all-in on the O'Kane shit these days, you and Finn. Brotherhood, booze, and cute little

Hawk found Jeni in the crowd again. Her hair was half up, pulled away from her face to cascade down her back in soft waves. Her endless variations fascinated him almost as much as the way she could disappear behind wigs and makeup. He'd learned to hide his expressions behind a single blank mask, but Jeni had a hundred of them, and the truth of her was in the precious, rare places where they all overlapped.

"She's not mine," Hawk replied softly. And because it was Shipp, who wasn't quite a father but was so much more than a friend, he added the truth. "Not yet."

"No?"

"I'm working on it."

Shipp was silent as he finished his cigarette. Then he crushed it out on the bottom of his boot and turned to Hawk. "Sometimes you have to take a chance. Go ahead and jump, even if you're not sure how you're gonna land."

From anyone else, it would have been casual advice. But Shipp *knew*. The whole sordid story, the reason Hawk had been chased away from his home to begin with. Damn near half his life ago, but the pain of it still surprised him sometimes. Like a bruise he forgot was there until someone slammed into it just right.

O'Kanes didn't do jealousy, but Hawk sure as fuck did. And this was a hell of a bad time to piss off the O'Kanes. "It's complicated, man."

"Isn't everything?" Shipp jerked his head toward a small cluster of cars just outside the circle in the field. "I want to show you something."

Hawk followed him, nodding when people broke off to greet him and returning the hugs from sisters and shoulder slaps from brothers. The crowd surged around him, ebbing and flowing, so familiar the sense

53

The tension plaguing Four seemed so distant. The people here weren't partying harder as they stared down oblivion. They were just partying. The war was still abstract to them. They had their solar power, their chores, the same lives they'd been living all along.

Hawk could fool himself into thinking he'd lure them to safety, but they wouldn't hear him. Not while their illusions of peace held strong.

The men who stood around the cars here weren't farmers, strictly speaking. Their cars were a little beat up, and everything that wasn't essential had been stripped out of them to make room for hauling. Half the cars had engines that were too big for them, so they'd had to weld counterweights to the back frame to maintain stability.

The cars were rough, but they ran like a dream, and so did the men who drove them. This was Shipp's crew, his family, and it showed.

"Big John." Shipp caught his towering friend in a one-armed hug. "Hold down the fort okay while I was gone?"

"Still here, ain't it?" Big John grinned and tossed Hawk a nearly empty bottle of liquor. "If you can stand to drink anything but O'Kane's finest these days."

Shipp grimaced. "Don't do it, Hawk. You have too much to live for. John's moonshine tastes like shit."

Not drinking wasn't an option. Big John wasn't just Shipp's oldest friend—he was Shipp's *oldest* friend, a legitimate badass who'd been orphaned during the Flares and had still come through the aftermath kicking.

The bottle was a test. A dangerous one—the worst of the rotgut the O'Kanes peddled still went down smooth compared to the shit John cooked up. Hell, from twisting off the top and letting the moonshine burn through his tongue on its way to his stomach.

"All right, all right." Big John retrieved the bottle with a grin as the rest of Shipp's team hooted and cheered.

"That's enough." Something serious lurked beneath Shipp's lazy amusement. "It's time to show the boy our Plan B."

Big John nodded and popped open the trunk of his car. Inside were wooden crates and weathered jugs, all packed in there as tightly as possible.

Shipp pried open one crate. At first, Hawk thought there were weapons nestled amongst the hay. Then he looked closer and saw that they were *flare* guns, the simple kind that were nothing more than large tubes and triggers.

He whistled as he lifted one from the crate. "Where'd you get your hands on these?"

"A man's gotta have his secrets," Shipp answered flatly. "If city forces breach the sector, we need a way to warn the others. We'll distribute these to the farmers and settlers, make sure they know how to use them."

It was a clever solution, one Eden couldn't thwart. And Shipp wouldn't just be distributing them. By the time he was done, everyone would have an evacuation plan in place. They'd know what to grab, where to go, how to get out.

If only that was enough. Hawk set the tube back in the crate and made himself say the damn words. "If it comes to that, you know what you have to do. The whole damn sector has to burn."

"What do you think these are for?" Shipp thumped a jug, then grabbed the bottle from Big John's hand and swirled it around, one eyebrow raised. "Least this

"I was drinking that," John said mildly.

Shipp relinquished the rotgut with a snort. "It's your liver, old man."

They were still cracking jokes, and Hawk couldn't tell if they didn't believe the danger was real, or if they'd skated past horror and straight into laughing in the face of the inevitable. He was still stuck in between, having to imagine Shipp hauling a screaming Alya away from her burning farm.

It was gonna take a while for that mental image to stop hurting.

Shipp sobered, his morbid humor fading. "Go," he told him quietly. "Enjoy the rest of the party."

Hawk squeezed his shoulder again, then turned toward Jeni. She still stood in a tight knot with two of his sisters. Not even that far away, but *getting* to her...

In Sector Four, folks melted out of his path. It only took one glance at the O'Kane ink on his wrists to clear the way. Here, the crowd contracted. People were eager to see him, to ask questions about the world beyond the farm, about the O'Kanes, about *him*. It was a welcome that warmed his heart and tried his patience at the same time.

He broke free of the final circle—three of his youngest brothers begging him to come look at the car they were working on—after promising a longer visit in the morning. Then it was just Bethany and Luna, and he braced himself for whatever stories they had to be telling Jeni. Especially Bethany—she'd been born the week before him, to their father's second wife, and had witnessed the most spectacular embarrassments of his childhood.

"—is amazing," Bethany was saying as Hawk slid up next to Jeni. "Where did you *find* it?"

answered. "I can get you a copy."

"We'd owe you big." Bethany grinned at Hawk. "You brought us a smart one. She's going to cure your mama's horse."

Of all the conversations he'd been imagining... He quirked an eyebrow at Jeni. "You know about horses?"

"God, no." She laughed and shook her head. "I read a book."

And clearly remembered it well enough to impress Bethany, which was its own miracle. Bethany might not be Alya's daughter by blood, but she was heir apparent to Alya's empire and took the farm seriously.

Luna bumped her shoulder against his. "If you're thinking about stealing your girl away, forget it. We're having a discussion here."

His girl. No matter what he said to Shipp, the words felt right. Hawk looped his arm around Jeni's waist. "She'll still be here tomorrow, but the dancing won't be. You gonna spoil her first rally?"

Luna dropped her head back with a disgusted noise. "Ugh, fine. Still plenty of time to tell stories, I guess."

Hawk made a mental note to keep Jeni *far* away from his sisters for the rest of the night. Maybe for the rest of the trip. "Behave," he shot back, already tugging Jeni toward the shadows. "I know stories, too. Stories I could tell a certain smuggler..."

Luna's face went red, and she muttered something under her breath, something foul enough to make Bethany burst out laughing.

A momentary victory, but enough of one to make their escape. Hawk caught Jeni's hand and led her between two cars and out into the darkness. "Horses, huh?"

is nice."

"Most of 'em, most of the time. But it's not much like Sector Four."

"No, it isn't." Her voice was low, almost a whisper. "It helps, though. I might even be starting to figure you out."

He turned them both toward a gentle rise covered with trees—the closest thing to privacy on a rally night, when the barns would be full of people stealing kisses. "And what are you figuring out, Jeni?"

"Too early to say," she demurred. "Where are we going?"

"Someplace quiet." He rubbed his thumb over the back of her hand. "Someplace where I don't have to share you."

She fell silent, following him as he crested the hill. Then she sucked in a breath and stared out at the horizon, away from the city, at a sky heavy with stars. "How did you ever leave this place?"

Hawk gave in to temptation and stroked his fingers lightly over her hair. "I didn't have a choice the first time. My father kicked me out. It happens a lot with sons who disappoint."

She looked up at him with questions in her eyes, her gaze sliding over his face like she could find all the answers there if she just stared long enough. Eventually, she smiled. "But you came back. And then you left again."

"Because someone had to help Trix and Finn get back to Sector Four." He wrapped a lock of her hair around his finger and tugged lightly. "I stayed for the wrong reasons at first. And then I stayed for the right ones. Dallas is worth supporting."

Her smile deepened, and she turned her face back

That smile tugged at the parts of him he didn't like, the jealous, dark parts. She'd smiled at Dallas like that during the last meeting, as sweet and affectionate as the touches they'd exchanged. Dallas had stroked her hair, just like Hawk was now. Jeni had kissed his cheek.

And Hawk had seethed with envy.

"Is that the reason?" he asked, not wanting to know the answer and still unable to stop himself from asking. "Dallas and Lex. Are they why you're not ready?"

Jeni stiffened. "I wasn't thinking of them at all, actually. I was laughing at myself a little. For a minute, I thought..." She exhaled sharply. "I thought you might say that part of the reason you stayed in Four was for me."

He let his thumb drift to her cheek and traced down to her jaw. "I can't say it. I'm already worried about scaring you off. If you find out how long I've been watching you, you'll run for it."

"You offered me a collar, Hawk. I assume you've been thinking about it for a while." A breeze blew strands of hair across her parted lips, and she brushed them away as she turned to him. "Show me."

She was so small. He never really noticed until they were this close, until he was staring down at her lips, calculating how long it would take to close the distance between them. He wrapped an arm around her waist and hauled her firmly against him and up, until she was balanced on her toes, and he still had to bend down to claim her lips.

Jeni wound her arms around his neck and tilted her face to his, upsetting her already precarious balance. But she didn't cling to him for support. Instead, her hands skated over his back, slowly exploring as she

She was at his mercy, even if only in the tiniest way, and it felt *good*. Dangerous, because reveling in that small victory twisted into craving more, and he was moving before he could stop himself. Kissing her harder, sinking his fingers into her hair as he bent her back over his arm.

Her tongue traced over his, teasing more than stroking. Licking and then dancing away, inviting him deeper. Daring him to *take*.

He groaned and caught her lower lip between his teeth, but that wasn't enough, either. Panting, he bit her jaw next, mere heartbeats from spilling her to the ground in a tangle of grasping hands and rent fabric.

"You're both," he whispered instead. "I stayed for you when it was wrong. And when it was right."

She was panting too, soft, maddening puffs of breath against his ear, and her hands trembled when she touched his face, held him there. "Thank you."

The moonlight filtered through the trees in teasing patches. He could see her eyes, her smile, the masses of hair curled around his fist. But so much was in shadow, just like that night in the courtyard behind the warehouse.

Except no one would see them here. No one would witness the fracture in his self-control except for Jeni.

He claimed her mouth again, rougher this time, driving his tongue between her lips before she could tease him. So she teased him in other ways, gliding her hands down to the small of his back. She made a low, approving noise in the back of her throat when her fingers encountered the bare skin beneath his shirt, and another when he tightened his hand in her hair.

Three steps behind them was a flat, knee-high rock, a popular place to sit and stare up at the night

her astride his lap. The thin skirt of her sweet cotton dress rode up her thighs, but he was focused on the ties at her shoulders. One firm tug and her dress slipped open on one side, baring the swell of her breast.

He still had one hand buried in her hair. It was so easy to guide her head back, to stroke his other hand down the soft skin of her exposed throat. Her pulse raced beneath his fingertips, and he lingered there for a moment before sliding lower, scraping her skin lightly with his nails. "You're so beautiful."

She wiggled closer, pressing her hips tight against his. The contact made her shudder and flush beneath his touch.

Slow down. His brain knew the right thing to do, but his body wouldn't listen. He tugged at the cute little bow on her other shoulder and pushed the fabric down to her waist. Her skin was far too delicate to suffer his work-roughened touch, but she only squirmed harder as he circled the tight peak of one nipple.

He'd watched her touch herself on that damn stage night after night, had gone home hard and aching only to close his eyes and imagine his hands in place of hers, stroking and teasing and pinching. But he of all people knew that the Jeni who danced on that stage was a character. An act that stood a little off-center, holding parts of her but never all of her.

The command bubbled up from deep inside him, slipping free before he could stop it. "Touch your nipples. Show me what you like."

She obeyed with whisper-soft caresses, her fingertips barely skimming her flesh. In the darkness, it could have been an illusion that she was touching herself at all, except for the way her nipples hardened more with every delicate brush of her fingers.

enough to drive her teeth into her lower lip and elicit another, longer shudder.

Fucking *hell.* "Again."

She dropped her hands to her lap—and dangerously close to his dick. "No."

Not a denial, but a challenge. He recognized the spark in her eye, the mischief, the dare. How many parties had he attended where Noelle sassed Jasper with that gleeful light in her eyes, only to end up over his knee or over his shoulder, hauled away to some private, far more intimate punishment?

Hawk imagined it. He couldn't fucking stop himself. Jeni, across his legs, her little pastel plaid skirt tossed up over her ass. Squirming and whimpering as he spanked her until her skin was red and her thighs were slick with arousal, and he barely had to touch her to have her sobbing with relief and release.

When had his imagination gotten this damn vivid?

"Jeni," he growled, dragging her head up with his grip in her hair. "Do. It. Again."

She wanted to push him. He could see it in her eyes, lurking beneath the glazed pleasure. But she did as he commanded, cupping her breasts and squeezing her nipples between her fingers until he couldn't stand just watching anymore, so he bent his head and licked her fingers.

Jeni muffled her moan against his temple. "Please."

The plea shot through him, straight to where she was rocking against his dick like she was going to grind herself to orgasm. A part of him he hadn't realized was there drove him to drop a hand to her hip, stilling her restless movements, forcing her to endure the tease of his breath feathering over her. "Tell me what you want."

against his lower lip. "I ache. And it doesn't matter how many times I get myself off, it never goes away."

He dragged his tongue across the straining tip and relished her tiny, desperate noise. She was electric under his touch, so responsive he knew he could get her there. "Put your hands on my shoulders."

Her fingers dug into his neck and shoulders, clenching, as if testing his strength through his thin T-shirt. He left one hand on her hip and slid the other up to tease his thumb over the nipple still wet from his tongue. "Try it now. Make yourself come."

Her eyes locked with his. She held his gaze, even when the first tiny rock of her hips had her lashes fluttering down in pure, agonizing pleasure. She watched him, riveted, as she did it again, and again—nothing as coordinated as the way he'd seen her move on stage, but something new. Desperate.

Something that was only *his.*

Need throbbed in time with the rhythm of her hips, an ache that warned him he was too far gone to come back. But he didn't give a shit if he exploded in his jeans like an anxious teenager—as long as she kept moving, kept moaning, kept trembling like she felt just as lost, just as untried.

He rolled his thumb over her nipple again, earning a hitch in her breath. But soft wasn't what either of them wanted.

His head swimming, he brought his thumb and finger together and pinched until she choked out a curse and covered his hand with hers, holding his fingers to her ravaged skin.

Pain and pleasure. She wanted both, *needed* both. And it felt so very, very good to give it to her.

Jeni ground against him, harder with every

their clothes, so seductive he had to grit his teeth. She threw her head back like she was going to scream, so he started to cover her mouth, but all she did was breathe his name, one syllable wrapped in a whispering sigh and a groan of sheer, absolute relief.

His heart pounding, Hawk dragged her close to his chest, wrapping both arms around her to protect her bare skin from the cool evening breeze. "You okay?"

"Yes." The word left her on a soft laugh, one that tickled the crook of his neck. Her teeth scraped his skin, and she sat back, as if she couldn't even feel the night chill.

Then she dropped her hands to his belt. She unbuckled it without looking away from his face, and the only thing more arresting than what she was doing was the way she was *watching* him—waiting, a question in her eyes.

He could stop her. Maybe *should*. But every brush of her fingertips across the denim covering his straining cock stoked his arousal, and he was flesh and blood. Just a man, unable to resist temptation when it stared at him with huge, pleasure-glazed eyes.

He cupped her cheek and pressed his thumb to her lips. The soft command he uttered was absolutely wrong—and so, so right. "Use your mouth."

She slid off his lap, rising before dropping to her knees at his feet. Every movement was careful, deliberate. Perfect obedience, a submission that went beyond the illusion of power and straight into the very heart of it.

Unbuttoning. Unzipping. By the time she wrapped her hand around the base of cock, he was grinding his fists against the rock to keep from tangling his hands in her hair and jerking her mouth down.

her tongue in a lush, wet circle around the head of his cock.

"*Fuck*." It was better than his imagination ever could have painted it, better than any goddamn thing he could remember. Because she was on her knees for him, her clothes askew, so disheveled she looked like he'd already fucked her, and he wasn't going to last if she kept teasing him.

His self-control snapped, and he laid one hand on the back of her head. "Now." He tried to whisper, but it came out rough and dark instead, a snarl. "Suck me."

Her lips slid around him, slick and hot and soft. She didn't tease, exactly—she didn't hesitate or hold back—but she took her time. Up and down her mouth worked, taking more of him with every advance, gently increasing the pressure until her cheeks were hollowed out, and Hawk couldn't resist her.

He didn't have to. This might be his first taste of Jeni and the dark passion that sizzled between them... but it wouldn't be the last.

The thought undid him. He stopped fighting the pleasure and gave in with a groan. Fire flooded him, and he spread his fingers wide at the back of Jeni's head, holding her in place as his hips jerked and he came on a rush of satisfaction.

She swallowed him with a moan, then soothed him with gentle flicks of her tongue. And while he gasped for breath, she laid her head on his thigh and waited.

As if he could catch his breath with her curled at his feet, sweet and patient. He stroked her cheek and ran his fingers through her tangled hair. "That was perfect."

She smiled and bit his thumb.

"Brat." Lazy pleasure spiraled through him as

willingly, settling across his legs with her head tucked under his chin. He took his time running his hands up each leg, brushing away the dirt and pine needles, rubbing at the tiny indentions where pebbles had dug into her skin. "Still okay?"

"No." Her fingers clenched in his shirt. "You make me want to stay here, where everything is so far away."

Hawk wrapped both arms around her and rested his chin on the top of her head. "I wish everything really was far away. It's easy to forget here, but it's dangerous, too. I don't want them to forget."

Jeni touched his arm. "I know."

The wind picked up, stirring through the trees above them. Jeni's skin broke out in goose bumps beneath his hands, and he urged her upright. Working in silence, he eased her dress back into place and tied it securely at each shoulder.

"So serious," she whispered.

"I'll always be serious about taking care of you." He smoothed her dress one last time and touched her chin, tilting her head back so she had to meet his eyes. "You deserve it."

Her sudden smile was impish. "Are you starting to regret the fact that your mother banished you to the bunkhouse with the rest of Shipp's crew?"

He laughed and brushed a kiss to her lips. "Not even a little. This means I get to sneak you out to the barn tomorrow night."

"Dirty." Jeni glanced back toward the field. "We should probably rejoin the party. They're going to miss you."

They already had, without a doubt. There'd be even more razzing when he hit the bunkhouse tonight, and his sisters would be unlivable, but he didn't give a

to his. "I'm not done kissing you."

Jeni leaned into him, warm and pliant, as he captured her mouth with his. If he'd thought a couple of orgasms would ease the tension between them, she proved him wrong with the slow, lazy caress of her tongue and the eager heat of her body.

They'd barely scratched the surface of what they could be together. Now Hawk knew in his bones that she'd take him all the way down into his darkest, basest desires, and she'd love every minute of it.

Lord help him, so would he.

5

Hawk's sister liked to talk.

Jeni already knew that, of course. The night before, Luna had dominated her conversation with Bethany, asking a million questions, mostly about what life was like outside of Sector Six. She was irrepressible, so full of life, and so *young*.

Jeni could barely remember ever being that young.

Luna moved down another row of the large, fenced plot that served as their herb garden and beckoned for Jeni to follow. Besides the typical herbs used in cooking, like basil or thyme, they grew an impressive array of plants and flowers she'd only seen in illustrations and pictures.

"We have plenty of aloe, of course—that's good for burns and scrapes," Luna said. "Marigolds, goldenseal, fenugreek, comfrey..."

orized. With them, they could possibly treat a number of common ailments or complaints, though they'd have to be careful. Dosages had to be monitored closely, just like the medications manufactured in Sector Five. Too much could mean organ damage, even death.

"We have a few willow trees around the farm, mostly down near the creek on the eastern side," Luna went on, "but Alya prefers feverfew when it's in season." She stopped beside an elderberry bush and idly traced its leaves. "How long have you known Hawk?"

Jeni had expected the interrogation, but not from his baby sister. It took her a moment to answer. "A few months."

"But you just got serious." It wasn't a question.

Jeni answered anyway, just to have something to say. "Yes."

Luna smiled. "It's nice. I don't think anyone's seen him like this since—" She cut off abruptly and turned away. "Purple coneflower—that's echinacea. You can make a tincture out of the roots. Bethany swears by it. Says it'll knock out a cold quicker than anything."

The conversation was clearly over. Jeni swallowed the urge to question the girl further, but she couldn't entirely quell her curiosity. No one had seen Hawk like this since...what?

Since who?

Luna pointed to a row of tall hedges at the edge of the garden. "And those are barberry bushes. The fruit's kind of sour, but it makes good jelly. Careful of the thorns, though."

Barberry. It snagged against a memory, and Jeni closed her eyes. She could picture the pages she'd read, and she focused on one, from an old, dusty book Dallas had kept in storage, one filled with hand-drawn

wheat rust?"

"The strains of wheat we grow here are resistant to fungal infection," Alya said from behind them. When they turned, she was studying Jeni again—the same measured assessment from the previous day. "Did you grow up on a farm?"

It took every ounce of self-discipline she had not to squirm. "I'm from the city. But I've been helping out with the gardening projects in Four."

"Ah." Alya didn't look away from her. "Luna, love, they need help getting the babies settled down for lunch. Could you run in and give them a hand?"

"Sure." Luna spared Jeni a quick wave before weaving her way through the beds toward the house.

Just like that, she was alone with Alya and her withering scrutiny. The urge to laugh at the ridiculousness of her own nerves almost overwhelmed her, but Jeni pasted a polite smile on her face instead.

Alya tilted her head. "I was listening to the last little bit. You're looking for medicinal herbs?"

"Dallas thinks it would be a good precautionary measure in case of supply shortages." The truth, such as it was, since he'd readily agreed with her when she'd brought it up.

"I see." Alya turned and waved a hand. "Walk with me. I'll show you around."

She headed around the side of the house, past a large, cabin-like structure closer than the other barns and sheds. It was huge, with several chimneys dotting the roof at regular intervals. "That's the smokehouse. We mostly cure pork, though we keep some cows and chickens to fill our own tables."

Silence fell again, so heavy that Jeni's palms actually started to sweat. Which was the absolute height

71

proved of her? He was a grown man, for Christ's sake. And Jeni had never been ashamed of herself, or of anything she'd done, and she wasn't about to start now.

So why did it matter so much?

Alya stopped at the top of the next rise. Down in the gentle valley before them, people clustered around the new, yellow framework of a small building. The sounds of sawing and hammering drifted up, along with the low drone of conversation and the occasional laugh or shout.

They were too far away for easy recognition, but Jeni spotted Hawk immediately. The way he moved was unmistakable, all leashed strength and control, whether he was raising a support beam into place or climbing into the cage for a fight.

Or touching a woman.

Jeni's cheeks heated. She'd never be able to look at another cluster of trees without picturing the moonlight filtering through the leaves or the shadows melding together to form the illusion of privacy. The association was imprinted on her brain now, along with all the things she'd discovered about Hawk—like the fact that he didn't just crave her submission, he got off on it. Hard.

The whole collar thing made a lot more sense now.

Alya shaded her eyes and stared down the hill. "They're putting up a new house. One of Shipp's boys finally coaxed one of Hawk's sisters into marrying his sorry ass, and we're out of bedrooms again. Bethany and her family are next up to get their own space, so that one'll be hers."

Jeni still couldn't wrap her brain around how huge the families were. "There are so many children here."

"My late husband took ten wives. Between us,

brothers and sisters who made it to adulthood." Alya dropped her hand and turned back to Jeni. "We didn't have Eden messing with our water, but the bastard still gave us fertility drugs. Twins and triplets were more efficient. More dangerous, but worth the risk. To him."

It fit all too well with that Hawk had told her about his father. "But you only have Hawk?"

"Oh, they're all my children, more or less." She smiled, but banked protective fury burned in her eyes. "We say it, and we mean it, for the most part. But I worry about him a little more than the rest. I always will."

"Right." Jeni rubbed her hands on her jeans. "You probably have questions."

"Not so many." Alya looked back out over the valley. "Hawk's been on his own for damn near twenty years now. So whatever has you so nervous, you should know I don't give a shit. All I care about is seeing him happy."

There was an unspoken question in there some-where—or maybe Jeni only heard one because she expected it. "The O'Kanes have a reputation for casual," she said carefully. "But I think people just don't under-stand. None of it is casual. Ever."

"Good, because neither is he." Alya looked away, her lips tight, her eyes shuttered. "Hawk won't tell you this because he's loyal to a fault, but I was no kind of mother to him. I was too young, and then I was too broken. By the time I was strong enough to protect him, he didn't need it anymore, so no one's ever taken care of him. That's all I want, Jeni. Someone in his life who can take care of him."

The man she knew was an island, a rock who kept

whether through preference or necessity or sheer force of habit. "I can try," she offered, "but I can't make him let me."

"No," Alya conceded. "He brought you here, though. That means something."

"I think so. I *hope* so."

"I know so." Alya finally smiled. "You're the first one, honey. Ever."

The first woman he'd brought home, maybe, but Luna's words played over and over in her mind. *I don't think anyone's seen him like this since—* "There was someone else once."

"Someone—" Alya cut off with a sigh. "Who was it? Luna?"

The easy answer, but it wasn't the whole truth. Luna's slip was a piece of the puzzle, one Hawk had laid out for her himself, back in Four. *Not having you is bad. Not getting to keep you would be worse.* "Don't worry, she didn't tell me anything private."

"I wish it *was* private, for his sake." Alya gripped her shoulder. "Ask him, Jeni. You should know. Because it's not a pretty story, and he's the only one who doesn't come out of it looking like a villain—but that's never been how he saw it."

"I will." It was a promise she could make, because it was as much for her as it was for Hawk. If she was going to wear his collar, belong to him, then they had to be able to talk about things that had hurt them. It was the only safe way to exist in that space between sex and control, desire and pain.

"Good." She ran her hand down to Jeni's and squeezed it. "Come on. I'll show you our setup for making medicine."

"Thanks, Alya." Jeni lingered for a moment

when Hawk turned, spotted them, and lifted his hand to wave.

She waved back, wishing they were back at the rally, hidden away in that little grove of trees. Sex was simple, easy. No matter how emotionally charged it was, in the end, it was about physical intimacy, giving and receiving pleasure.

There was nothing simple or easy about confronting the past.

She'd almost given up on Hawk when the pebble hit the guestroom window.

Jeni slid from beneath the covers and tiptoed across the floor. When she parted the curtains, he grinned up at her, one eyebrow raised in teasing challenge.

God help her, she couldn't resist that smile. She opened the window, wincing when it squeaked loudly, and stuck her head out. "You're late."

"I had to make sure the coast was clear." His grin only got wider. "C'mon, Jeni. Sneak downstairs so I can steal you away."

There was no way she'd say no, and he knew it. She left the window open as she stripped off her nightgown and grabbed the sundress she'd laid out for the next morning.

Carrying her shoes in one hand, she crept down the stairs, careful to avoid the one that creaked. The last thing she needed was to start a chain reaction of crying babies and Hawk's sleepy-eyed relatives spilling out of their bedrooms.

He met her at the front door, holding it open as she slipped through and easing it shut in silence. His fingers brushed her shoulder and slid down as he leaned

cold like this."

Was there anything more delicious than when he unbent enough to tease her? "No, I won't," she whispered back. "You dragged me out of bed, so it's your job to keep me warm."

"I can do that." His kiss was the barest caress, another tease. His lips found her chin next, then her jaw, and traced a slow, lazy path down her throat as he sank to one knee. Silently, he tugged one shoe from her grasp and held it for her.

The night air had nothing to do with the goose bumps on her flesh as she slipped her feet into the flats. "I'm glad you came. I missed you."

"Nothing could keep me away." Hawk caught her hand as he rose and twined their fingers together as thunder rumbled overhead. "Come on. I don't know how much time we have."

It didn't take Jeni long to figure out what he meant. In the middle of their sprint through a field, the sky opened up. Rain pelted them, unexpectedly warm but relentless. Unforgiving.

They were drenched by the time Hawk pushed open the barn door and ushered her into its dry, dark refuge. Squeezing out her braid sent another torrent of water rushing down her arms, and Jeni bit her lip to hold back a laugh. "This is sexy," she said as she turned. "We both look like drowned—"

The words died on her tongue. Hawk didn't look waterlogged or bedraggled or anything else that would have been just and fair. He looked perfect, even with water dripping out of his hair and plastering his shirt to his chest.

His gaze drifted down her body, lingering on all the places where her dress clung to her curves. "I'm not

"But we should get you out of this wet dress anyway. Just to be safe."

His hands burned where he touched her. "You didn't have to lure me out into the rain to get me naked, you know."

"I know." He gathered the fabric at her hips and worked it up slowly. "But I like you like this. A little disheveled."

"Or a lot." She spun out of his grip. "You're distracting me."

"Am I?" He caught her with a low laugh and dragged her against him so tightly that his erection pressed against her lower back. "From what?"

His bold arousal shook her resolve. It would be easy to let it slide, to slip back into the pleasure and discovery they'd enjoyed the night before. But what Hawk wanted—what *she* wanted—was something beyond sex, and this was the only way to make that happen.

She turned and looked up at him. "Why did you have to leave Six?"

Hawk froze. His mouth pressed into a stern line and his brow furrowed, but after a moment he ran his fingers through his wet hair, shoving it back from his forehead. "Let's find some blankets. I don't want you catching a chill."

He led her deeper into the barn, pausing to gather a few blankets tossed over the dividers between stalls. He spread one over a low platform of hay bales and wrapped a second around her shoulders. "Do you want the long story or the short one?"

"Whichever one matters to you."

"The long story, then." He sat and tugged her down beside him. "Remember that farm I pointed out

Remembering the place did what the rain and chilly air couldn't, and Jeni shivered. "Yes."

"When I was...I don't know, nineteen or twenty? There was a drought that year, and Anderson's southern wheat field caught fire. We all had to go out and try to contain it, because it could have swept onto our land. Everyone was out there, men and women and any child old enough to carry a bucket." He sighed. "And that's how I met her. Caroline. Anderson's seventh wife."

It was the last, breathtaking piece of that puzzle. Suddenly, the whole awful story stretched out in front of Jeni like a movie, a thousand possibilities and eventualities playing out in her mind at once. "Oh."

"Oh," he echoed. His lips curved into a wry, tired smile. "It's not unusual, you know. One of my elder brothers fell in love with my youngest stepmother. They never moved past longing looks and hand-holding, but my father found out and ran him off the farm."

Pain wreathed the words, the kind that clenched around the pit of Jeni's stomach and squeezed. "I'm sorry."

He wrapped one hand around hers. "You can probably figure out the rest. Caroline and I went way past hand-holding. Got away with it for almost a year. But when we were caught out..." Hawk trailed off with a shrug. "I tried to get her to run with me, but she was too damn scared. Scared we wouldn't make it, or that it would just make the punishment worse when Anderson finally got his hands on her."

Jeni would have bet all her money that the penalty for adultery—no matter the circumstances—was steep. "What happened to her?"

"I don't know." His voice roughened. "I mean, she's still over there. I see her sometimes, once or twice a

recognize me. They did something terrible to her. And it will always be my fault."

"Why? For the unforgivable sin of falling in love?" Jeni gripped his chin and turned his face to hers. "You lost your home. Do you blame her, or is that one on you, too?"

His tiny smile broke her heart. "For a lot of years, I blamed Alya. I was cruel to her the day he drove me out. I *knew* how that bastard treated her, that he had hurt her and would keep hurting her. But I told her it was her fault, and she believed me."

"Well, I hope you've apologized to her for that. A lot."

"For the last fifteen years, give or take. Doesn't mend what broke." He cupped her cheek, his touch soft. Almost tentative. "Now you know, Jeni. Why I move slow, why I have to be careful. When I'm not, people get hurt. And sometimes *I'm sorry* can't fix it."

There were so many conclusions she could draw from his revelation, so many things that fit—why it mattered to him that she wear his collar, a blatant symbol of ownership. Why every move he made was calibrated, calculated, as if he had to consider every angle before allowing himself to want something at all. Even why he'd been fixated on her involvement with Dallas and Lex, the two people with the power to turn him out of a sector for the second time in his life.

Her heart ached for him, for the things he'd lost and the weight he still carried. She couldn't ease his pain, but there was one thing she could do, one thing she could give him.

Trust.

She took a deep breath, the sound almost lost under the thundering rain on the barn roof. "I want it

The thumb tracing back and forth across her cheek stilled. "The collar?"

"The collar."

"Why?"

So many reasons, but only one that mattered. "Because you trusted me enough to share this with me, even though it made you vulnerable."

He rested his forehead against hers. "I told you, I've been hanging out with Noelle and Jas. Maybe that ink is supposed to mean that she belongs to him, but he's just as much hers. And that's what I want. To be yours as much as you're mine."

Her heart thumped painfully. She'd seen it before, all around the O'Kane compound, but she'd never felt it. Not like this. "I won't hurt you."

"I know." He brushed his lips over hers. "Check my back pocket."

The wet denim clung to his skin. She worked her fingers into his pocket and closed them around warm, supple leather. "Oh."

"I brought it. Just in case."

Jeni pulled it free and studied it. It was simple black leather set with silver and a few glinting green jewels that looked like emeralds. In the center was a beautiful, delicately wrought Celtic tree, just like the one inked on Hawk's chest.

It was gorgeous, and it was too much. "Are these real?" she asked, holding up the collar. "Hawk, I can't."

"Why not?" He took it from her, his large fingers deft as he worked the delicate clasp at the back. "What else am I supposed to spend all that fight night money on?"

"Your family?"

"They get most of it." He paused with the collar

he could wrap it around her throat. "Let me be selfish, just once."

She lifted her braid, and he fastened the leather around her throat. It fit snugly, hugging her skin without being tight enough to constrict. "A perfect fit," she whispered.

He rubbed his thumb over the silver tree. "It *is* selfish, you know."

"Because everyone will know." His shirt was wet enough to be transparent, and Jeni traced the tattoo on his chest the same way he was touching the medallion at her throat. "They'll never have to wonder who this collar belongs to. Who *I* belong to."

"No, they'll never wonder." His gaze finally met hers. "I'm learning to be okay with how badly I want that."

"You think you shouldn't?" She tugged his shirt up. "It's an animal desire, nothing civilized about it. But that doesn't make it wrong."

"So you O'Kanes keep telling me." He lifted his arms so she could strip away his shirt, revealing hard muscles and vivid, elegant lines of ink.

She completely lost her train of thought, but that was okay. All that really mattered was leaning in, her mouth on him, and tracing all those beautiful lines with her tongue.

Hawk hissed in a breath, his head falling back as his eyes closed. But his hands were already moving, finding their way beneath the blankets to tug at her dress. She climbed into his lap as he pulled it up, and she shivered when the wet fabric rasped over her breasts, hardening her nipples to tight, aching points.

He tossed her dress aside and bent his head. He closed his mouth around the tip of her breast, blazing

sucked hard enough to make her hips buck and leave her shuddering above him.

Jeni gripped his hair, his shoulders, anything to *hold on*, but it didn't matter. The storm outside was nothing compared to this one.

"Jeni." He groaned against her skin, his hands sliding down to grip her bare ass. *"Fuck—"*

It was all the warning she got before he rose and laid her down on the blanket spread over the hay bales. Hawk sank to his knees between her legs, running his hands up the insides of her thighs to push them wide. He was on her before she could drag in another breath, that blazing mouth covering her pussy, his tongue thrusting deep.

It should have been too fast, but she was primed for this. For weeks, *months*, she'd lived on some shaky edge where all it took was a word or a glance to coax thwarted arousal into biting, throbbing life. Ever since the first party where Lex had leaned over her, her skin as hot as the breath against her ear, and told her that Hawk was watching her.

Now, with his tongue nudging her clit and his fingers biting into her thighs as thunder crashed outside, it felt like destiny. Fate. Two objects in different orbits drawing closer and closer together until they collided.

He lifted his head, panting, and she felt his fingers on her. Parting her pussy lips, baring her completely to his gaze. He stared at her with such intensity, such possessive satisfaction, that she had to clench her fists in the blanket to keep from squirming away.

Whatever had been chained up in him before, carefully, meticulously contained, had been set free. Like the storm outside, his lust raged, and she was at his mercy.

over her clit. She lifted her hips, chasing the caress, and moaned as pleasure zipped up her spine.

His moan joined hers, low and muffled as he bent his head again. His tongue replaced his thumb, wet and firm, lashing against her without mercy.

Jeni tried to hold back a groan. It slipped out as a whimper, one she muffled with her hand. But Hawk growled against her—an unmistakable, wordless command—and she dropped her hand to the blanket.

Then he touched her again, two fingers gliding over her sensitive flesh. She grabbed his other hand and held on tight as he worked his fingers into her in slow, maddening increments.

More. Jeni tried to form the word, but all that came out was a strangled plea. Hawk must have understood, because he gave it to her—thrusting fingers, the delicious rasp of his tongue, gentle suction that turned rough when he drew her clit between his lips.

He fucked her with his fingers and his mouth, searching for the right rhythm. Jeni helped him, riding his hand and his tongue until the tense heat began to unfurl around the edges and the first threads of bliss snaked through her.

Her shocked cry echoed through the stillness of the barn, louder than the storm outside, but she didn't hold back. She couldn't, not when this was *Hawk* touching her, drinking in her pleasure as it wound tighter and tighter, holding her as the tension shattered into a mind-melting orgasm.

He carried her through it, his touch gentling until she slumped back against the blanket, drained and dazed. His thumbs moved in slow, soothing strokes over her skin, coaxing her back to sanity. "Are you with me?"

wearing pants." Christ, she sounded as dizzy and giddy as she felt. "Unacceptable."

Hawk rose and tugged his belt open with a slow smile. "Are you ready for what happens when I'm not?"

"Nope." She inched back, making room for him on their makeshift bed. "Take 'em off anyway."

He did, kicking off his boots and then stripping off his pants. No more teasing, no more slow seduction. He came over her in a rush, his knees driving her legs wider, his broad shoulders and powerful chest blocking out the world. His cock slid against her, as hard and thick as she remembered, grinding against her clit.

She shuddered and almost jerked away. Instead, she pressed her nails to his shoulders in warning. "Hawk—"

He rocked again, gaze locked on hers. "Tell me."

There was only one word that mattered, more than *yes* or *please* or any of the other things dancing on her tongue. "Yours."

"Yes." He rocked back again, and this time when he returned, the head of his cock pressed against her—*inside* her. He nudged deeper as his lips found hers, then claimed her with one long, relentless thrust. "*Mine.*"

The sheer rush of sensation cut off her breath, and her eyes burned with tears. Not of pain or helplessness, but at the intensity of the moment. She'd had sex before—*lots* of sex, for money and fun and affection and even what she'd thought might be love.

But it had never been like this.

Hawk froze, buried deep inside her, and cupped her cheek. His thumb caught a tear at the corner of her eye. "I got you, Jeni."

"I'm not—" Her voice broke. "I'm good. I'm very,

"You promise?"

They were both trembling with anticipation. Jeni turned her head and licked the inside of his wrist. "I swear."

"I'm glad," he murmured, a heartbeat before his lips found hers again. Soft, sweet, a kiss she could have floated on forever if she hadn't needed so desperately for him to *move*.

And then he did, and it wasn't sweet at all. Hawk braced his weight on his arms and drove into her—*hard*. Pleasure streaked through her like a bolt of lightning arcing down to earth, leaving fire in its wake.

She gripped his hips with her legs and urged him on with her hands on his ass. There was nothing hesitant about the way he touched her now. Nothing careful. For one precious moment, all his deliberations and plans had vanished, leaving her with the one thing she'd wanted from the start.

Hawk, above her, his face tight with pleasure as he fucked her deep enough to curl her toes.

Another thrust scattered her thoughts, and she cried out. No one had ever touched her like this, with single-minded desperation, as if the world could fall around them and it wouldn't matter, as long as he was still inside her.

"Yes." It was a snarl, a *demand*. He shifted his hips and found a new angle, deeper and starker. "Come around me, Jeni. Just like this."

It was too soon, too fast—and it was happening anyway, the kind of blinding, volcanic pleasure that started in her core and rolled outward. She shook with it, shuddered, *screamed* as it broke through her in rough, breathless waves.

"Oh, *fuck*—" His rhythm faltered, and his lips

trembling. His cock throbbed inside her in perfect time with her racing heart, and she clutched him closer, willing the moment to last forever.

But it couldn't. Hawk pushed up on his arms and dragged in a deep breath. "Goddamn."

His hair was drying in odd angles, his eyes were glazed, and his face was flushed. He looked wrecked, and Jeni loved it. Loved that even with all his expectations, she'd managed to surprise him. "Is it my turn to ask if you're all right?"

"Maybe." He rested his forehead against hers with a soft, wry laugh. "I meant to take my time, but I wasn't ready for how good it feels to make you come. Or how fucking *perfect* it is being inside you."

Her breath caught. "Say it again."

"You're perfect." His lips grazed her cheek on their path to her ear, and his low whisper curled through her. "And you're mine."

Outside, the storm raged on. Jeni wrapped her arms around Hawk. "Unless you want to make a mad dash back, I think we're stuck here for the night."

"If we go back, I'm sleeping in the guestroom with you." His laughter was warmer this time. Wicked. "And we'll both be in trouble when you can't be quiet next time."

She ran her hands over his back, memorizing the way his muscles flexed beneath her touch. "Let's stay here instead. We don't have much time."

"Even if we don't get any sleep?"

Especially if they didn't get any sleep. She'd been so nervous about coming to Sector Six, but now it seemed like an escape. Another world away from the constant tension that thrummed in Four, a place where she could stare at the grass and green fields and

But time was slipping through her fingers now, each moment faster than the last, and her only consolation was that she wasn't going back empty-handed. Her work could help them survive this war, and then...

And then.

nessa

Nessa's earliest memories were the rumble of her grandfather's voice and the pungent smell of molasses mash. She could remember the gleam of their lantern off the giant metal vat, and the way his body swayed as he stirred and stirred.

She remembered being so, so proud the day she turned six, and her grandfather trusted her enough to let her measure out the sugar. The huge jars had been almost too heavy for her, but she'd taken her job seriously. She'd held them aloft, one by one, and as her grandfather waited for the molasses to dissolve in the simmering water, he'd quizzed her.

"What are we making now?"

"Rum."

"And what would we make if we had potatoes?"

"Vodka."

On and on, drilling it into her mind, into her blood and bones. She'd learned math in ounces and cups and teaspoons. She'd learned to read by sounding out recipes long-since committed to memory. The distillery had been her schoolroom, liquor her alphabet.

A is for Apple Cider. B is for Bourbon. C is for Corn Whiskey...

That had been their first setup. Back on the ranch in Texas, before Dallas had sent for them. They'd brewed and distilled whatever they could get their hands on, because there was never enough of the right things, never enough of *anything*, but Nessa was the only person she knew who never went to bed hungry. Because booze meant forgetting, and forgetting was gold.

She was thirteen when they arrived in the sectors. Pop had been old then—old when they started out, and even older after the harrowing drive north. Too old to do more than supervise from his chair as Nessa surveyed the sorry state of Dallas O'Kane's newborn business.

That had been in the earliest days, when the warehouse that now hosted fight nights was the one thing Dallas owned. When it had been empty and echoing, filled only with the equipment that Dallas and his earliest followers had been able to scavenge and rig together. They'd been limping along for a few years, churning out rotgut from inferior supplies, just enough to let them afford one shipment of good ingredients.

Molasses. Sugar. Yeast.

The O'Kanes were famous for whiskey, but Nessa knew the truth. Molasses and her grandfather's undeniable skill were the true origin story. Under his direction, she'd prepared their first batch of quality booze, and the credits had swept in like the tide.

bottles. The rum bought the supplies they needed for more efficient distilling equipment, bigger vats, better ingredients.

Rum bought the first supply of grain fine enough to turn out a batch of whiskey that burned in all the right ways. The whiskey had cemented the O'Kane legend, but Nessa still had a weakness for rum.

She had a weakness for the aging room, too. When the loneliness got to be too much, she took the freight elevator down to the basement and savored that first moment of revelation, when the doors slid apart to reveal rack after rack of oak barrels.

Her grandfather's legacy. Her life's work.

Who needed a grand fucking romance when you had a thousand barrels of priceless liquor to keep you warm at night?

The elevator shuddered to a halt, and Nessa held her breath, waiting for the first glorious sight of her empire stretching out before her. Instead, she got a first glorious look at something else entirely.

Jas was standing in the main aisle, pointing toward one of the barrels. And the man next to him...

Oh sweet Jesus, glorious didn't cover it.

Dark brown skin. Beautiful brown eyes. Chiseled features that belonged on a pre-Flare movie star or some artist's masterwork. Even his fucking eyebrows formed a perfect arch that only enhanced all that seething, serious intensity.

He was almost as tall as Jas, but he was *built*. Like Bren, or even Hawk—except Bren and Hawk topped out at jeans and leather in the style department. This stranger was wearing a suit as casually as Jared, one that had been cut to show off his wide shoulders and lean waist.

casually violent warriors the sectors had to offer. Her crush on Jared's sleek sophistication had been the closest thing she'd managed to teenage rebellion.

That crush had been mild. Fleeting. The sudden eruption of butterflies in her stomach and tingles in parts of her that had been sadly neglected was something far, far more serious.

God help her, she *wanted* him. And that was terrifying enough to have her praying the doors slid shut before they noticed her. If life was kind, if it was fair, she'd be back upstairs in a few minutes. She'd tuck herself away in her office until the handsome stranger was gone, and she'd be safe from temptation and this intolerable, aching *yearning*.

But this wasn't a fair life. It was Nessa's life.

Jas turned as the doors began to close. The stranger turned, as well, his gaze clashing with hers, and sudden, flustered panic made her shove her arm out. The elevator door bumped her elbow and slid open again, and there was no helping it. She could stand there gaping like a fool, or she could try to play it cool.

As if *Nessa* and *cool* had ever been within screaming distance of one another.

Still, this was her territory. So she stepped out of the elevator and let her pride of ownership stand in for confidence. "Hey, Jas. Can I help you find something?"

"Nah, I was just showing Ryder around. I'm glad you're here, though." He held out his arm, ushering her closer. "Nessa, this is Ryder, the guy who took over Five. And this is Nessa."

Of course he was. Of *course* he fucking was, because if her hormones were anything, they were reliably self-destructive. Why fall for a nice, boring boy loyal to Sector Four when she could get the hots for a

ous he'd taken over Sector Five from the inside.

Touching him was out of the question. She shoved her hands in her pockets and nodded in greeting. Cool. Collected. Then she opened her mouth, and words fell out. "So you're the drug dude."

He blinked at her. "I make them, yes. So do you, it seems."

"What? Hell, no. I make liquor. Excellent liquor."

He inclined his head. "Of course you do."

Nessa couldn't tell if he was agreeing with her or humoring her, but the spike of temper was exactly what she needed. Pride overrode hormones, and she tilted her head. "I was going to check out some of the seven-year, Jas. If you're showing him around..."

Before Jasper could answer, Ryder folded his hands behind his back. "I'd like to see it."

"Then follow me."

She led them down the aisle and to the left, past hundreds of barrels labeled in her burned-in block letters with the date, the cask number, and her coded notes. Near the back of the room on the last few racks, the handwriting shifted to her grandfather's scrawl, legible only to the people who'd worked with him for years.

As long as these barrels were down here, she'd still have a part of him.

There was a sink against the far wall, next to a tasting table stacked high with glasses. She scooped up the whiskey thief and hauled the stepladder down the row until she found the cask she wanted.

In the old days, there'd been laws about bourbon. Hell, there'd been laws about everything, more and more every year. Her grandfather had sworn they were on the verge of another Prohibition when the Flares

came before sounded more like an old man's rage at a world that had fallen apart.

Pop might not have had much use for most of the old government's laws, but the sanctity of his bourbon was something else altogether. She could still remember the screaming match when he'd insisted Dallas had to find him *new* oak barrels and everything he needed to char them right.

The shit they're paying for now is practically jet fuel. They won't know the fucking difference between new and used barrels. They might not know the difference if you pissed in it.

I'll know. And a decade down the road, you'll be thanking me.

Her grandfather had gotten his barrels. He'd gotten every damn thing he ever asked for—not that it had taken a decade to make good on his promise. There was that, at least. Even though he'd died before her fifteenth birthday, he'd lived long enough to have Dallas thank him for holding the line.

And Nessa had bottled the first batch of straight bourbon without him.

Her eyes stung, and she hurried through drawing the sample and blinked away any hint of tears as she hopped back to the floor. Jas had already upended three glasses, and she watched the liquor as she distributed it between them, all too aware of Ryder's gaze on her.

"What is this?" he asked in that sinful rumble of his.

"Straight bourbon whiskey." The flutters were back, and she fought them with facts. "Sixty-five percent corn. It's been aging seven years now, and I think it's getting close."

"To what?"

offered it to him. "You guys ever get the good stuff over in Five?"

"I wouldn't know." He accepted the glass with a tight smile. "I don't drink very often."

An odd stance for a man who peddled a goddamn glittering rainbow of mind-altering recreational pharmaceuticals alongside his more sedate medical offerings, but Nessa supposed she was just as much a hypocrite.

Except *her* mind-altering recreation tasted better.

She passed a glass to Jasper before raising the final one. "Well, here's to the finer things in life."

Ryder saluted her in return, then tossed his whiskey back like a shot of cheap grain alcohol. His throat worked as he swallowed, and it would have been one of the hottest things she'd ever seen if it hadn't been so infuriating.

Offended on behalf of her liquor and her grandfather, she snatched the glass from his hand and replaced it with her own. "That is *not* how you drink good bourbon. Jesus Christ, did you even *taste* it?"

"*Nessa.*" Jas looked scandalized.

"What?" she shot back. "Where's your fucking pride?" Without waiting for a response, she curled Ryder's hand around the glass. Then, because Jas didn't deserve it if he wasn't going to stand up for her, she plucked his glass from his hand and lifted it to her lips. "Watch. Bring it up like you're going to drink it, but first you smell it. With your lips parted, like this."

She rested the glass against her lower lip and inhaled slowly—and couldn't for the life of her tell what the hell she was smelling. Because Ryder's gaze was fixed on her mouth, and the butterflies were elephant-sized and stomping all over the place.

95

told him, and at least she didn't sound breathless. Yet. "*Sip* it. Let it roll across your tongue. Taste it."

He followed her instructions, his gaze locked with hers as he sipped the whiskey. Then, just when she was ready to break eye contact to save herself, he licked his lower lip. "You're right," he murmured. "I stand corrected."

Oh, she'd correct him. She'd climb that hard body like a tree and lick his lower lip herself, see what else he was willing to let roll across his tongue—

No. No, no, *no.*

Nessa set the glass on the table, untouched. "Good. Enjoy the rest of your tour." She pivoted before they could stop her and disappeared between two aisles of casks, striding away so fast that she could hear the murmur of Jas's voice, but not his words.

She had rules, good ones. No men with brains. No men with power. No men who might find themselves on the opposite side of the O'Kanes for any reason that mattered. And, most especially, no men who made her feel things that might make her forget the reasons she needed those rules.

Nessa had always been the key to Dallas O'Kane's power. She was the heart of his whole empire. And once, at fifteen, she'd almost brought it crashing down because a pretty man had said all the right things to make a lonely girl grieving her dead grandfather feel like someone loved her.

Everyone else got to take big risks in the name of love. She didn't have that luxury.

6

If the rooftop garden was the one place in Sector Four where Hawk felt on the firmest footing, the underground tunnels were the other extreme. Cold, sterile, and lifeless, the cement walls and artificial light were enough to give him a case of claustrophobia—even without the very real possibility that he could take one wrong turn and be lost down here forever.

But the new kid was in his fucking element.

"My grandpa used to do this," Tank told him as he used his boot knife to open a small bag of the cement mix. "Before the Flares. He helped build the factories in Eight."

It was a common story. So many of the people who scrabbled out their lives in the sectors were descended from people who had originally come here with a dream, following the promise of a grand future. A dream of

in the fruits of their labor.

A dream that had died when the lights went out.

Hawk held the mixing tub steady for Tank and watched Bren and Jas fix the frame into place in front of doors leading toward the city. Bren had already used Noah's instructions to disable the control panel next to the door, but a broken door could be fixed with enough patience. Noah himself was proof of that.

The project they were working on today was a lot more permanent. "Are you guys almost ready?"

"Just about." Jasper tested the makeshift wooden wall with the heel of his hand and squinted when it gave just a little. "You sure this'll hold it?"

"The stuff is light." Bren tossed his hammer aside and knelt to check the charged air compressor. "The wood'll hold." He jerked his head toward the large black bag he'd brought. "Don't forget the putty."

"Right." Jas retrieved a block and pinched off a piece, working it between his fingers until it was malleable. "This expandable shit freaks me out."

"Dallas O'Kane's right-hand man?" Tank teased. "Never."

"It should," Bren said flatly. "I saw a guy get pumped full of it once. They were reinforcing the wall over by Three after it was damaged by the firebombs. Poor fucker got impaled by a nozzle—"

Jasper groaned. "Stop."

"—and they didn't shut down the pump fast enough."

Tank grimaced. "Get the fuck out."

"No, really." Bren rose. "The worst part is that this shit takes a minute to expand. Literally—sixty seconds. Longest fucking minute of my life. His too, I guess."

minute dragged out. "I'd take sixty seconds over what happens when you wind up on the wrong side of a tractor. You get on toward the end of harvest, with Eden breathing down your neck and everyone around you hopped up on illegal stimulants, and shit gets ugly, fast. Limbs all mangled, trapped and waiting for someone to find you..."

"And people think running illegal booze in the sectors is dangerous." Jasper held out a clump of the putty. "Patch the other side, Hawk. I want to finish and get the hell out of here."

Hawk took the putty and set about his task. "So if this works, how many of these do we have to do?"

"Seven more," Bren answered. "One for each sector. There are a few main tunnels that we know have collapsed over the years, but Dallas wants the doors sealed anyway. Just in case."

Eight main doors. The hubs connecting the underground network between Eden and the sectors. Hawk hadn't even known they existed before coming to Sector Four, but it sure the hell explained how the military police had been able to appear in Six without warning and disappear just as fast.

Not for much longer, though. Not if Dallas pulled off his crazy plan to bottle the city up so tight it popped.

"Ready?" Bren asked. Tank nodded, and together they closed and sealed the mixing tank. The air compressor hummed idly as Bren slid the slim nozzle into the hole they'd bored through the wall and roughly caulked the edges with more putty.

The compressor firing up reverberated like a shot in the enclosed space, rattling Hawk's bones. The ground trembled beneath his boots, and he slapped a hand against the nearby wall to reassure himself it was

being lost in a labyrinth of tunnels was replaced by the vivid image of being buried beneath the rubble.

Christ, his thoughts were grim.

The mixing tank began to churn, followed by a liquid hiss. The tube running to the nozzle wiggled like a trapped snake, one that could break free and turn on them at any moment.

They were all thinking it, even Bren, whose severe expression was set in even harsher lines than usual. And it wasn't just the uncertainty of this plan or process, either. It was the fact that they needed to do this, block off every one of Eden's possible access routes into the sectors.

It was another reminder that this was *war*.

Bren checked the readouts on the mixer, then cut the compressor. The sudden silence was deafening, and Hawk checked the urge to rub his ears.

"Now what?" Tank asked quietly.

Bren pulled the nozzle from the hole and quickly covered it with the surrounding putty. "Now we wait."

"For?" Even as Jasper spoke, the wooden wall started to creak. As they watched, it bulged slightly, like an overfilled plastic bag. "Oh, that's not good."

But it didn't explode. It stayed like that, bowed but sound, and they all held their breath until Bren looked up from his watch and nodded. "Now."

Tank picked up a crowbar and proved that he deserved his nickname. Massive arms that put even Flash and Zan to shame bulged as he pried at the wood. His face had turned red by the time the first board gave with a snap, and Hawk jumped out of the way, still half-expecting the concrete mix to splatter out.

But the empty space revealed a concrete wall, looking as solid as if it had been there the whole damn

wall, Bren's story took on a new, horrifying light. "Shit."

"Yeah." Jas took the crowbar and swung it at the new wall. It bounced off without so much as chipping it. "Okay, I think we can call that a win."

Bren ran his hands through his hair. "They can break through it, but it'll slow them down long enough for us to have some nasty surprises waiting for them when they do."

Jas shook his head and shouldered the crowbar. "Let's report back. Tell Dallas and Lex it's a go."

There were benefits to not being the new guy anymore. Tank gathered up most of the supplies with a good-natured grumble. Hawk fell in next to Jasper, eager to get the hell above ground. "How'd things go while I was out in Six? Any more trouble on the wall?"

"It's been pretty quiet." Jas slanted a look at him. "Your visit went all right, I guess."

The comment had nothing to do with Shipp's trunk full of flares. Hawk and Jeni had arrived back in Four just in time for a status update meeting, and every eye in the room had gone straight to Jeni's throat.

Even Dallas's raised eyebrow and assessing stare hadn't been able to crush Hawk's savage satisfaction.

Mine.

The whole damn compound would know by the time they got back, and Hawk nearly smiled in spite of the stifling air and claustrophobic walls. "Yeah. I'd say it went pretty good."

"Uh-huh. Can't decide if you move too fast or too slow."

Too fast at the things the O'Kanes were used to taking slow, and too slow at the things they always took fast. "Probably both. But she said yes."

Bren caught up to them with his big black bag

"Jeni," Hawk replied, and that damn smile broke through on a fresh wave of satisfaction. "I offered her a collar, and she said yes."

"Yeah? Congratulations. She's a nice girl."

It was damn close to *sweet*, and slightly surreal, coming from a man who'd been recounting death by expanding cement only a few minutes ago. Then again, Hawk had seen Bren's girlfriend cheerfully break half a man's fingers before tossing him face-first into the street, so maybe Bren didn't have to compartmentalize these things. "Yeah, she is."

"Man, I've been out of the loop over in Three," Bren said. "I didn't even know you two were a thing."

"Oh, you're all caught up." Jasper grinned. "Hawk went zero to sixty on this shit."

Hawk jabbed an elbow into Jasper's arm. "You're the one who told me that's how you show you're serious. I'm fucking serious, okay?"

"No kidding."

Bren stepped between them. "He's busting your balls. Don't listen to him. He did the same goddamn thing with Noelle."

"Oh, *really*?" Hawk laughed. "I always wondered how that went down. I mean, it was big news even out on the farms. Everyone was talking about how Dallas O'Kane had a councilman's daughter dancing in his bar." It had been the moment Hawk had started paying attention, the moment he knew O'Kane had balls of steel and wouldn't hesitate to spit in Eden's eye.

"It was fast," Bren confirmed. "And I say fuck yeah. When it feels right, why wait?"

Right didn't begin to cover the way his heart raced when Jeni sank to her knees, touched him for the first time with her tongue, or rested her cheek on his thigh, come close to covering how it felt to thrust into her, to ride her orgasm while her moans turned to screams.

"Fuck right," Hawk replied. "It's perfect."

Jasper laughed before turning to Bren. "Was I this bad?"

"We all were," he answered solemnly.

"Then I eagerly await my turn," Tank said, his voice strained by the weight of the equipment he carried.

Hawk grinned. It was easier now to joke, to laugh, as if the collar was an O'Kane ritual and now he truly was one of them. "Carry all that shit around the back way so the ladies can admire you, and your chance might come sooner rather than later."

"On it." He hitched his load higher and walked faster.

Hawk had to bite the inside of his cheek to keep from laughing at the younger man's earnest enthusiasm. Hawk had been just as wide-eyed in his earliest days in Four—but he'd also had responsibility weighing him down. Tank was diving headfirst into everything the O'Kanes had to offer, including dancers who appreciated flexing muscles and fight night victories.

Tank disappeared around a corner, and Hawk let his laughter out. "He's gonna run the whole way back, isn't he?"

"Probably." Jasper sobered quickly. "I didn't want to mention it in front of the new guy, but stay sharp, okay? The chance that Eden doesn't have spies in the sectors is slim to none."

"We would have noticed a plant," Bren argued.

"Maybe, but not someone who's been here for a while. Someone they managed to get to." At his friend's startled look, Jas shrugged. "None of the O'Kanes. No vest for a while anyway."

Hawk considered that. "Smart, after what happened to Gideon." The leader of Sector One had come damn close to dying at the hands of a man he'd known most of his life. If there was one thing Eden was good at, it was ruthlessness. Anyone with family in the city could end up facing an impossible choice—turn spy, or watch your loved ones die.

Bren rubbed his jaw. "There's another option, you know. We could leak something, and see if it gets back to the Council. If it does, we start our search."

"Take it to Dallas and Jared," Jas advised. "I don't have the stomach for that shit."

"What about that councilman that Lili was so worried about?" Hawk asked. "Any word from him?"

"Nope. Hell, we don't know who's in charge anymore inside that wall. We're just..." Jasper trailed off.

Waiting. Waiting, even if it drove them all crazy, because every day that passed was a day not only where Eden got a little hungrier, but where Dallas grew a little stronger. They'd finished the hospital and were stockpiling weapons and medicine. The only rational, tactical thing to do was drag this stalemate out as long as they could.

Hawk blew out a rough breath. "Am I the only one ready to climb that fucking wall to get this over with?"

"No." Jasper stopped walking and waited for Hawk to turn. His face was harsh in the artificial light, tense lines and anger. "We could. Count up all the men and women we have ready to go, and we might even outnumber the MPs. But there's one thing we'll *never* get from Eden, and that's a clean fight. Those Council bastards will hide behind a load of little kids if it means saving their own asses. So we wait."

relief tangling in his gut. Waiting might be hell, but it also meant *time*. Time for him to make new lists about Jeni. He'd cataloged her masks, her smiles. Now he wanted to learn every way she laughed, every way she sighed and moaned and begged.

Every way she got off.

Jeni was his bright spot in the darkness, the outlet for all his mounting tension. They could burn it off together, burn through everything until they were too exhausted and sated to worry about tomorrow.

And they could start tonight.

The warehouse was bustling with activity and conversation. Jeni sat around the assembly table, placing full flasks of alcohol into bags before passing them along.

It wasn't the usual packing that went on at O'Kane Liquor, and it wasn't the usual alcohol. This stuff was high-proof, clear and pungent and fresh out of the still. No need for Nessa to age it, because drinking it wasn't a priority. But it would make an excellent antiseptic— and, along with the other medical supplies they'd collected, it could save lives.

Jeni looked across the large square of tables to where Jyoti stood, double-checking the filled bags before setting them aside on a pallet. "How many medics do you and Doc have in training?"

"Fifteen senior medics, as of this week. All of them with some sort of rough training." Jyoti smiled, the pleasure in her dark eyes offsetting her weariness. "And almost seventy nurses. I've had to open a second house for the school."

Sometimes, all they could do was look for a sense

impressive."

"It helps that Rose House trained its initiates in first aid. Some of them have gone straight to advanced training." Jyoti's smile turned wry. "The former Orchids are better at taking men apart. We might need to give them a way to do that, Lex."

"What do you think, Six?" Lex glanced over and arched an eyebrow in challenge. "You up for running some guerrilla warfare training in your new sector?"

"Hell, yeah." Six's grin was downright feral. "Bren's been whipping our new guards into shape. A little competition from girls who can kick their balls halfway to their ears might keep them sharp."

"You should check out the warehouse on Halstead," Scarlet suggested. "My band used to practice there all the time. Good acoustics. Lots of room for ass-kicking, too."

Six passed another bag to Lex. "I can work with this. Hell, we have the women who are always hanging out at fight night, waiting for Dallas to give them a shot. I could bring them over, too."

"Knock yourself out, honey."

"What about you, Jeni?" Jyoti glanced up from the bag she was checking. "Did you find much of what we need in Six?"

"I did. We'll start planting tomorrow." It was the first time anyone had mentioned her trip, and *no one* had breathed a word about the leather fastened around her throat—which could only mean that Lex had warned them off.

A quick glance at the woman in question yielded a sheepish wink, and Jeni sighed. At least this explained why Nessa in particular had been so quiet today.

Jeni tucked a flask into another bag and squared

it?"

Nessa let out an explosive sigh. "Oh thank God, I was actually, *literally* going to die."

"Literally?" Jyoti teased. "Nessa, it's been an hour, if that."

"I know!" Nessa planted one elbow on the table and rested her chin in her hand, her eyes alight with excitement. "Come on, Jeni. Details. *Please.*"

With Nessa, it could have meant anything from *tell me how romantic it all was* to *describe the dick, if you will, using no fewer than four adjectives.* "There's not much to tell," she demurred, her cheeks heating. "Last fight night, Hawk asked me if I'd consider a collar, and—"

"Wait, wait." Nessa raised both eyebrows. "Last fight night, like when you went to climb him for the first time?"

Lex's stare wasn't sheepish now. It was sharp, assessing, and even though she wished she didn't, Jeni knew what she was thinking. She was wondering if Hawk had finally given Jeni what she wanted—but with the collar as a condition.

"I didn't," she said, as much in response to Lex's unspoken question as Nessa's voiced one. "We didn't, I mean. He asked me to go to Six with him, and some things happened. Some things...changed."

"Are you happy?" Jyoti asked softly.

It was all so new that she'd barely had time to consider it. But now the shock of the situation, the *surprise*, had begun to fade, taken over by a sense of something very much like wonder. None of them knew how much time they had, but what *she* had, she could spend with Hawk—getting to know him, all the things beneath what he would share, what he even realized

"Yes," she whispered. "I'm happy."

"Oh man, look at her face." Nessa sighed again. "His dick must be solid fucking gold."

Scarlet elbowed her in the side.

"What! I'm jealous." But she leaned over the table to squeeze Jeni's hand. "I'm glad you got him. We need happy right now. All the happy we can get."

"Yes, we do." Lex stopped working and looked around the table. "Ford and Mia's reports out of Seven aren't good. Things are breaking down, and people are fleeing—mostly to Eight. Gideon sent some of his Riders in to try and restore order, but I think the losses will be considerable."

A hush fell over the room. There were so many ways people could die in the sectors—lack of access to food, clean water, security, basic medical care—and the issues were compounded considerably when you were talking about refugees. Eden's military police force didn't even have to set foot outside the walls for its Council to cause enough chaos to kill people.

Six's jaw tightened. "People coming in off the farms in Seven won't know shit about survival close to the city. They'll be easy prey."

Just like Hawk's family. The thought of Bethany and Luna trying to navigate the dangerous sector streets made Jeni's stomach clench. "There must be something we can do."

"There is," Lex replied evenly. "We can win this fucking war."

Six tapped her nails against the table, her gaze fixed on empty air. "Maybe we can do more. Jyoti, you still need help clearing the roads in Two, right?"

"We need help clearing *everything*."

"We're the same over in Three. And hell, it doesn't

we can pay them..."

"I can feed them," Jyoti replied. "And you can find them someplace to live."

"Probably." Six glanced at Lex. "It's a start, right?"

Lex smiled slowly, her eyes bright. "I think it's perfect."

Jyoti nodded. "It is. We just have to figure out how to get them over here."

"Ha." Nessa waved a hand. "Leave that to Mia. You tell her what you want, she makes it happen. Sector Eight doesn't know what hit it."

Rachel opened another box of wrapped bandages and started stacking them in front of her. "Nessa and I were talking about the herb garden, and I think we have a decent idea of where and how to convert part of the distillery for processing."

"Yeah, it'll be great." Nessa raised her eyebrows at Jeni. "Are you going to take over organizing that part? Dallas says you can keep it all straight in your head."

She'd assumed she'd be gathering the information, then passing on the actual project to someone else. "I don't know. I guess that's up to Dallas."

Nessa snorted. "Do you *want* to?"

The possibility seized her and, for a second, Jeni couldn't breathe. The idea of something that was hers, built from the ground up and nurtured rather than handed off, would fulfill every dream she'd barely dared to have. "Yeah, I do."

"So..." Nessa tilted her head toward Lex.

The moment hovered in the scant space between confusion and awkwardness, and Jeni couldn't blame Nessa. For as long as Jeni had known her, Lex had handled O'Kane business as much as Dallas. But this was different. *Jeni* was different.

109

ended. Some people could turn it on and off, the dominance they brought to the bedroom. Hell, some never took it out of the bedroom in the first place, so it was easy to let it go. Others, like Dallas, figured they owned everyone on some level, so it didn't matter.

Lex might not ever be able to issue another command to Jeni, no matter how far removed from sex the situation was. It wasn't about lingering feelings, but the associations. For some people, control was inextricably entwined with how they expressed it, so simple words that used to come easily to Lex might be lost forever.

Hawk would be the same way.

Jeni touched the medallion at the hollow of her throat. No matter how or why their relationship ended, on terrible or even the very best of terms, there would be no going back. A part of Hawk would always see her with this collar. As *his*.

Before the awkwardness could twist and grow, Lex grinned. "Don't underestimate Dallas, Nessa. You of all people should know that he's probably got the whole thing set up for Jeni already. He just hasn't gotten around to letting her know yet."

"Yeah, that sounds like him." Nessa rolled her eyes and went back to filling the small bottles. "But that's good. It'll be nice to have you there with us. We have fun, don't we, Rae?"

"Sure." Rachel chuckled. "It's extra fun when Ace and Cruz show up to remind me not to lift anything heavy."

Scarlet shook her head. "Poor boys are losing their minds."

Six threw up her hands. "Hey, I keep telling them pregnancy is normal and natural and to leave you the

doesn't want to wrap you up in blankets and lock you somewhere safe."

"He listened to Hawk when he said ginger might help my morning sickness." Rachel peeked over at Jeni. "Maybe more than his dick is pure gold."

This time, the laughter didn't make her cheeks flame. Jeni pasted on her most innocent look, shrugged, and said, "His mouth is pretty magical, too."

And she wouldn't elaborate for the rest of the afternoon—no matter how much Nessa begged.

7

Hawk had tired muscles, an empty stomach, and dripping-wet hair when someone knocked gently on his door.

The hair was easy to fix. He rubbed a towel roughly over his head as he walked to the door, unable to stop the anticipation stealing through him. By the time he reached for the doorknob he didn't give a shit about his aching back or nagging hunger.

Jeni was on the other side of that door. Weeks of planning ended here, in this moment, where months' worth of guilty fantasies had started.

Jeni, in his room. Jeni, in his bed.

Jeni, his.

He hauled the door open, and anticipation melted into slow, lazy satisfaction as she looked him up and down and swallowed hard, her fingers tightening on

After a suspended moment long enough to stretch into delicious tension, she held up the basket. "You missed dinner."

"I did." He took a step back and waved her in. "Dallas had us crawling through the tunnels all day. I needed a shower."

"Mmm." She brushed past him. "And you still look good wet. It's not fair."

Few things in life had ever sounded as good as the soft *click* of the door closing. It was just the two of them now—no teasing friends, no nosy family. He turned and watched her size up his room, suddenly conscious of how stark it must look. Plain, utilitarian furniture crowded one side, while a gun rack and punching bag took up the other.

Not exactly the cozy, luxurious love nest she was probably used to.

She set the basket on the table and waved a hand to indicate the room. "It's bigger than mine."

That was the sole benefit to the new third-floor rooms. The downsides were ugly cement walls, bare lightbulbs, and cramped bathrooms tacked on when they'd hastily started expanding. For the first time, Hawk wished he'd held out for one of the nicer rooms instead of passing it off to newer arrivals. "Yeah. I've been meaning to fix it up a little, but..."

"You've been busy." Her brow furrowed. "Hawk, I don't care what your room looks like. I'm a little shallow, but not *that* bad."

"I don't think you're shallow." He crossed the room and brushed one knuckle over the medallion at her throat. "I just want you to feel comfortable here."

She slipped her hand into his. "Then stop looking at me like you think I might leave."

114

skin. He tugged them up and kissed them. "If you left, I'd find a way to lure you back."

Her pulse thumped a little faster. "Dinner."

The tiny hitch in her breath had him ready to say *fuck dinner* and hoist her onto the table, but the basket was big enough to hold food for both of them, which probably meant she hadn't eaten, either. So he pressed a final kiss to her palm and pulled out a chair. "Have a seat."

Jeni did so, then smothered a laugh when the first thing he retrieved from the basket was a cluster of candles tied up with a red ribbon. "Someone in the kitchen is either very practical or very *impractical*. And a hopeless romantic."

The single sad light hanging from his ceiling already left most of the room in shadow. And since the power required to keep the Broken Circle and the stills running tended to monopolize the generators more nights than not, candles were plenty practical. But after he passed Jeni his lighter and she lit the first few, he adjusted his assessment.

Solar-powered lanterns were practical. Candlelight was magic.

"Maybe we should turn the light off anyway," he murmured, watching her skin take on a golden sheen from the flickering light. "Since the breaker usually pops after dinner."

"Good thinking." She rose, reached for the switch along the far wall—which was usually damn inconvenient but perfect right about now—and flipped it off. "Be straight with me. Tell me what's really churning behind those eyes of yours."

That was the only way it could be now. He'd learned enough from watching the O'Kanes to know

but only if you were willing to say it out loud.

He edged his chair back from the table and held out a hand. "Come here."

Jeni slid onto his lap, her face mere inches from his, shadowed by candlelight. "Talk to me," she whispered.

Hawk settled his hands on the gentle curves of her hips and let out a soft breath. "It's still hard sometimes. These are urges I've fought against my whole damn life. Things I thought were fucked up and wrong, proof that I'm just as twisted as my old man was. I didn't even have words for this stuff before I came here, because you don't talk about this shit on the farms. Hell, I don't know if *anyone* talks about this shit."

"I do," she offered quietly.

"O'Kanes do," he replied just as softly. And, because it was the truth, he closed his eyes. "That first night, up on the bluff... You said *no*. And all I could think about was turning you over my knee and..."

His voice roughened as he remembered the only time he'd seen Lex spank Jeni at a party—right before Jasper warned him to stop *watching* so closely. He could still remember her moans, her squirms, the way her skin had turned so delightfully, hypnotically red.

Her fingers brushed his cheekbone. "And?"

He slid his hands lower, until he could cup her ass. They were just words, words she *wanted* to hear, but they had to fight their way past a lifetime of inhibitions and came out as a growl. "I wanted to spank you until you were so turned on you begged me to get you off."

"Then we need a safe word." Her fingertips trailed down the side of his neck. "A way for me to say *no* or *stop* so you'll understand I mean it, and it's not just part of the fun."

own uncomfortable tangle of guilt and fascination—especially when he imagined the pleasure he could take in watching her pant and writhe, in listening to her pleas for mercy. Mercy he could grant...or withhold.

Twisted, but maybe not wrong. Not if they did it like this, where he could be sure he was giving her exactly what she wanted. "What's the word?"

She paused, licked her lips. "Strawberry."

"Strawberry," he echoed. He tightened his fingers, savored the softness of her flesh under his grip. Fabric still separated them, but it wouldn't soon. Knowing he was so close gave him the patience to ask the questions that mattered, the ones that would make it good. "Tell me how you like it."

"Hard," she answered immediately. "And rough—I like it when it hurts. Does that shock you?"

"Maybe at first," he admitted. "But I've been here a while, Jeni. I see Bren in the cage and Noelle at the parties. I see all the ways people fit together. You like pain. I want to be the one who gives it to you."

"Don't forget this." She ran the tip of one finger between his eyebrows, smoothing the furrow he hadn't even realized was there. "I want this intensity, too. All over me."

He could give her that. He'd give her every goddamn thing she wanted, anything she'd ever dreamed of. But he'd start here, with something a little bit selfish—something he wanted, too. "Then stand up."

She held his gaze as she slipped off his lap and stood in front of him. Simple, sweet obedience.

His heart beat faster. "Take off your clothes."

Her shirt went first, falling away slowly, one button at a time. When it hit the floor, she reached for her jeans, undoing them with the same careful attention,

She stepped free of the denim and her shoes at the same time and kicked both away, then paused in her underwear, as if knowing he'd want a moment to admire her.

There was plenty to admire. The white lace was teasingly innocent but so transparent he could see the darker tips of her nipples through the sheer fabric. A tiny black bow between her breasts matched the one perched beneath her belly button. Her lips curved gently upward as she reveled in his appreciation.

She was beautiful, but he'd had his fill of confining himself to simply looking at her. "All of it, Jeni."

She eased one strap off her shoulder, letting it slink down her arm as she reached back and opened the clasp. The fabric clung to her breasts, and she peeled it away before dropping her hands to her panties.

She stopped there, her thumbs hooked under the satin, and stared at him.

They were back in the woods again, her quiet defiance a crackle of electricity between them. A game, only this time they'd discussed the rules in advance.

This time, he could play it. "Last chance, Jeni. Take them off, or I'll do it for you."

Her breath caught, jagged and loud in the quiet darkness, and she dropped her hands to her sides.

Little lacy panties were probably expensive as fuck in the sectors. That was the only thing that kept him from tangling his fist in the fabric and tearing it from her body. Instead, he caught her around the waist and dragged her to him.

He snapped his legs shut, pinning her between them, and rubbed his thumb across that little black bow. "This is what you wanted that night up on the hill, isn't it?"

ing the tiny flex of muscle every time his thumb moved. "Show me how much you need me. How you'll take it if you have to."

That was what she wanted, to be *taken*, hard and rough. It gave him perverse pleasure to do the opposite, to tease his fingers across her belly and edge her panties down with the softest of touches. "I'll take you when I'm ready."

"Will you?"

A gentle challenge, but he refused to rise to it. He skimmed her underwear lower, until he had to shift his legs to let it fall to the floor. Before she could move, he trapped her again. "You'll see, won't you?"

"I guess so." Her hand drifted up, over his shoulder to his damp hair. "I missed you today."

"Yeah?" Her breasts were temptingly close. All he had to do was lean forward, and his lips grazed one tight point. "Thinking about you got me through it."

"The tunnels?"

"Mmm." He traced his tongue around her nipple, then drew it in his mouth and sucked hard enough to arch her back and elicit a whimper. "There. That's what kept me going."

Jeni bent her head to his. "It had to be more."

He hid his smile against her skin as he trailed his fingers down her back and across her hips. "No, it was mostly the noises you make. The noises I *make* you make."

She laughed softly, her breath stirring his hair. "I like being a little silly with you."

He liked it, too. Not just the laughter, but the *trust*. Nothing left you more vulnerable in the sectors, more utterly exposed, than joy. All your weaknesses on display, your heart naked and begging to be shattered.

of his lips over her wet nipple. "Be silly with me. Be *Jeni* with me."

Her amusement faded as she gazed down at him and touched his face. "I've never been anything else. Not with you."

"I know." He tightened his grip on her hips and eased her back a step. "Sweet, beautiful Jeni. Give me what I want, and I'll give you what you need."

She regarded him for a moment, her eyes burning with anticipation, then nodded quickly—and he knew this was one time she wouldn't fight him, wouldn't make him push.

Instead, she stretched out across his lap. She lifted her bare feet, crossed at the ankles, and braced herself on his leg and the edge of the chair, precariously balanced—but perfectly arranged for whatever wicked things he might care to do to her.

His heart thumping, Hawk smoothed his hand along her spine and down, tickling her legs. She shivered under his touch, so eager for what came next. The power of the moment swelled inside him as he gently repositioned her, tugged her closer, and braced an arm across her back to hold her in place.

She wanted this, *needed* it, and yet she was probably still wondering if he had it in him. If the slow stroke of his fingers or the tenderness as he squeezed her ass meant he couldn't be rough, couldn't be mean in all the ways she wanted him to be.

He was meaner. Mean enough to get off on making her wait for it.

And *that* was an uncomfortable enough thought to prompt action. He caressed her one last time before raising his hand and bringing it down in a gentle slap. Not hard, just enough to sting, but the sound cracked

He repeated it on the other side, savoring the sound and her reaction. "Here's what we're going to do." He rubbed her pale skin, though it held only the slightest hints of pink—so far. "After each time, you can say *harder, please* or *thank you.* Do you understand?"

She squirmed on his lap. "Yes, sir."

Sir. A word for commanders. For leaders. A word that screamed power, and it fell from her lips like a prayer. He was already so fucking turned on that her squirming would be a special sort of torture, but it was nothing compared to how hot it was to bring his hand down again and have her release the breath she was holding on a sharp exhalation.

"Harder," she gasped. "Harder, please."

He tightened his arm around her, holding her more firmly in place, and let his hand fall again. Color rose where he struck her, bright pink that he knew would deepen to red, and he craved it with a guilt she banished every time she begged for him to hit her harder.

She needed it. It couldn't be wrong if she needed it.

Everything outside the flickering circle of candlelight slipped away. There was only Jeni, her body responding to his touch as if he'd been made for this, to hold her tight and hurt her just the way she wanted. His blows came harder and her pleas broke on ragged sobs, but when he slid his hand down to her thighs, they were wet with her arousal, and every time he struck her, she said the same thing.

Harder, please.

The words came farther and farther apart, punctuated by tremors that shook her whole body. Her head fell forward, baring the back of her neck as her hair cascaded down. She was tense but somehow also limp,

"Jeni?" When she only whimpered, Hawk scooped her upright on his lap and snuggled her against his chest. Her head tipped back on his arm, revealing dazed eyes and tear-stained cheeks. "Hey. Look at me, honey."

Her eyelashes fluttered, and she turned her face to his shoulder instead.

"Jeni." He made his voice firmer and caught her chin, tilting her face up. His heart still raced, but more from fear than excitement. "You need to stay with me."

"I can't..." Her voice trailed away as she wiggled, then shivered through a moan. "Your jeans—"

Oh *fuck*. He shot to his feet, cradling her to his chest and cursing himself. Rough denim against spanked skin—it had to chafe like hell. He carried her to the bed and kicked off his jeans before stretching out next to her. "Better?"

"Shh." Her fingertips brushed his lips. "It wasn't bad."

"No," he agreed, smoothing the damp strands of hair back from her forehead. "You were liking it just fine, I could tell. But you worried me, not answering."

"Sometimes I go a little woozy." Jeni trailed her fingers down to his collarbone and scratched him lightly. "It's all right."

He caught her hand and held it against his chest, unable to let go of his concern. If she was too dazed to look at him when he asked, how could he trust that she'd stop him before he took things too far? "Are you still woozy?"

"Yes." She shoved at his shoulders, but not to push him away. When he rolled to his back, she followed, climbing over him with a predatory gleam in her eye.

Woozy, maybe—but not out of it. When her hips

with need and grinding down against his cock, it took everything in him not to flip her over onto her knees and drive into her. To ride her fast and hard while he admired the marks he'd left on her skin.

Soon. When he understood her well enough to know when she'd had enough and when she needed more. For now, he was content to grip her hips to steady her. "You did good, Jeni. So good. You would have taken more for me, wouldn't you?"

"Yes." She rocked her hips until the head of his cock rested perfectly against her pussy, then stopped. She hovered there, one heartbeat away from driving down against him. Waiting.

Waiting for him to decide. To take or deny, reward or punish. The tangible weight of the responsibility pressed in on him. If he wanted her to, she'd balance just like this—thighs burning, body aching, nerves overloaded. She'd do it until she collapsed, because of the piece of leather wrapped around her throat and the promise it represented.

Everyone was right. He'd understood what the collar symbolized, but not what it *meant*. There was knowing what Jeni liked to drink or how her mood impacted her hairstyle, and then there was *this*. Knowing when a whimper meant *too much*, and when it meant *keep going*. When glazed eyes and a trembling body called for gentle handling, and when it called for *more*.

He'd asked for too much, but he wasn't giving it back. He'd learn to be worthy of what she'd given him, even if it meant asking for help.

And he'd learn by watching. He tightened his grip and flexed his hips, watched her face as he pushed up into her.

smiling down at him. "See?" She met his thrust as she leaned over him, so close that her hair spilled across his chest. "It's all right."

It was better than all right. She was hot and tight, and their bodies fit together as if they'd done this a hundred times already. He splayed one hand at the small of her back and guided her in another lazy rock, shuddering almost as hard as she did when his thighs brushed the heated flesh on her ass.

She hissed in a breath and followed him down, grinding against him. "Hawk..."

He gathered her hair with his free hand, wrapped it around his fingers, and urged her to look at him. "I got you," he rumbled, forcing every word past gritted teeth. Her pussy clenched around him, tempting him with selfish oblivion, but he kept his thrusts slow and guided her into each one. "Come on, Jeni."

Thrust after thrust, the sizzling tension built. But instead of speeding her movements, Jeni slowed even more, until all that was left was the flex and sway of their joined bodies as she stared down at him.

Sheer, beautiful agony. He dragged her closer and groaned against her cheek. Her skin tasted of salt, of tears, and he licked his way to her ear before nipping it sharply. "Let me feel it. I want to know how hard you come when you can still feel my handprints on your ass."

She whimpered and buried her face against his neck. Her hands skated up his sides, then beneath him to grip his shoulders as she tilted her hips. It turned the slow grind into something charged and fervent, a fire that blazed out of control a heartbeat later.

She came with a moan she muffled against his skin, the sudden bite of her teeth burning through him.

hot and wet around his cock, and he almost followed her over the edge as swiftly as he had last night in the barn.

Too easy. Pride rioted, and he was moving before he could stop himself. Jeni was still shaking when he spilled her to the bed and flipped her onto her stomach. He barely had to touch her hips—she came up on her knees willingly, desperately, so eager that his hands shook as he dragged her thighs wider and drove deep into her still-clenching pussy.

She cried out with relief and something darker, something almost like anticipation. The cries melted into words as she closed her fists around the blanket—the words he'd demanded of her. "Harder. Please."

The paler skin of her back brightened to red on her ass. The marks of his hand, vivid and raw, and he ran his fingertips lightly over them just to feel her shudder again before he gripped her hips and eased back.

Then he drove into her. *Hard.*

Jeni moaned. She begged, pleaded, but it was her silent reactions that strained Hawk's control. The way her skin flushed, the fine tremor in her thighs that only intensified as he kept fucking her. The way she arched back every time he pulled away, as if she couldn't bear to have a single moment of contact end.

They were the key to the puzzle that was Jeni, everything he needed to learn her. To understand her.

To master her.

She bit her arm as another orgasm swept through her, the sharp bite muting even sharper cries. His rhythm faltered as she tightened around his cock, coming so hard that the clench of her inner muscles turned into the sweetest torture. Pleasure arced down his spine and settled as a knot at the base, a pressure he could barely deny.

Grinding deep, he slipped his hand beneath her to find her clit. She squirmed, gasping, but trying to escape the demanding press of his fingers only rubbed her tender ass against him. "Keep coming," he commanded, increasing the pressure of his circling fingertips. "I don't even have to fuck you, Jeni. I'll get off just like this, feeling your pussy squeeze tight because you can't stop getting off on me."

"Hawk—" Her voice had gone rough, hoarse.

She pulsed around him, hot and irresistible, dragging him down. He clenched his eyes shut and tried to hold back. Just a little longer, just a little—

"Thank you. *Thank you*—" The words dissolved into a shriek. She bucked back, so hard that he had to drive her hips to the bed to hold her in place. The dam inside him burst, flooding him with pleasure so razor-sharp it cut to the bone.

He'd have scars from this, marks no one could ever see and he'd never stop feeling. Because with Jeni trembling beneath him and his head swimming with relief, with *satisfaction* so deep it reached places he'd never even known were there—

There was no going back.

She sank to the bed, exhausted, her tangled hair spread across his pillow. Hawk used the last of his strength to shift his weight before he crushed her. He collapsed on his side next to her and stroked her hair into place before moving his soothing touches down her spine.

Her shaking eased as he caught his breath, but she was still limp beneath his hand. When she shivered, he caught the edge of the blanket and dragged it over her before resettling close enough to watch her back rise and fall with her breaths. "You with me, honey?"

"I'm here." She turned her head, then rolled to face him. "We have so many things to figure out."

More wild strands of hair were stuck to her temple, her cheek. He took his time brushing them away. "Not just about the sex."

"*Mostly* not even about sex." She touched the collar at her throat and smiled. "Practical concerns. Things people usually have figured out before...this."

He tucked the blanket more firmly around her and tried to ignore that it was plain cotton, and that the sheets were as utilitarian as the walls. Not much of a palace he was offering her, but he could make it finer if she gave him a reason to. "You can stay here, if you want. With me."

"You could demand it." Her fingers slowed, lingering on the silver medallion on her collar. "That's what this means."

The truth of the simple reminder settled over him, another layer of responsibility he'd seized without realizing he was asking for it. She'd sleep wherever he told her to, because she'd agreed to be his.

A huge promise for a tiny scrap of leather. "I'd rather not have to."

"I want to be here." Her other hand settled over the tattoo on his chest, the one that matched her medallion. "I do."

"Then stay." He slid his hand over hers and twined their fingers together. "I don't know how long we have before the sectors explode. I don't want to spend any of

She answered by snuggling closer, trapping their joined hands between them. Her head fit neatly under his chin, and he tracked her gentle drift toward sleep by the slowing of her breaths.

Jeni, in his bed. The sectors might explode any day, but tonight, he didn't care.

8

The first order of business with the herb garden was to get the seedlings Alya had given them transplanted into the beds and tiers up on the roof. Once that was finished, Jeni's next job was to get the seeds they'd also been given into containers so they could start them inside the greenhouse.

The second part was really fucking hard, considering she could barely sit down.

Jeni set a fully planted sprouting flat on a shelf inside the greenhouse's protective structure, then slid gingerly back onto her stool at the high worktable. Her bruised ass throbbed in protest at being unceremoniously perched on hard wood for the third time in less than an hour, but she refused to give up.

Part of being an O'Kane was not letting your recreational activities interfere with your duties.

The best thing about Ace was how much he cared about people. The worst thing was how much he cared when you didn't want him to. "Good afternoon to you, too."

Ace made an amused noise. "Good's relative. Rachel woke up starving, ate, puked, and cried because she was still hungry. So Cruz tried to take her over to the hospital in Three, Six yelled at him to stop hassling Rachel and find her some damn food, and Rachel got so upset that Lex kicked us all out."

Jeni hummed her sympathy and pulled out the stool next to hers. For all his complaining, Ace wore an air of smug satisfaction like a second skin these days. It fit him as casually as his faded jeans, his ink, or the long, dark hair spilling across his forehead. It was a part of him, had been since the day he'd first opened his heart to Rachel and Cruz.

He dropped to the stool and studied her, his gaze sharp and knowing. "I'm not gonna let it go."

"I figured as much." Jeni pushed away the bucket of soil and turned to him. "Go ahead."

Ace tilted his head. "You gonna get snarly if I ask to see how bad it is?"

Christ, things really were dire—he wasn't even flirting with her. "Relax. It's no worse than some of your handiwork."

"Not exactly the same, darling. *I* know what I'm doing."

There was no quick retort to that, no snappy rejoinder. The truth of his words was a constant weight on Jeni's shoulders—not because Hawk was new to the delicate dance of dominance and submission, or to the even more delicate interplay between sadism and masochism. But because she'd known he was new...and

It was reckless. No, it was something beyond reckless. It wasn't *safe*, to put herself completely in the hands of someone who didn't know how to handle that responsibility. It wasn't a failing of his, just reality. He didn't know better, but she did.

Hawk would never hurt her, not on purpose. But it was tragically easy to go too far without even realizing it.

"We're being careful," she said finally. "Going slow until he gets his bearings."

"Good," Ace drawled. "Because if he fucks up, which one of us is gonna stop Cruz from taking him out back and breaking a bunch of his bones? Or maybe we should just let him, because that'll be slap on the wrist compared to Dallas and Lex coming down on him."

The mental image of that beatdown came all too readily, and Jeni scrubbed her forearm over her eyes to banish it. "No one's more worried about Hawk fucking up than Hawk, okay?"

Ace sighed and tossed an arm around her shoulders. "I know, Jeni. Christ, if I wasn't sure that was true, *I'd* be beating his ass down. That's why you gotta do this shit right."

"So what do you suggest?"

"I suggest thinking like an O'Kane."

Which meant asking for help. "Ace, darling? You may have forgotten—what with your blinding, happily-ever-after kind of threesome—but I've fucked most of the people Hawk could talk to about this. That could get awkward."

"Maybe." Ace kissed her temple. "Or maybe you're underestimating him. Six isn't a fan of anyone getting their hands near Bren, but she wasn't going to learn how to give him what he likes spontaneously. Besides,

some of these tightly wound motherfuckers. Trust me."

He loved to brag about how much Cruz had loosened up. "Uh-huh. You still owe me for that one, by the way."

"I know. And trust me, cowgirl, if Rachel wasn't puking and Cruz wasn't ready to stab anyone who gets too close to her, she would have already invited you both over for dinner and some light flogging."

But she was, and he was, so that left them out. And Dallas and Lex weren't even an option. "Jas and Noelle?"

"Now *that* has potential." Ace tilted her face up. "And if it doesn't work out and you need me, it doesn't have to be a party. I can be there for you like I was there for Bren and Six. To show him how it works, and to make sure you're *both* safe. Rachel and Cruz understand."

"Thanks, Ace." She hesitated, then forged ahead. "I know I probably shouldn't have taken the collar. But things are so crazy now, and Hawk..." Her voice failed her. She swallowed hard and tried again. "It just felt like the right thing to do."

"Hey, hey now." Ace slid off the stool and tugged her into his arms. His hand smoothed over her back. "I know, Jeni. I know. The world's fucking upside down. But we're gonna put it right again, because that's what Dallas does. And I want you to come out the other side whole and happy. That's all."

"I will." She *would*. Somehow.

Hawk had been braced for a private summons from the leaders of Four from the moment he'd rolled back into the sector with Jeni wearing his collar.

covered with maps of Sector Six, he knew this meeting was something else.

Something worse.

Dallas nodded, acknowledging his realization, then pointed at the chair next to Lex. "No one wants to have this talk, but it's too important *not* to have."

Hawk sank into the chair and studied the map. He'd helped Ace with the details, penciling in the individual farms and distances based on a decade of driving between them to deliver smuggled goods and stimulants. They sprawled out to the west of the city, following the line of the reservoir and the river beyond. Miles and miles, creeping out more every year as Eden's demands heightened and eldest sons drove past the borders of the farthest farms to try and reclaim more of the desert. To squeeze a living from the land as much as to satisfy Eden's hunger for *too much*.

"I talked to Shipp." Hawk traced his finger over the cluster of buildings that represented his family's farm. "They're used to keeping in touch with the other farms via radio, but he knows the first thing Eden will do is take out the towers."

"We were ready to offer them tech," Lex murmured, "but I'm guessing they found a better early-warning system all on their own."

"Rocket flares," Hawk confirmed. "They go up loud, burn bright, and drift down on little parachutes. Everyone who sees them will fire their own, which should spread the message fast."

Lex leaned forward. "Will they be able to do it?"

And there it was, the crux of the issue. No more evasion, no more pretending they were talking about a fight to defend the land or a simple, orderly retreat.

They were talking about burning his home sector

Hawk leaned across the table and picked up a marker. "Shipp will get it done," he said, circling their farm in red ink. Old man Anderson was hit-or-miss, but once Alya's fields went up in flames, it would be impossible to stop the spread. He skipped over that one and circled all the farms he knew Shipp could sway, the men who had been angry enough to put down their tools and face starvation if Eden kept taking everything from them.

When he was finished, twenty-nine circles covered the piece of paper, scattered from the border with Seven all the way down to the edge of Five, from the farms closest to the wall out to the very edge of the territory. "Some of the others might, but these are the ones I'm sure of. Just over half."

Dallas studied the map before tracing his finger over one of the blank spaces between circles. "Will it spread?"

It probably would have on its own, but Shipp wasn't taking any chances. "They're distributing accelerant with the flares. It'll burn fast and hard, and Eden isn't equipped to stop it."

Lex studied him, then sighed. "Are you all right?"

He couldn't answer her question without thinking about what those red circles really meant, and that hurt too fucking much. The practicalities of war were easier. "If Jyoti has the communes and illegal farms under control, this is the only option. We don't need Six, but Eden does."

"Hawk."

He ignored her and stared at Dallas. "Does my family have a place here?"

"Yes," Dallas said without hesitation. "Finn's already organizing the new recruits to expand your

"Then I'm all right."

Dallas leaned back in his chair, one eyebrow raised. "That's nice, but I'm not the one who asked."

Hawk didn't want to look at Lex. Dallas was casually ruthless, cold enough to keep this safely impersonal. Lex's ruthlessness ran hot, her passion so tied up in protection that she seemed a hundred times more dangerous.

And she reminded him of his mother. "It's gonna break her, Lex. Shipp's gonna have to torch the place and drag Alya away and it's gonna break her fucking heart."

"Yeah." She reached across the map and touched his hand. "I know what it's like to make something out of nothing, Hawk. And I would never, *ever* ask someone to tear down what they'd built with their own fucking hands unless I was willing to do it myself."

"I know." He exhaled and finally met her eyes. "It's been coming. I've known it for years. I'm all right because you guys made a place for them. That's all you can ask for in the middle of a damn war."

"We all know what's at stake here," she agreed. "If we win, Alya can rebuild. And if we lose, none of it will matter. So we're going to win."

When she said it like that, matter-of-fact and confident, it was impossible not to agree. "Yeah, we are. Tell me what I have to do to help."

Lex rose. "What we need most right now is information. Noah can get anything we want from Eden, but it could be a one-shot deal. We need to keep that ace tucked up our sleeve for now. Which means doing this the hard way. Human intelligence."

"Eyes open. Ears open." Dallas rolled up the map. "Gideon's helping Jyoti maintain a presence in Two, in Three. We'll be spread thin until the new recruits are ready to fly solo."

A month ago, Hawk would have nodded and taken his leave, content to be an obedient foot soldier with his eyes on the distant prize. But that map and its vivid red circles made the future seem a lot more immediate, the stakes impossibly high.

And he could be more than just another foot soldier. "Can I make a suggestion?"

Dallas raised an eyebrow. "Sure."

"I haven't had time to make a full round of all the roof gardens since the wall went hot. I got to know the people in all those buildings while we were setting up. I fixed a few leaky faucets, patched some broken furniture." He shrugged. "I helped out where I could, and they talked to me. They'd probably keep talking if I came back around."

Lex eyed him before shrugging. "It's worth a shot. We have a few other things in motion already, but we need everything we can get, Hawk. *Everything*, no matter how silly or inconsequential it might turn out to be."

"Hell, it might be good for morale." Dallas shoved his chair back and gathered the maps. "If we're still worried about growing food, that means we think we'll be around in a few months to eat it. I need every goddamn person in this sector to believe that. So go convince them."

No big challenge, just fight back the swell of desperation devouring the sector. But oddly, Hawk felt encouraged. If life in the sectors taught you anything, it was how to get back up every time you'd been kicked down. How to dig in hard, stubborn even in the face of the impossible.

she'd sweep it clean and rebuild. Sector Four would do the same—but they'd all fight easier with a little hope in their lives.

And Hawk could give them that.

ashwin

By the ninth anniversary of his birth, Ashwin had learned the fundamental truth of humanity: people are irrational.

Irrational behavior in and of itself wasn't the problem, though. Even the DNA modification they'd performed on Ashwin before his birth couldn't erase all his emotions. That would have been counterproductive. Too much of what made a soldier elite was rooted in instinct, and instinct was nothing more than evolution's slow honing of the basest human emotions—fear, mistrust.

Rage.

Ashwin had been angry when anger served no practical purpose. He'd felt the sharp prickle of fear urging him to alter course, to fall back and protect himself from pain. He'd been trained to recognize those

nothing more. Most of the time, he considered them, processed them, and proceeded on a logical course.

Sometimes he didn't. Sometimes Ashwin was irrational. But the difference between him and the people around him was that Ashwin never lied to himself about it.

Breaking into the clinic on the Base was irrational. He numbered the reasons to himself as he overrode the electronic lock and slipped inside, the layout so familiar he barely had to look around him.

Three reasons this was a bad idea. One reason it bordered on madness.

And one reason to do it anyway.

He heard the unmistakable sound of a pistol's safety being disengaged in the darkness, followed by a long-suffering sigh.

Ashwin supposed there had been a time—a time before training and harsh conditioning—when he'd felt fear the way everyone else did. A shiver up the spine, a clench in his gut. Now, it was almost a taste, bitter and sharp. Unwelcome.

But not unwarranted. The man behind him was the closest thing Ashwin had to a friend—and Samson wouldn't hesitate to put a bullet in his skull.

Ashwin turned slowly, raising both hands as he moved. Palms open, forward. An almost universal sign of surrender—and a good position from which to launch an attack, if Samson hadn't been smart enough to stand out of reach. "You're not on guard duty tonight."

"What can I say? I had a feeling. Lights." The bulbs in their recessed fixtures obeyed the command immediately, flooding the room with a harsh glare that drove away the darkness. The light glinted off Samson's sandy hair, as well as the polished nickel of the

Ashwin."

"I'm not forbidden." Which was simple fact. His bar codes provided access to every exterior door on the Base, and his retinal scan and fingerprints could get him into plenty of classified areas. But scans left a record, and Ashwin couldn't afford that.

That was one reason this was a bad idea.

"There's a hell of a wide stretch between *not forbidden* and *supposed to be here*." Samson flicked the safety back on, holstered his gun, and sighed again. "If this is official business, spit it out."

Spit it out. So casual. Samson had always been like this, even when they were young. On the rare occasions they'd been allowed free time to mingle with the other children on the Base, the unmodified recruits had avoided Ashwin, dissolving any game or contest he tried to join, abandoning any table when he sat down. He couldn't mimic their slang or their informal speech, and the comfortable rhythms of their banter eluded him.

But Samson could make himself one of them. No, not just one of them—their king. The other young soldiers had flocked to him, shown off for him, done anything it took to win his regard and respect. And they'd been fools, assuming that Samson must be different from the rest of the Makhai trainees simply because he could smile and joke.

That was how Samson trapped you. He put away his obvious weapons and acted like you were old friends, and you never saw the death blow coming. The only reason Ashwin hadn't closed in to attack was the fact that they *were* old friends. Ashwin didn't want to kill him. But he'd have to, if he couldn't talk Samson around.

couldn't, the truth was a calculated but necessary risk. "It's not business. I'm trying to recalibrate."

"On your own?" Samson asked skeptically.

"I can't afford to be taken out of the field right now." Not now that the O'Kanes had locked down the tunnels. Eden had lost any hope of resupply, no matter how minor. The councilmen would be looking at the food in their increasingly sparse pantries—and plotting action.

"And how exactly do you plan to *recalibrate* yourself?"

Distaste flavored the word. Ashwin couldn't blame him. Recalibration was merely a polite word for carefully regimented torture.

Moving slowly, he unsnapped one of the pockets on the leg of his pants and withdrew a glass bottle and a syringe. "I need to disrupt an obsessive thought pattern."

Samson stared down at the vial in Ashwin's hand, not bothering to hide his horror. "You can't be serious."

Ashwin ran his thumb over the label on the bottle. Not the worst drug available on the Base, but it would go in like acid and get worse. He'd feel like his blood was boiling free of his veins, eating its way through his organs. Men injected with it had betrayed brothers, lovers—even their own children.

If he remembered that kind of pain every time he thought of Kora, maybe he wouldn't tear the sectors apart trying to put his hands on her. "I'm serious."

"Well, then you *need* to be yanked out of the field, because you've lost your fucking mind." Samson stepped closer. "There's a reason they only use that shit with telemetry and a dozen goddamn doctors clustered around. It kills people."

He'd have the psych team. And they'd drag the truth about Kora out of him, because those doctors were nothing if not efficient. Even if he managed to hold back the secret of what she was, they'd know that she *mattered*. They'd see another chance to experiment with a Makhai soldier in the throes of a fixation.

They'd find her and use her against him. In his worst nightmares, they found her and *gave her* to him. They wouldn't care if he ravaged her, if she was unwilling or terrified. If he hurt her.

Ashwin was an expensive, malfunctioning asset. Kora's fear and pain would be an acceptable price if she provided a solution.

"I can't," he forced out. "There's too much at stake."

Samson's eyes narrowed. "Is this about her?"

His friend's hands were still relaxed, but close to his weapon. If this went wrong, Ashwin would have to move fast. "Yes."

The word erased the last of Samson's easy demeanor. "Are you the reason she's missing?"

"No." That was the truth—Kora had abandoned her home and her life on her own. "And I don't know where she is."

Samson stared at him for several long moments, his gaze searching and sharp. Finally, he nodded, then gestured to the items in Ashwin's hand. "If you're determined to do this, you will. But I can't let you do it alone."

Gratitude was an alien sensation. Few things in his life had mattered enough to provoke it. But when he handed the drugs and syringe to Samson, it spilled through him, the sweetness of relief mixed with the sharp tartness of dependency.

He didn't like needing other people.

third door on the right. The exam room was clean and sterile, identical on the surface to the others and the ones in the city. But this was the one they always sent Makhai soldiers to.

There was a panic button near the door, another on the edge of the counter, and a third under the cabinet where a retinal scan allowed access to the strongest sedatives on the Base. Ashwin had once had a nurse apologize to him for their prominence, as if hiding them would be preferable. As if the Makhai soldiers wouldn't still know they were there.

As if they had the kinds of feelings that could be wounded.

Ashwin rolled up his sleeve and slid onto the exam table. If he closed his eyes, he'd see her against the backs of his eyelids. Blonde hair swept up into a messy ponytail. Her lab coat clean and so *white*, the kind of white that didn't last in the sectors unless you were rich enough to pay for expensive soap.

She'd sutured lacerations and administered tests and removed bullets from Ashwin's body in this room. She'd run her gloved hands over him, searching for bruised ribs and broken bones and internal injuries, oblivious to the effort it took for him not to lean in, bury his face against her neck, and inhale.

She'd teased him. She'd told him jokes, bizarre, inexplicable ones that sent him to the Base's reference library to puzzle out the logic behind them. He'd spent three solid weeks researching knock-knock jokes after she'd tried to tell him one, just in case she did it again.

Every part of this room sparked memories. A hundred times she'd put him back together. A hundred times she'd stirred something in him—not something safe like interest or affection or the chemical lie

Base hadn't dared dig out, the primal survival instincts they'd dialed up so, so high.

Ashwin thrust out his arm, closed his eyes, and let the memories flood him. Kora seeped into his cells, filled him with the driving urge to tear through the wall and find her, claim her, *keep* her—

It swelled until it was all he could feel, until the edge of the metal exam table bent under the grip of his free hand. "Do it."

"Ashwin..."

"*Now.*"

Fire flooded his veins. Torment chased after it. His back spasmed, and he ground his teeth together, because he couldn't scream, he couldn't get caught—

Kora, touching a bruise on his chest, her brow furrowed.

Acid in his blood.

Kora, her expression serious as she violated protocol and used med-gel to ease his pain, because she couldn't stand to see him hurting.

The acid burned through his veins. Ate away at his flesh.

Kora.

Pain.

Kora.

Agony.

It went on and on until he couldn't separate the two, until his internal organs felt vaporized and his bones felt crushed into pebbles. Kora and pain and Kora and pain—

Ashwin pushed his thoughts of her away and let the fire consume him.

9

Hawk looked at the limo idling in the alley behind the Broken Circle and then down at his clothes. He'd donned his best pair of jeans—dark denim with no rips—and had tucked in his black T-shirt. His boots were mostly clean, his belt buckle was shiny, and his leather jacket had only a few scuffs.

He'd felt damn dressed up until Jeni appeared in a white gown with a plunging neckline and a slit up the side that revealed her entire right leg with every step. And now there was a fucking *limousine* pulled up next to the bar, and he honest to God hadn't even known they existed outside of the city. "You said we were meeting your friend for dinner."

She draped her sheer wrap over one arm. "We are."

"Doesn't she live about six blocks away?"

with four-inch heels. "You gonna make me walk it in these?"

The shoes were impractical as fuck, barely more than sandals balanced on tiny little spike heels. But the leather straps that crisscrossed her skin and looped around her ankles were so hot that he could think of a few things he'd like to see her doing in them.

Walking didn't rate high on the list, though.

He reached for the door, but the driver beat him to it, pulling it wide in silence. Jeni slipped into the car as if being chauffeured by stone-faced men in suits was nothing unusual, leaving Hawk to follow her awkwardly.

Inside were two bench seats facing each other, with plenty of room to stretch out his legs and a little divider between the back and the front that offered at least the illusion of privacy. He was probably the first person to park a denim-clad ass on the pristine leather seats since before the Flares. "How long have you known Gia?"

Jeni crossed her legs, leaving them both bare nearly to the hip. "Almost eight years. I met her fairly soon after I left the city."

The bared skin was entrancing, but not as much as the peek at her past. Plenty of people in the sectors had pasts so ugly that asking about them was danger-ous, especially people from Eden. Hawk slid his hand onto her knee and stroked his thumb over her skin. "How did you come to leave?"

"I just...walked out." She wrinkled her nose at him. "Does that sound ridiculous? I wasn't in trouble. Didn't get kicked out. But I didn't like who I was turn-ing into, so I split."

It sounded a lot of things—decent, honest,

into?"

"My mother," she said softly. "You could call her a professional husband-hunter, I guess. Always on the lookout for an upgrade." She brushed her hair behind her ear and sighed. "It worked for her, but I decided that if I was going to whore myself, I was at least going to be real about it."

"Seems like your way would be easier," he murmured. "A job to pay the bills instead of a life you're stuck living."

"I've been a lot of things, but never trapped." Jeni laced her fingers together with his. "I'm glad you understand that. I wasn't sure you did at first."

He squeezed her hand. "You mean because of your job?"

"Because of the assumptions people have made about it." Her eyes met his. "They thought I'd only be selling my body if I was desperate or abused or brainwashed. That I needed to be rescued from my horrible fate. It was so fucking backwards. They could come to me for sex, guilt free, but there had to be something wrong with *me* for being willing to provide it? Fuck that."

He'd been through all the sectors over his years with Shipp. He'd been to Three, where if the pimps didn't stab you, the dancers would. He'd been to Eight, where they managed prostitution with the same orderly, businesslike efficiency as any of their factories. He'd seen the drug dealers in Five with their drugged-up mistresses, and he'd seen the elegant, delicate flowers of Sector Two, whose gilded cages came equipped with impenetrable locks.

People bought and sold sex in a million different ways, but it always seemed to come with baggage.

149

at themselves for needing something so basic, hate directed at the men and women who provided it for a fee.

Maybe it was the only thing Six and Seven had gotten half right. Compared to the dawn-to-dusk manual labor on remote farms, life in the brothels that lined the edge of the warehouse district was downright posh. The farmers had good reason to support and protect the people willing to barter for sex. It kept their unmarried sons satisfied—and away from all their nubile young stepmothers.

"It's different in Sector Six." He felt a wry smile tug at his lips. "You don't rescue girls from the brothels there. Hell, women run *away* from the farms to try and get jobs in them."

"Based on what you told me about most of the farms? I'm not remotely surprised."

"One girl told me she was gonna be on her back either way, but at least she got paid for whoring and didn't have to have kids unless she wanted them."

"Not always an easy life," Jeni agreed, "but better than some."

She looked so serious that he cupped her cheek. "I want to protect you, not save you. As for the rest... I have some jealousy in me, Jeni. I've got a lot of things that aren't so civilized going on. But—"

"No one else is you." She laid her hand on his thigh and leaned in until she was almost close enough to kiss. "And you're the one I want. Remember that."

Oh, those words felt good. So good that he dropped his hand back to her bare leg and stroked his fingers up the inside of her thigh. "You didn't let me finish. I was gonna say jealousy can't cut so deep when you stop fighting all those uncivilized things and embrace

"That's all you have to do?" she whispered. "Just let go?"

He rubbed his thumb in a slow circle. Just a little higher and he'd be touching her pussy—and possibly defiling the back of Gia's limo.

Probably not the first time it had happened.

He brushed his lips over hers and smiled. "Knowing you're mine helps."

Her lips parted—and so did her legs. "Hawk..."

The car coasted to a stop. The driver's door creaked open. Jeni didn't jerk away, so Hawk stayed right where he was, sliding his thumb back and forth as her lips trembled against his.

The door next to him opened, and Jeni smiled. "Come on." The words feathered over his mouth. "I bet Gia's dying to meet you."

At this point, he was pretty fucking curious about her, too.

Hawk eased away from Jeni and slid from the car. The driver was holding the door but staring straight ahead, as quietly functional as a piece of furniture. Hawk reached out to help Jeni from the car, then let her draw him toward the ornate front door of the sprawling brick building.

The man who opened the door was *huge*, bigger than any of the O'Kanes, and dressed in a fucking tuxedo, of all things. He bowed his head wordlessly and ushered them into—

Actually, Hawk didn't know what to call the room they were waved into. It didn't seem to have any purpose short of giving new guests a place to stand while they gawked. And there was plenty to gawk at. The stone floors were covered with thick, woven rugs. A goddamn chandelier hung above his head, the glittering

tricity, considering the current power crisis.

A staircase curved toward a balcony that lined the second floor. Gilded mirrors sparkled on the walls next to art that looked fucking expensive, and the spaces in between doors held potted plants and vases on carved wooden stands.

Hawk was pretty sure his mouth was hanging open.

"Jeni, darling." A tall, gorgeous brunette who *had* to be Gia stepped through one of the doors, pausing as if she knew that the carved doorway framed her like another piece of art. Her crimson skirt was slit just as high as Jeni's, but the top of her dress was a leather corset that looked more like armor, and even in heels damn near as tall as Jeni's, somehow she managed to cross the room in a swaying prowl.

She stopped in front of Jeni and reached up to stroke the leather wrapped around her throat. Her fingertips lingered over the silver tree, and Hawk felt a swell of entirely uncivilized satisfaction as Gia stroked the symbol that made Jeni *his*.

"So it's true," Gia murmured. "Congratulations, love."

"It's true." Jeni framed her friend's face with both hands as a brilliant smile curved her lips. "It's good to see you."

"You too, sweetheart. We've missed you." Gia brushed a quick kiss to Jeni's lips before turning to study Hawk. Her gaze started with his face and drifted down with a level of casual, shameless appraisal that brought heat to Hawk's cheeks. When her gaze slid back up, she noticed—and laughed. "Oh, bless you, Jeni. He blushes."

She sounded so delighted, Hawk resolved himself

out of his depth here, but Jeni seemed right at home—and that gave him an opportunity to see a new side of her.

Jeni, casually glamorous. Maybe even Jeni as she'd been before she left Eden.

Gia was still watching him like she was waiting for him to melt into the floor from embarrassment. He summoned a challenging stare instead—maybe not Bren at his most intimidating, but at least Jasper on a good day. "I only blush when people are staring at me like I'm for dinner."

Gia's perfectly arched eyebrows went up. "You should warn him not to tempt me."

"He can handle you." Jeni dropped one hand to the small of his back, stroking lightly through his shirt. "Hawk, this is Gia. She grew up with Ace and Jared, so she had to get scrappy."

Hawk didn't know what the proper greeting was when you were meeting someone who had diamonds dripping from her ears. Thrusting out his hand seemed like the safest bet. "Nice to meet you, Gia."

She clasped his hand, and even though she had smooth skin and slender fingers, her grip was hard enough to feel like a test—or a challenge. "Welcome to my home."

Oh, there were layers to this one. The word *my* rolled off her tongue like it was her favorite word in the whole goddamn language. She'd met him covered with jewels and a dress that may as well have been a weapon. This was her territory, the place where she ruled as undisputed queen...

And Jeni had once been one of the subjects kneeling at her feet.

Hawk tightened his grip just a little, to see what

and she glanced at Jeni. "I think you've found a diamond in the rough, darling."

"*My* diamond," Jeni emphasized with rueful amusement. "Are we having dinner on the terrace tonight?"

"I thought one of the upstairs alcoves might be cozier." Gia tilted her head toward the stairs. Hawk released her and settled his hand at the small of Jeni's back, ignoring the way Gia smiled at the gesture before turning to lead them upstairs. "Dinner should be ready. The cook made all your favorites."

Her heels clicked on the hardwood as she started up. "She didn't."

"Mmm. She must have bribed someone to get salmon on such short notice." Gia laughed softly. "She wouldn't even give me the full menu, so I expect she bribed a *lot* of someones."

The *cozier* room Gia had mentioned turned out to be almost as big as the warehouse where the O'Kanes held their fight nights. Another chandelier graced the high ceiling, shining down on the couches and circular ottomans scattered throughout the room, along with a huge, polished piano that gleamed in the glittering light.

Two walls were lined with mirrors, creating the impression that the room went on forever. The other two walls were inset with alcoves, all with the curtains drawn back. Some held tables or seating arrangements, and others had only plush cushions and pillows scattered on their carpeted floors.

All the leather and crystal and art in the world couldn't hide the fact that it was a party room, just like the one Dallas presided over from a sagging leather couch. A room where *party* meant debauchery of the

Gia led them to one of the alcoves with a sleek black leather booth that curved in a half circle around a table sporting candles, wineglasses, and three elaborate place settings.

Jeni slid onto the leather and moved over, then patted the seat beside her. "It's not as sinful as it looks." she murmured. "It's just easier to have a conversation here than at the monstrous table that seats forty-eight."

It was intimate, though. The angle hid the back of the booth from the rest of the room unless you were right in front of it, and a flick of the wrist could swing the curtain into place and remove even that visibility. And the shadows were deep enough that Gia wouldn't see him slip his hand under the table to squeeze Jeni's knee lightly. "Nothing wrong with sinful, though."

She smiled and unfolded her napkin into her lap, lingering to brush his hand.

Gia sat across from Hawk and reached for the bottle of wine chilling in a bucket in the middle of the table. "I hope you don't mind that I had them keep things simple tonight, Hawk. I wanted a chance to talk without servers coming in and out endlessly, but that means a simple affair. We'll have to do for ourselves."

He'd wager money that his idea of simple and hers weren't even within shouting distance of one another. "I grew up on a farm in Sector Six. Doing for myself is pretty much the status quo."

"A farm boy. Good Lord." Gia filled Jeni's glass. "Now I think you and Ace are just competing to ruin my life."

Jeni raised one eyebrow. "Don't tell me you've run through all the pretty, wide-eyed boys in the sector already."

Gia leaned across the table to pour wine into the glass in front of Hawk. "What do you think?"

None of his coping strategies for dealing with the O'Kane women were going to work on Gia. She wasn't a pestering younger sister or a friend. She was a wolf, sizing him up to see if he was a respected adversary or prey.

Not so different from how most of the men in the gang had treated him during those first weeks. So he told her the same thing he would have told Ace. "I'm just glad you think I'm pretty."

"She's teasing you." Jeni leaned over and kissed his jaw. "It's Gia's specialty."

"And he's putting up with it," Gia replied with a smile. "You'll do, Hawk. You'll do just fine."

Something sparked in her eyes, a fire that went beyond casual interest. And Hawk realized that Gia wasn't a wolf stalking her prey. She was a guard dog with one sweet, helpless little lamb. If he didn't prove to her tonight that he could take care of Jeni, she'd be even fiercer than Lex and Dallas. She wouldn't have bonds of brotherhood and ink holding her back. She'd come for him and tear him to pieces.

Which could make her the greatest threat to his fragile new relationship—or his greatest ally. Because she clearly knew Jeni better than he did, maybe better than anyone. No doubt she knew all the things Jeni wanted, and all the things she *needed*.

If Hawk asked nice, she might tell him.

Hell, if he asked *real* nice, maybe she'd show him.

10

The wine was going to her head.

Everything about the dinner went past delicious and straight into sumptuous—from the delicately glazed fish to the creamy rice and oak-aged chardonnay. Positively exquisite, and Jeni could barely taste any of it. She was too focused on the man beside her, and the subtle but distinct tension brewing between him and Gia.

It was almost as intoxicating as the wine, and even more provocative, because it was unpredictable. Wine was easy. Drink another glass, get a little fuzzier, a little freer. But this...

It could go nowhere—or *everywhere*.

Hawk was smiling, his eyes alight with amusement, and Jeni struggled to keep her mind on the story she was telling. "So anyway, the guy has tons of money

"And *I* only speak Spanish. And Italian. And some Russian and German, I suppose…" Gia trailed off and wrinkled her nose. "But the only French I know is one *very* dirty joke."

Hawk frowned. "Where the hell do you find someone who only speaks French?"

"North." Gia refilled her glass from the second bottle of wine and rolled her eyes. "He made an absolute fortune with…something. Now I can't even remember what it was. Do you, Jeni?"

"Mining. This big operation, just him and his brothers." Jeni tipped her glass toward Gia, who poured the rest of the second bottle into it. "So I came up with this brilliant plan—I'd just learn. What's the big deal, right? I had three days to get it done."

Hawk tugged on a lock of her hair. "You were going to learn a whole language in three days?"

"Oh, she learned a lot of it. She knew tons of words." Gia tapped the side of Jeni's head lightly. "This little brain of hers is a wizard at memorizing things. She can probably still read French. But when she tried to *pronounce* it…"

"It was a disaster." Jeni's cheeks heated as she recalled trying to stumble her way through the simplest of conversations. "Neither of us could understand a goddamn thing the other was saying. We were communicating with notes when Gia stepped in."

"There is one universal language," Gia murmured. She stroked a finger down to curl another lock of Jeni's hair around *her* finger, and the embarrassed heat in Jeni's cheeks turned into something else entirely. "He was actually sweet once I got him on his knees. Especially when he saw the flogger. Begging is downright *poetic* in French."

maman—and loving every second of it." Hawk was watching her with a warm, lazy smile, and Jeni cleared her throat. "So he bankrolled the entire expansion, and Gia paid him back in record time. With interest."

"Naturally." Gia sighed wistfully. "Business was good in those days. Everything in Eden was so placidly dull. Sneaking out here to enjoy fine wine, good conversation, and a little mild perversity was practically a rite of passage for anyone who wanted to *be* someone."

Hawk tugged at Jeni's hair again, but beneath the table his other hand found the slit in her dress and eased the fabric aside. "Only mild perversity? That's disappointing."

"Maybe I have a different definition of *mild* than you do," Gia replied, running the backs of her fingers over one of Jeni's flushed cheeks. "Or maybe not. Does he tease you terribly, Jeni?"

She gulped the rest of her wine, then looked at Hawk. He stared back at her, his expression as tight as his hand on her leg, laden with unspoken command.

Answer her.

She couldn't look away as she obeyed. "Sometimes," she whispered. "If I get too greedy."

"So all the time?" Gia smiled fondly as she glanced at Hawk. "Ace talked to me, you know."

"Oh?" Hawk's earlier unease had vanished. Something about the silent undertones to their conversation tonight had grounded him, and it was more than just Gia putting him at ease.

The darkly confident Hawk who'd flipped her onto her stomach and fucked her breathless had returned.

And Gia could tell. "He thought you might need some guidance, like Cruz did in the early days. Someone to show you how good it can be to put a sweet,

voice dropped to a husky whisper as she stroked Jeni's flushed cheek again. "But that's not what you need at all. You know exactly what you want."

Hawk's fingers slipped up Jeni's inner thigh. "I want her."

Jeni's heart thumped harder. It would be a strange sensation for most people, she supposed, listening to a conversation that was *about* them but not *for* them. A discussion that had everything to do with their needs and desires, but didn't require their input, not yet.

For her, it was like the wine. It flowed through her, warming places that even Hawk's touch couldn't reach.

Gia touched the collar at Jeni's throat. "You already have her. So tell us what you really want, Hawk."

No, Gia wouldn't be like Ace, blunt and confrontational, challenging Hawk's claim and undermining his feeling of control. Gia was too clever, too subtle.

Gia would make him admit the truth.

His hand rested heavy on Jeni's thigh, his fingers spread wide. The silence built between the three of them until the tension *hurt*, but when Hawk's voice came, it was rough with desire. "I want someone to help me find the lines."

"You want to learn how to hurt her without *hurting* her." Gia sat back and reached for her wineglass. "How to do it just right."

Hawk finally looked at her, his eyes intent. "Does Gia know how to do it just right, Jeni?"

What she knew was both simpler and more complex. She knew the places pain could take someone, how the mind and body would react in different ways. How some people would scream, and some would cry,

religious in its transcendence. When you put lash to flesh, it stripped away all pretense and left behind only the purest bleeding truth.

Hawk could take her to that truth with a word or a look. It was a different sort of trust, the kind wrapped up in dominance and submission, something Jeni craved as much as the pain. But if she could have both, and have it with *Hawk*—

"Yes," she said breathlessly. "Gia knows."

He cupped her cheek, turning her so that she couldn't see Gia, only him, as he leaned in close. "Would you like it, Jeni? If I asked her to show me. To *help* me."

It wasn't a question, not really. But she nodded anyway.

Hawk swept his thumb over her mouth, then teased at her bottom lip. "Is there someplace private we can go?"

Everything was private tonight. Gia wouldn't have invited them over if she were open for business, and her staff knew exactly when to make themselves scarce. But there was one place Jeni needed to go. One place that meant something. "My room."

"Why don't you show him there?" Gia slipped out of the booth. "You two can discuss things, and I'll be along once I've settled the place down for the night."

Her room was in another wing of the house. Jeni gripped Hawk's hand and led him down the quiet, dimly lit hall. Her stomach fluttered, even through the relaxing edge of the wine. "Now I know how you felt," she confessed.

"About what?" He squeezed her hand. "Showing you my room?"

"Yes." She paused at the door, then pushed it open. Inside was the same as the day she'd left. White that Gia had imported from somewhere, white furniture, and a huge bed that took up the entire center of the room.

It was nothing like her room back at the compound, which was draped with mismatched silks and pillows in bright, clashing colors. But it was still a part of her, and having him here felt like showing him every secret she hadn't realized she was keeping.

He tilted his head, his gaze drifting slowly across the room, cataloging everything. "It's not what I expected." He laid his hand on the back of her neck. "But it fits you."

She wanted to turn to him then, feel his hands slide down, all over her—but she'd seen the questions in his eyes at the table. "What do you need to know?"

His fingers tightened slightly—possessive, pressing the leather of the collar closer to her skin. "I need to know if there's anything you don't want to happen. Any way you don't want her to touch either of us."

She wasn't accustomed to being on this side of things. If this question had been asked before any of her previous sexual encounters, it had never been directed at her. She'd always been the temporary visitor, the guest. The reason they needed the rules.

It was arousing as hell. "No," she whispered, tugging at his jacket, watching his eyes. "I know what's mine."

His lips curled into a smug smile. "You'll use your safe word if anything is too much?"

"Yes." She clenched her hand in the warm leather. "You should, too. If you need it."

He dragged his fingers down her shoulder and hooked one under the edge of her dress, pulling it down. "How would you wait for Gia, if I wasn't here?"

162

Hawk leaned down until his lips brushed her ear, and his words came on a low, sexy-as-hell growl. "Then do it, Jeni. Get naked."

The shoes had to go first. Jeni bent to unbuckle them, acutely aware of Hawk's gaze on her. Then she straightened, stepped out of them, and reached for the side zipper of her dress. A slow, sexy unzipping was hard at the best of times, and her hands were already shaking. It only got worse when Hawk shrugged out of his jacket, his shoulders flexing as he moved, and dropped to the padded bench at the foot of the bed.

Her dress hit the floor, and she left it there. She had things to do—things like kneeling beside Hawk, the plush rug soft under her knees.

He stroked her hair, his touch as tender as the look in his eyes. "Tell me one thing you want from tonight. One fantasy."

A gentle flush was already sweeping through her, warming her until her skin prickled and her nipples hardened. "I want to make you feel this good. I want to show you that I can."

"How good do you feel? Show me."

Jeni shivered as she eased her legs wider, baring herself a little more to his gaze but mostly to her own touch. She glided two fingers over her slick pussy, shivering again when she grazed her clit. Then she raised her hand, showing him the wetness that clung to her fingertips.

"So ready." He caught her wrist and dragged her hand up, close enough for him to swirl his tongue around her fingers. "Does it turn you on so much, imagining trying to please both of us?"

"Yes." She glanced at his lap, at the hard length of his cock still trapped in his jeans, and swayed closer.

"You." Hawk caught her chin and tilted her head back. "Knowing Gia will see how sweet and obedient you are for me. Because no matter who's touching you, you're mine."

There it was, the very edge of the darkness she craved. "That's it," she whispered. "If I could have one thing tonight, it would be for you to let go. Whatever filthy thing you want, I'll make it beautiful for you."

His chest heaved. His eyes blazed. But before he could respond, a soft knock sounded at the door. Hawk held her chin, held her gaze. "Come in."

The door opened, but Jeni couldn't turn her head. She heard it close again, then the soft click of Gia's heels as she circled the edge of the carpet. "My, what a lovely sight."

Jeni had been naked in front of Gia—*for* Gia—hundreds of times. But she'd never knelt for her. This was entirely new territory, and having it all happen under Hawk's hot, watchful gaze...

There it was again, the tingling, plucking at the parts of her that needed so much to *give in*.

"We talked," Hawk said, his voice beautifully dark. "Jeni wants to be a sweet girl, do anything that pleases me."

"Of course she does." Gia's footsteps became muffled as she stepped onto the carpet, and Jeni could *feel* her behind her. "What would please you first?"

His thumb edged up over her lower lip, but this time he worked it into her mouth, onto her tongue. "Having you show me how hard I can fuck this sweet mouth."

Jeni moaned, the sound subdued by his thumb, and laid her hand on his knee.

A light touch drifted over her hair, a moment

the brush of Gia's skirts on her bare back, sensuous silk that slid over her as Gia circled her and sank to the bench next to Hawk.

She was waiting, too. Not for Hawk to command her, but for Hawk to give her permission to command Jeni. Because they might be under Gia's roof, enjoying Gia's hospitality...

But Jeni belonged to Hawk.

The same realization flared in his eyes. His lips curved into a smug smile as he eased his thumb away and sat back. "Be good for Gia," he murmured. "Obey her. Can you do that?"

There was nothing he couldn't ask of her. "Yes, sir."

"Oh, Jeni." Gia's voice held nothing but warmth as she stroked Jeni's cheek. "You shine for him, don't you? It's beautiful. Now open his pants, and we'll show him how much brighter you can glow."

Her fingers skipped over his belt buckle. She stroked the soft fabric of his T-shirt, and he dragged it over his head. The warm lights burnished his skin, and Jeni stared at him as she undid his belt.

Gia's touch shifted to the collar at Jeni's throat. She traced the silver medallion with a smile. "I understand this now. It's charming, the way she matches you."

Hawk's chest rumbled with something too low to be called laughter. "*Charming* isn't exactly what I'd call it. Hot as fuck, more like."

"I imagine so." Gia reached lower, stroking over the swell of Jeni's breast to circle one nipple. Jeni arched reflexively, seeking more, especially when Gia's next words rolled over her. "You should get her some clamps. They look so beautiful on her, and she *squeals*

165

Hawk stared at her breasts, already locked deep in the fantasy, so deep that Jeni felt it pulling at her, too. He could be so gentle, but there was another part of him, one that could be so deliciously rough. One that would pinch and tug and twist until she was sore as hell, *on fire* with possibility.

She popped open the button on his jeans and smoothed her hand over his caged erection as she reached for his zipper.

Gia's thumb and forefinger pinched tight without warning, turning the pain from her fantasy into shivery reality. Jeni's eyes fluttered shut, and her hands fumbled.

"Shh," Gia soothed, rubbing away the sting with the pad of her thumb. "You see how little it can take to get a reaction? Pain isn't always about *how much.* Especially with someone so desperate to please."

Hawk reached for Jeni's other breast, his fingers broader and rougher than Gia's, though they mirrored her slow caress. "Then what's it about?"

The toe of Gia's shoe nudged the inside of Jeni's knee, commanding her silently to spread her legs wider. "Knowing her, darling. When she needs you to break through what's holding her back, and when she's already so exposed that you can shatter her with the lightest touch."

Hawk slid his free hand over Jeni's, pinning them both in place against his open fly and the erection straining behind it. "Open your eyes."

She obeyed, her ears ringing, her heart thudding painfully.

His thumb circled her nipple, slow and taunting. He teased it to a taut, aching point, his gaze locked on her face as if she was the most beautiful thing he'd

going to play with until you can't take another second of it and beg to stop coming." His fingers pinched tight, sparking bright pain through her. "And then I'll make you come one last time, just to please me."

Jeni didn't fight it. She fell into it, embracing the way the pain buzzed along her nerve endings. She didn't make the choice to move, not consciously, but somehow she freed Hawk's cock, wrapped her hand around the thick base, and shuddered when he groaned and *twisted*, jolting her with another delicious wave of stinging pain.

Gia's fingers were cool on her flushed cheek. "Beautiful girl. You know what he wants. Don't make him tell you again."

Tell, not *ask*, because nothing about this night would be as polite or simple as a request. Jeni bent her head and touched her tongue to the head of Hawk's cock. She licked him in long strokes and short flicks, leaving him wet enough for her hand to glide easily, following as her tongue retreated.

Every caress trembled through him, but he held back until she looked up, met his eyes, and closed her lips around him.

"*Fuck.*" It exploded from him on a growl, and he thrust his hands into her hair, tangling the strands around his fingers until her scalp tingled.

Gia placed her hands over his. "Tighter. Sometimes the sweetest gift you can give her is to put her exactly where you want her to be. Don't make her guess. Let her relax and know she's pleasing you."

He hesitated. They were poised at the edge of something, another cliff where he might turn away from his darker desires instead of indulging them.

Please. Jeni uncurled her fingers from his cock

167

He clenched his fingers, and the tingle in her scalp turned into a burn. He held her gaze as he guided her head down until his dick was almost—*almost*—choking her and kept her there for an endless moment. When he finally pulled her back, it was with a harsh command. "Suck."

His voice was equal parts desire and demand, only this time they weren't warring for control. They were in exquisite harmony as he pushed her down and hauled her up, teaching her the right rhythm, the one that would turn his wicked desires into perfect pleasure.

It was Gia who tilted the balance, luring Hawk deeper into fantasy with a husky suggestion. "You want to know how hard you can fuck this sweet mouth?" She dragged her nails lightly down Hawk's arm. "Stand up, darling, and find out. Because you're not there yet, not even close."

Hawk dragged Jeni's head up as he rolled to his feet. She almost fell over, but steadied herself with one hand on his bare hip. He gave her a moment to settle herself, then cupped her cheek. "Is Gia right? Is it a gift, not having any choice now that you've decided to please me?"

Did he really not understand how arousing it was to be exactly what he needed? "The gift is having you trust me this much," she told him softly.

His lips curved. "That's what I was going to say." He pressed his thumb to her chin and guided her mouth open. "Gia?"

"Yes, darling?"

His smile widened. And even though he was speaking to Gia, the crude words were all for Jeni. "Hold her in place for me. I don't want her distracted from sucking my cock."

nails up Jeni's spine as she settled at her side. "Arms back."

Jeni was so entranced by Hawk's expression that she didn't move fast enough. Gia slapped her hip, forcing her to attention, and she folded her arms behind her back.

"I know, love." Gia pinned her arms. The supple leather of Gia's bodice brushed Jeni's naked skin, evoking a shiver. "I know that's a beautiful cock, but you have to earn it, don't you?"

She was caged, trapped, but she still had her voice. "Every delicious inch."

Hawk made a low noise. "Good girl," he rasped, gripping his cock with one hand. The other pulled tighter in her hair, holding her head in place as he rubbed the crown across her lips. He groaned when he slid between them, pushing forward until her mouth grazed his fingers where they curled around his shaft.

It was nothing she couldn't handle, not even as deep as before. But there was something provocative about being held still while he moved. He could choke her, overwhelm her in pursuit of his pleasure, and she'd be helpless to stop him.

It was painfully erotic.

He eased back and then forward again, watching her face as he fucked into her. His speed increased, his fingers still around his shaft as a guard, but his thrusts were sharper now. Rougher. He dragged her to meet his advances, forcing her to sway with his rhythm.

"How wet is she?" he growled.

Oh, God.

Gia slid her free hand down Jeni's body, her touch familiar and knowing. She teased two fingers over her clit, just hard enough to leave Jeni chasing the caress,

The sudden rush of pleasure screamed through Jeni. She whimpered and fluttered her tongue over Hawk's dick, silently begging him to *hurry, please, hurry.*

But Hawk had something else in mind. He waited as Gia worked a third finger into her, fucking them in and out until the slick sound of it filled the room. He *waited,* until Gia finally answered him. "She's so wet you'd drive all the way home with the first thrust."

His chest heaving, Hawk dragged Jeni's head back. "Show me, Gia. Wrap those fingers around my dick and let me feel it."

Jeni licked her lips and held her breath. Gia had slapped men for far less presumption than this—but now she only brushed a kiss to Jeni's temple and eased her fingers from her body. Her fingers glistened as she curled them around Hawk's cock and stroked him lazily.

Hawk hissed, and Jeni exhaled sharply. She'd never seen him so close to giving in. It was like every command he issued was a test, a tiny step further to see if she and Gia would balk. And when they didn't...

His face was tense with lust, every muscle in his strong body quivering. Jeni leaned in, pulling against his grip on her hair, and circled her tongue around the slippery head of his cock.

He shuddered. "Jeni—"

Gia dropped her hand. "Go on, Hawk. Give her what she wants."

He did, dragging Jeni into a slow thrust that went on and on. He tasted like hunger, like *her,* and her rough moan was cut short when he drove deep enough to choke her. She swallowed him instead, working her throat around his cock.

the tension palpable as he let out a tortured groan. Gia stroked her cheek, murmuring encouragements and compliments that faded into white noise. Jeni stayed— her lungs burning, tears streaming out of her eyes. Willing the moment to last forever.

But it couldn't. Hawk pulled back with a hiss of loss, then thrust forward again, over and over, fucking her throat with a wildness that proved the last of his control had shredded away.

"Fuck—" The words began with his next thrust, short and breathless, filth falling from his lips with the fervency of a prayer. "So fucking good, taking all of me. Your hot mouth and pretty lips. Take it, Jeni. Take—*fuck*—"

So close to the edge. Jeni wanted to reach for him, to hold him as he tipped headfirst over it, but she was still trapped in Gia's arms. Hawk came with a harsh groan, spilling hot and thick across her tongue with every desperate, jerky thrust.

He stilled finally, and Gia stroked Jeni's cheek, wiping away tears. "There you go, sweet girl. You did so well. Didn't she, Hawk?"

His knees folded, and he sank to the carpet in front of her. "So perfect," he agreed in a hoarse voice, cupping her other cheek. "Better than any fantasy."

She tilted her face to his touch and let the peace of the moment wash over her. She knew she was a wreck—tangled hair, smeared makeup, a sheen of sweat covering her skin—but when he looked at her like that, it didn't matter. Nothing did.

She *felt* perfect.

He kissed her, teased his tongue over her lower lip, coaxing her to open for him. She floated on the slow, lazy kiss until he gripped her chin and turned

Softer lips. A quicker tongue. Gia kissed with an edge, with scraping teeth and the bite of fingernails at the back of her neck, promising pleasure inseparable from pain. They traded her back and forth, kissing and stroking and petting and praising, until—

Jeni opened her eyes. Hawk was kissing Gia, his open mouth slanted over hers. His tongue flashed as he coaxed her lips wider, and a quick pulse of lust rocked Jeni. Watching him like this was a kind of torment, one that came with its own reward. She was always so wound up when he touched her, aching for relief, that she could never fully appreciate his raw animal appeal.

She appreciated the hell out of it now, watching him turn it on Gia. Gia, who had been touching her all night, who had given Hawk more than anyone could have asked for already.

Gia, who had done it all just for Jeni.

Her head was tilted, baring the vulnerable line of her throat. Jeni licked a path up the side of Gia's neck, over her jaw, then touched her tongue to their joined lips. "This is what I want now."

Hawk broke away. "What, sweetheart?"

She tangled her fingers in his hair, then stroked the back of his neck. "It's Gia's turn."

Gia shook her head. "That's sweet, love, but unnecessary. Tonight isn't about me."

"Bullshit," Hawk rumbled, rising slowly to his feet. He loomed above them as he lazily refastened his pants, then extended a hand to Gia. After a pause, she accepted it and allowed Hawk to help her up. Jeni stayed where she was, watching as the delicate moment played out.

Hawk stroked Jeni's disheveled hair. "Tonight is about Jeni. She wants to get you off. I want to get you

172

Not quite an order, but more than a request. And Hawk meant it—he wanted to see Gia satisfied. Not just because Jeni wanted it, but because he wasn't the type of person who would use someone in pursuit of his own pleasure without offering pleasure in return. Not even if they were willing.

Not even if they expected it.

Gia framed his face, her lips softening into a sweet smile. "No wonder you're wild about him," she murmured. "He's exquisite, Jeni."

"I know." He was gorgeous—and he was *hers*.

Gia moved toward the bed, and Hawk extended his hand again. When Jeni slipped her fingers into his, he pulled her up against him. The hair on his chest chafed over her breasts, and his jeans scraped teasingly against her bare thighs. "Did you leave things here? Floggers, whips?"

Her breath seized in her chest. "All of that."

"Show me."

She walked to the cabinet set along the far wall. It was just another piece of furniture in the same sophisticated style as the rest of the room. But inside lay all the items the O'Kanes displayed so brashly—leather and suede and steel, all locked away, waiting.

Hawk traced the supple leather of one whip before dragging his fingers through the falls of a deerskin flogger. "Join Gia on the bed. I'll pick something."

"Do you need—?"

He smiled at her. "I know what I want tonight. Go."

Gia was standing by the bed, her hair gathered up off her neck, clearing the way for Jeni to reach the clasps along the back of her bodice. "Who helps you with these dresses now that I'm gone?"

Gia smiled over her shoulder. "He's getting downright possessive of my wardrobe. I had to ease him back before he terrorized the washwomen."

Lance could terrorize anyone just by existing. The man was *huge*, and it was hard not to laugh at the idea of his massive fingers trying to navigate tiny buttons, tricky zippers, and gauzy fabrics. But he was painfully loyal, completely devoted, because Gia had picked him up off the street and given him a job, a purpose. A life.

That was Gia. She gathered people who'd been tossed aside, thrown away, and she made them her own, just as Dallas did.

The thought sobered Jeni as the leather parted, revealing Gia's smooth skin. "You know I'm still here, right? Just because I left the job behind doesn't mean I left you."

"I know, love." Gia turned and took Jeni's face between her hands the same way she had Hawk's. But her smile was softer this time, her eyes warm with affection, and her voice dipped to a whisper. "I always thought Dallas and Lex would be the ones to take you away for good. They'd care for you and keep you safe. But Hawk will make you his world."

Jeni had never been anyone's world before. She waited for the panic, the fear—she wouldn't be enough, no one *could* be—but it didn't come. Instead, what flooded her was strength and certainty.

Jeni matched Gia's smile as she eased the leather straps from her shoulders and let the heavy dress drop. "Then I'll have to return the favor, won't I?"

In Hawk's earliest days as a member, Dallas had sent him out with whoever needed backup.

174

hazing all rolled into one, because brotherhood was something you had to earn.

Ace had always been the worst. Not because he liked to haze, but because he liked to *talk*. Hawk and Jasper could cover the entire market plus another ten blocks without feeling compelled to exchange more than a few necessary words.

But Ace? He never shut *up*.

Even that might have been tolerable if they shared an interest—any interest. Finn and Bren loved to talk cars, Cruz and Zan liked to talk weapons. But Ace only seemed to have three settings: art, booze, and kinky fucking. And Hawk had still been trying to convince himself *so damn hard* that that last one wasn't a shared interest at all.

Jeni's cabinet was a goddamn treasure chest of delicious perversion. Leather cuffs that would fit around her wrists and ankles, connected to delicate lengths of chain. Equally delicate looking strands of pearls that his imagination could already conjure uses for. Vials and bottles stacked in neat little rows, some recognizably products of Tatiana's robust business in massage oil and lube, some tiny and elegant, *screaming* money.

And hanging on a row of hooks in the back...

Ace would probably call it a modest collection. But Ace was the one who'd dragged him into the leatherworker's shop in the marketplace on every fucking trip. Ace was the one who waxed fucking poetical about choosing the right tool for the job.

Ace was the one who'd had a shit fit the day Hawk had wanted to get the fuck out before temptation overrode his good sense, so he'd gone ahead and asked how many fucking floggers one man could possibly need.

the types of leather and the weight and the width and why it mattered. About the *art* of knowing when someone needed something sharp and stinging, and when they needed deep and solid. And there might have been a few jabs about how a man would have to be a boring-ass lay if he thought a partner always wanted one or the other.

Hawk had tried to let it roll off, but some part of him had hoarded every precious scrap of knowledge. Deep down, in the same place where he'd locked away his lust for Jeni and all the urges he'd never considered indulging. So he knew he wasn't ready for the whip, and that the flogger made from thin strips of oiled leather would sting more than he wanted when she was still tender from the other night.

He picked the other one—soft, supple leather in strips almost as wide as his thumb. As he gripped the handle, his heart thudded faster, which should have been fucking impossible. His heart had stuttered when Jeni slid to her knees, and shattered the first time she swallowed his cock, so desperate to please that she'd let him fuck her. Use her. *Violate* her.

Except it hadn't felt like a violation. It had felt joyous, and he was a walking dead man who'd somehow ended up in heaven.

He turned back toward the bed. Jeni and Gia were curled together, their limbs entwined. Gia had shed her dress and shoes, leaving her clad only in sleek black lace lingerie that sure as fuck hadn't come from one of the factories in Eight. It was probably irreplaceable.

And Jeni was goddamn close to ripping it.

Gia slipped a hand into Jeni's hair, and Hawk tightened his fist until he could feel every subtle ridge of the flogger's handle. He waited for that dark pit of

braced himself to fight back, to deny it, to rise above it.

What rose instead was even less civilized. Certainty, raw and undeniable. Jealousy fed on insecurity, thrived on doubt, and Hawk had none tonight.

Jeni was utterly and completely his.

As he crossed the room, she proved it by breaking away from Gia's kiss. She stared up at him, like a compass swinging back to north. He brushed his fingers over her flushed cheek and couldn't stop the smile that curved his lips. She was disheveled and so aroused she had to be aching for release, but no frustration showed in her expression. Just bright, shining trust.

Even heaven couldn't be this sweet.

"Keep going," he murmured. "You have about sixty seconds before I get my pants off and my fingers inside you. Think you can make Gia come first?"

She muffled a laugh against Gia's shoulder. "Hell, no."

Gia's laugh was deeper. Warmer. She watched Hawk over the top of Jeni's head as he tossed the flogger on the bed and reached for his pants. "I wouldn't be so sure. The two of you are hot enough to get *anyone* off."

The two of you. That's what they would be, if they managed to survive this war. If Jeni kept his collar—or even exchanged it for his ink wrapped around her throat. They'd be an entity, their names flowing together into one word. Dallas-and-Lex. Jas-and-Noelle.

Hawk-and-Jeni.

He popped open the button on his pants. "Sixty... fifty-nine..."

Jeni smiled softly as her hand vanished beneath black lace. Gia's head fell back against the pillows, her lips parting on a soft moan. "Does he think he has sixty

"Shh, don't tell him all my secrets," Jeni whispered. "Not yet."

And there, at last, was the jealousy. Not a raging fire inside him, but a single blade honed so sharp it cut deep and left him quietly bleeding.

Gia could get all over Jeni, inside her. She could lick and stroke and fuck her past the brink, and Hawk could watch, smug in the knowledge that Jeni had placed her body firmly in his keeping. Everyone who touched Jeni did so at his command, because that was the arrangement they'd made when she'd allowed him to wrap that leather around her throat.

Maybe they'd rushed it. War made people rush to snatch at whatever they could get, just in case it all slipped away. Jeni had given him everything she could. Recklessly, even.

But she couldn't give him this. You couldn't rush the kind of easy affection she and Gia shared, the quiet understanding where Gia only had to lift her hips and Jeni was there, sliding her underwear off her hips and down her legs.

It wasn't choreographed. It wasn't a *performance*. Oh, they'd get off on knowing how hot they were making him, how tempting it was to wrap his hand around his cock and fuck his fist to the tempo of Jeni's fingers. But he'd cataloged Jeni's performances, all of her masks and how different she was when she wasn't wearing one. This was real, precious—an understanding of each other's bodies that had grown over months and years instead of days and weeks.

Hawk might not have years. Fuck, he might not even have months. He could spend every waking moment inside Jeni and it still might not be enough to get them to where he needed to be, to the unassailable

That it wasn't just her body he'd laid claim to, but her mind and heart.

He'd fooled himself into believing he knew her just because he'd watched her. Because he'd been a silent, longing observer. And he'd had to believe it, because the alternative was facing the truth.

They were running out of time. And he'd wasted *so fucking much* of it.

Jeni licked the curves of Gia's breasts above the delicate black lace that hugged them, then glanced up at Hawk. She held his gaze with one full of heat and desire—invitation. Challenge.

He'd wasted so much time. But wasting more wouldn't change that.

He slid onto the massive bed, hiding a smile at how easily the pieces fell into place. Gia might be humoring him with the illusion of control, but it wasn't stopping her from nudging them along. She'd reclined against the pillows at the head of the bed, with plenty of room for Jeni between her legs—and plenty of room for Hawk behind Jeni.

Hawk wondered how many men had gone to bed with Gia and walked away convinced they'd somehow gained the upper hand, oblivious to her quiet authority because those men equated dominance with bluster and show.

Ego was the enemy of control. And control was what he wanted more than anything.

He settled behind Jeni, savoring the view. Jeni, naked, her ass still sporting bruises from his hand, her skin flushed, her hair wild and her thighs wet.

Thwarted arousal. He trailed his finger up the back of one leg and thrilled at her shiver. "You've been so patient, Jeni."

inside of Gia's thigh. "That's an overly generous assessment."

"I don't think so." The flogger lay next to his leg, tempting as hell, but he kept stroking her, both hands sliding over her hips, up her back, down to massage her ass. Slow, gentle, precise—because she melted for him. No, not melted. Softened. Like clay under the heat of his hands, so easy to mold. He coaxed her ass higher, her knees wider. Nodded to Gia, who gathered Jeni's hair up into a shining rope she wrapped around one hand.

He didn't even have to give the command. Just a few fingers against the back of her neck, a slight pressure, and maybe she knew him a little after all, because she immediately lowered her open mouth to Gia's pussy.

Gia's throaty moan filled the room. Under Jeni's devastating tongue, she'd be writhing her way to orgasm in no time at all.

He planned to get Jeni there first.

But he was the one who groaned when he slid his hand between her legs. Slickness and heat greeted him, so much of both that he immediately pumped three fingers into her.

She tensed and shuddered. Her body tightened, gripping his fingers, as if silently begging him not to pull them free and leave her burning.

Giving her what she wanted meant his fingers were there to feel the helpless flutter of her inner muscles as he lifted his other hand to her clit. This time, she moaned huskily, and her fingers bit in to the soft skin of Gia's thighs.

Gia dragged Jeni's head up, her breathing rough. "Let me see it, Jeni. Show me how you come for him."

"*Fuck*, Gia—" Her voice broke on another moan. "You have no idea—"

He knew this about her, at least. That she liked firm, quick pressure. That when he thrust his fingers into her, slow and deep would get her going, but nothing would send her screaming over the edge like fast and rough.

As much as he craved control over her, she craved his loss of control over himself. So he gave her a taste of it, fucking her hard with his fingers as he worked her clit. "Show her, Jeni. Do it. Let go."

Jeni's legs shook, then gave way. Their hands were the only things holding her up, and that seemed to make her shake harder as she hovered in that fevered, blissful moment before orgasm. Then she was *there*, her pussy clenching around his hand as she cried his name.

Hawk eased back, not ready to overload her senses. Instead, he petted her hips and her back, leaned over her to kiss her temple while his cock ground against her ass. "Is that better?"

She answered with a soft noise of frustration. "Don't *stop*."

"Begging for mercy already?" He nipped at her ear and slid his fingers over Gia's, where they lay curled in Jeni's hair. "Focus, sweetheart. Focus on pleasing her for as long as you can, no matter what I do to you. Do you understand?"

He could almost feel the denial trembling through her. But when she spoke, it was with a seductive whisper. "Yes, sir."

"Good girl." He gripped her hip and straightened again. Gia had Jeni by the hair, so he stroked to the base of her neck and let her feel the bite of his fingers

Gia sucked in a harsh breath as Jeni's tongue glided over her spread-open pussy, but her dark gaze seized Hawk's. Watching him, assessing even as Jeni moaned and licked deeper.

Holding it together, coolly collected, while Hawk was scrabbling for the self-control not to drive into Jeni and send them both spinning into oblivion.

That sharp stab of jealousy eased. Every day with Jeni, every *moment*, shredded his defenses and threatened his discipline. The more he got to know her, the harder it was to resist falling into her, because every bit he uncovered only made him want her more.

Gia had the knowledge, the long-standing affection, and maybe she knew Jeni's body in ways it would take Hawk years to learn. But if she could hold herself above the pleasure of having Jeni on her knees, working to get her off with such sweet obedience...

Fucking hell. Gia didn't deserve her.

The corner of the other woman's mouth quirked up as if she'd heard the thought, as if she could read every damn emotion churning through him.

He didn't care. He slid his hand possessively down Jeni's spine and reached for the flogger. The handle fit perfectly in his palm, smooth and cool. He let himself get a feel for the weight of it. The balance.

Bringing it down against her skin would spark a reaction, fast and easy. But tonight wasn't about that. It was about feeling out Jeni's boundaries, knowing Gia was there, ready to stop him if inexperience pushed him too far.

He knew how she reacted to fast and easy. So he trailed the falls across her hips and gave her something far more devastating—anticipation. It made her twist beneath the flogger, chasing the tease as surely as she

As hungrily.

"Shh." He gripped her hip with his other hand, stilling her movements. Then he dragged the soft leather across her skin again, letting it tickle her sides and map the graceful arch of her spine. "Stay focused."

She dropped her hands to bed and clenched them in the luxurious sheets. The muscles in her arms tensed. Her body trembled.

Waiting was its own sort of agony, a gentle burn he could nurture until it consumed her. First a tiny flick of his wrist, just enough for the leather to kiss her skin. She started, just a little, the barest hint of movement. But the sound she made—relief and need and a longing so fierce he felt it stab through him.

He wasn't the only one feeling it. Gia's head tilted back and her back arched, her lips parting. She murmured something, obscene words of encouragement that melted past him. Nothing seemed as vital as watching Jeni's reactions as he went back to teasing her, not even Gia's sharp gasp or the shaking moan that heralded her first orgasm.

So Hawk focused on Jeni. On the way the leather fell against her skin—no easy rhythm she could anticipate, no pattern she could learn. Sometimes he teased until she stopped straining into it, then landed a gentle blow. Sometimes he gave her several in a row. But always light, never enough to bring more than the softest color to her skin.

More pressure than pain, but it didn't seem to matter. Before long, Jeni was reacting to every touch as though it was a blow, shivering and even lifting her head to gasp his name.

When she lowered it again, she laid her cheek on Gia's thigh and murmured something too soft for him

"We can't hear you, love." Gia reached for Jeni's chin, tilting her face up. "Say it again."

Her only response was a long, lazy moan.

Hawk dropped the flogger to the bed, wrapped an arm around Jeni, and flipped her onto her back. She sprawled languidly with her hair spread out across Gia's chest, her eyes full of the same glazed pleasure as the night he'd spanked her.

Gia ran her knuckles down Jeni's throat. "I've never seen her let someone this far inside her head."

Not the words he would have thought to use, but they fit. They *resonated*. And all of Ace's rants about choosing the right tool for the job clicked together to form a picture that was far bigger than pain and pleasure and physical sensation.

Those were the tools. The goal was this—Jeni, stripped bare and open to him. Needing him. Because, in this moment, she did. She'd trusted him so much that she had let go of the world, and until she came back to it, she was his responsibility.

His, in a way that truly did fracture his control.

He touched her knee, and she opened her legs and reached for him. Need and want and hunger and yearning tumbled over each other in her eyes—an actual impossibility, so maybe he was just seeing what he wanted. What he felt.

Desperate.

He leaned into her, and Gia was right there, the answer to the only question holding him back. "What do I do when she's like this? Do I stop?"

Jeni whimpered, and Gia stroked her throat again with a soothing noise. "You take care, Hawk. You remember that she might say yes to anything right now, just to please you. So you don't ask for anything

don't do it."

Simple, absolute permission to do the one thing he and Jeni both needed.

He had his hands hooked under Jeni's knees before her next whimper. Pushing them up and out, he drove into her pussy in one long stroke that forced a moan from him.

Jeni arched into him with a dreamy hiss. "Yes. *Yes.*"

Gia's hands covered his, and he let her take over, shuddering when she urged Jeni's legs wider. He gripped the headboard instead, trapping Jeni between their bodies, letting every rough thrust grind her back against Gia. Not just for the sensation of hot skin all along hers, but because Gia was right.

He was in Jeni's head. And he wanted to stay there forever. "Is this what you needed? Both of us fucking you?"

"Yes—" The word dissolved into a hitching breath as she touched his face. "Because you needed it."

They could spiral forever like that, each swearing they only craved what the other needed. It would be true, but also shallow. Someone had to be the selfish one, the one who let their partner give. The one who *took*.

For Jeni, he'd embrace selfishness.

And oh, it was so easy. To fall into the way she felt around him, the tight, hot clasp of her pussy, the primal satisfaction of the helpless, hungry noises she made when he fucked deep. "That's right," he groaned. "I need you just like this. Open and wet for me. All mine, to fuck as hard and as rough and as long as I want. Tell me, Jeni. Say it."

"Yours," she whispered, a hoarse sound that

185

Longer than you know."

That was a dangerous fucking thought, seductive in all sorts of ways that played hell with his self-control, and he had to cling to Gia's reminder. *Take care.*

Easier said than fucking well done, with Jeni squeezing his cock like just the thought of belonging to him was enough to get her off.

He dragged in a breath between clenched teeth. "Did you ever touch yourself, Jeni? Did you slide your fingers between your legs and pretend they were mine?"

"You know I did." Her glazed eyes sharpened. "They could have been yours. I tried."

So much wasted time. So fucking *much.* He drove into her again, as if the intensity of it could make up for all the weeks he should have been inside her. "Show me. Touch yourself, only this time you'll come all over my cock."

She traced her fingers over his lower lip. He opened his mouth and dragged his tongue around the tips before sucking them hard. When they were slick and wet, she slipped her hand down her body.

Even without looking, he knew the moment she touched her clit. She shuddered beneath him, exhaling roughly, and he could see the fantasy in her eyes, watch as this moment overtook the one in her memory.

It was almost as good as rewriting history.

He seized her mouth, spearing his tongue between her lips with the same ferocity as his next thrust. Rough and wild, because she was already tightening again, her pussy gripping him as she whimpered against his lips, and he couldn't hold on. He didn't want to.

Hawk gave her what she wanted, let her be what he needed. Selfish and greedy, he fucked her over the edge and kept fucking her. He rode her orgasm until

perate, continuous, one endless rolling peak that left her screaming.

And when he slammed into her one last time and let the fire consume him, it was because he wanted to come inside her, to fill her, to know he'd marked her in the basest way possible.

Jeni clutched at him, her fingernails cutting into his shoulders as the last of the tremors shook her, and whispered against his neck. Her breath was hot on his skin, carrying praise and promises and *vows*, all kinds of things he couldn't listen to when she was over the edge like this. Floating.

Take care. Not just with her heart, but with his, too. It was too soon to accept forever from her, even if he wanted it. Even if she was offering.

He kissed the words from her lips and eased away, feeling the tiniest dart of guilt as Gia gently coaxed Jeni's legs down. He'd damn near forgotten her in the end, which would have felt like even more of a shit thing to do if she hadn't been smiling like a satisfied barn cat.

They moved together, getting Jeni under the covers and snuggled down against the pillows. Hawk curled behind her, tucking her head under his chin, and watched Gia retrieve her underwear and slide it on. "Sorry," he felt compelled to murmur. "I lost it a little bit at—"

"Shh." Gia disappeared behind the wardrobe door and reappeared a moment later wrapped in a silk robe. She slid onto the bed and ran her fingers lightly through Jeni's hair. "If you want to demand power over others, then it's your obligation to learn when a moment is about you, and when it should be about what someone else needs. There's satisfaction in both, you know.

ate the latter can't be trusted with power."

Too bad the world seemed fucking full of them. "As long as you got something out of tonight, too."

"I got to see her happy." Gia smiled as Jeni turned her cheek toward her stroking hand. "Take care of her, Hawk."

Or else hung between them, unspoken but unmistakable, a threat no wise man would ignore. "Is this the part where you tell me you'll stab me in the dick if I hurt her?"

Gia laughed softly. "Of course not. I haven't done my own dick-stabbing in years, darling. I'd have one of the bouncers do it."

Jeni didn't open her eyes, but she did reach up and touch Gia's wrist reprovingly. "Be nice, Giovanna."

"I *am* being nice." Gia lifted Jeni's hand to her lips and brushed a kiss to her palm. "Are you staying here tonight?"

"If it's not too much trouble."

"It's your room, love." She settled Jeni's hand back on top of Hawk's before leaning over to brush a kiss to his cheek, too. "Just promise to have breakfast with me. And I have something for you to deliver to Dallas, if you can."

The corner of Jeni's mouth quirked up. "Anything."

Gia's lips were still close to his ear. "Keep an eye on her while some comes down," she murmured, before pulling back. Her nails trailed across his cheek in a shivery caress that could have been affection—or a reminder of her warning.

Hawk imagined the line between affection and violent protection was pretty thin where Gia was concerned.

She gathered her clothes and shoes and then

drowsily content woman. "You doing okay?"

"Mmm, perfect." Her eyelashes fluttered. "That's never happened before."

"What hasn't?"

"No pain." She turned in his arms and looked at him. She was still dazed, but the glassy look in her eyes was slowly slipping away. "I didn't know it could. Not for me."

"You mean getting fuzzy?" He smoothed a hand over her hair, trying to tame the tangled strands. It was impossible—she was disheveled, changed by what had passed between them even though he hadn't left a single mark on her this time.

"Never without the pain." She touched his jaw. "You *are* magic."

His lips curved up. "I'm not. I'm just the luckiest man in the world. Because you trust me."

"Yes, I do." Jeni snuggled closer, curling against his chest. "With my life."

Her life. Her body. So much already, but Hawk was greedy. Selfish.

And he was after her heart.

11

Jeni finished writing down the last name she'd committed to memory and handed the list to Dallas. "Gia said that's everyone who's been spending money like water at her place these days." The look on his face would have made her laugh—if the circumstances weren't so horrible. "Yeah, it's not exactly a small pool of spy candidates."

His gaze slid down the list, his jaw tightening. "Jesus fucking hell, Jeni. Damn near twenty, just from Gia?"

"And her girls don't come cheap. I should know."

Dallas snorted and passed the paper to Noelle, who nibbled on her lower lip as she studied the names. "It's not necessarily *that* dire. Some of them are probably just blowing their money now before Eden has a chance to get to them."

over his face. "So we have desperate motherfuckers who are about to be *broke*, desperate motherfuckers. We have people getting rich off Christ-knows-what behind our backs because we don't have time to chase them down. And somewhere in the middle of that mess, we have assholes selling us out to Eden."

Talk about your clouds with no silver linings. "Owen Turner," Jeni said quietly.

Dallas raised an eyebrow. "You got a feeling?"

Well, that was flattering. "Hardly. He's a talker, and he has a crush on one of Gia's girls. Keeps trying to steal her away. Last week, he told her she should take him up on the offer before it's too late." She rose with a shrug. "It could be nothing."

"Wait a second." He jabbed a finger toward the seat. "Park your ass."

She sighed but obeyed. "That's all I know, Dallas. You'll just have to run the leads, see where they go."

"That's not what I want to talk about." The full weight of his Dallas O'Kane, King of Sector Four gaze settled on her. "I wanna know if Hawk's taking good care of you. Because if he's not—"

"*Dallas.*" Noelle sounded exasperated. "Lex is going to kick your ass."

"Shut it, kitten." Dallas leaned forward on his elbows. "It's an easy question. Is he taking good care of you?"

When Dallas locked in on something, he didn't stop until he got what he wanted. Jeni's only defense was to make him *want* to end the conversation before he died of embarrassment.

So she relaxed back in her chair and let her eyes and expression go dark and sultry. "Oh, he's been taking very, *very* good care of me. You want the filthy

"Maybe." Without looking away, he reached to the side and dragged two glasses between them. The liquor followed, an inch in the bottom of each glass. He scooted one toward her. "You care about him this much, huh?"

"Enough to challenge you?" Jeni picked up the glass and sipped the liquor to hide her smile. "I'm wearing his collar, Dallas. What do you think?"

"I think you're wearing his collar." Dallas touched her wrist. "But you're wearing my ink, same as him. And this'd be a lousy time for me to have to kick his ass if he's not doing right by you. But I would."

"Understood. No one needs an ass-kicking."

"Until Lex hears about this," Noelle muttered.

Dallas slammed back his drink and rolled his eyes skyward. "Why did having an assistant seem like a good idea again?"

Noelle winked at Jeni over Dallas's shoulder. "Because you're going to get your ass out of here and go deal with business, and by the time you get back I'll have pulled files on everyone on this list and will probably know who to look at first. So scoot."

Dallas grumbled his way to his feet and circled the desk, letting his fingers trail lightly over Jeni's shoulder on the way. When he reached the door, he turned back and pointed to Noelle. "You say *scoot* to me again, and I'm telling Jas not to spank your ass for a month."

"Liar," Noelle shot back with a fearless grin. "You like watching too much."

Dallas muttered something Jeni couldn't understand and slammed the door behind him.

As soon as he was gone, the jovial mirth slipped from Noelle's face. She sank into Dallas's chair and rubbed her forehead, and Jeni's chest tightened. She'd been so distracted by her budding relationship with

must be going through in days.

She set down her glass. "How has he been?"

"He's..." Noelle sighed and shrugged. "Honestly, I don't know. I don't think anyone but Lex does. He's holding everything together, and she's holding *him* together, and all we can do is take as much of it off their shoulders as we can."

And Jeni had been cross with him. For a moment, remorse surged through her, but she shoved it aside. She knew Dallas, and the last thing he would want was to be treated *differently* right now, as though the world really was ending, and he wasn't so invincible after all.

Sometimes, all it took to make something true was for enough people to believe it.

She refilled her glass. "Is there any word on what the city has planned?"

"Nothing concrete." Noelle rescued Dallas's abandoned glass. "When I first got here, I wrote this program to track communications between the Sectors and Eden. I thought I was going to break the intel game wide open, give Dallas everything he needed to keep us safe." Her lips curved in a wry smile. "When Noah and I finally got a filter working for the data, guess what most of it was?"

"Petty arguments and porn?"

"Pretty much." She sipped her drink and shook her head. "Sometimes we found things buried under all the garbage, but now we don't even have that. The day the wall went hot, the data started coming out encrypted. Noah's been killing himself trying to crack it, but we need more processing power. Ford and Mia are working on something for us, but the factories weren't designed to turn out the parts we need."

"Maybe Noah will get lucky," Jeni offered. "Or

"If anyone can do it..." Noelle tapped the list. "This gives me something to work on, anyway. I have pretty hefty files on all the troublemakers. And I'll check out Owen Turner first."

"It could be nothing." Jeni hoped it was. Dallas and Lex had it hard enough. The last thing they needed was to deal with the idea of spies in their sector, of people who should have trusted them turning to the city instead.

"It's still a start. And hey—I'm glad you and Hawk are doing good. Forget Dallas, okay? He's snarly and protective, because you're..." Noelle smiled softly. "Not many people get as close as you did, Jeni. You're always gonna be a little bit his. Just like Jas."

"Not exactly like Jasper." It was more and less, but nothing so much as...different. "Anyway, if Dallas really thought he needed to be worried, he wouldn't ask me shit."

"That's the truth. But still, I'm glad. Hawk is sweet, and he cares about people so much. Jas respects the hell out of him, and that doesn't come easy."

Jeni's cheeks heated. "I didn't realize they'd spent that much time together."

"Jas grew up on a farm, too, you know." Noelle poured another shot into her glass and swirled the liquor. "Hawk comes to dinner with us sometimes. He and Jas can talk for hours, coming up with plans for his sisters' place. Cars, too, but mostly farming and family."

It sounded delightful, more intimate than friendship. It sounded like the family Noelle had mentioned, and Jeni found herself smiling.

This was what Dallas and Lex had built, what they were working so goddamn hard to shield and protect

195

hair was going gray at the temples, no matter how much stress they tried to take off of him.

She spoke without thinking. "You're from Eden, too. Do you think they know what'll happen to us if we don't win this war? Not *us*, I mean—not the O'Kanes or the other people the MPs would kill outright. But to everyone else."

"I don't know if they can imagine it." Noelle closed her eyes. "Hawk and Six can. Jasper. Anyone else who lived on the farms or the communes, the places that Eden needed to control. But so many of them think life is already as bad as it can get, and all they've ever known is being ignored, maybe swatted if they got in the way. They don't know how bad it can be when Eden decides to use you."

Jeni's fingers clenched until her nails dug painfully into her palms. "Then that's what we can do for Dallas. Make sure they never find out."

Noelle's eyes popped open, then narrowed. "You pulled that list out of your head. Lex told me you're good at that, remembering things you've read."

"Mostly. Also things like pictures or diagrams, it just has to be something I can look at." Noelle was staring at her in the oddest way, so Jeni tilted her head. "What are you thinking?"

Noelle twisted Dallas's chair around and came back with a large tablet in her hands. She dropped it on the desk and swiped the screen awake, her fingers flying. "I'm thinking I'm an idiot. Here..."

She spun the screen around, revealing a file full of documents labeled with dates and times. "It's the last of the filtered data we have from before the encryption kicked in. Just the stuff going between the sectors and Eden. Maybe you'll notice patterns we might have

Jeni opened one document and flipped through the first few pages. It all seemed mundane—letters, mostly, ranging from quick, dashed-off notes to formal correspondence. "You want me to look for things that don't fit?"

"Or just get an idea of what *normal* was before this happened, and then once Noah cracks the encryption…"

It seemed simple enough, though Jeni knew it couldn't be. If it was, Noah would have already written a magical program that could have done this for him. "Is this the part where we make a joke about how technology can't overcome the splendors of the human mind?"

"No doubt." Noelle leaned back. "We can tell it to look for patterns, but what about the ones we're not expecting? The ones we wouldn't realize were there until we saw them? No matter how smart you make a program, it finds a way to remind you how stupid we'd be without our subconscious minds and our gut instincts."

"How much is here?"

"Well, it *is* the filtered data."

"And that wasn't an answer." Jeni eyed her teasingly over the top of the tablet. "Come on, kitten. How bad can it be?"

Noelle wrinkled her nose. "Not *quite* five thousand?"

"*Pages?*"

"Not quite! Forty-eight hundred, at most."

"Oh, fuck." Jeni would need days—weeks, even—just to make a dent in it. "And what kind of time frame does this represent?"

Noelle lifted her glass again—and held it between them like a shield. "The last two days before the wall

Jeni felt faint. "How much shit did Noah's algorithms filter out?"

"You don't want to know, Jeni. Seriously."

"Well." Her fingers tightened around the edge of the tablet. It was a daunting task, one she wasn't even sure she could handle—but it was special, different from anything else she'd ever been asked to do.

She danced, and she tended the bar. She covered whatever needed to be covered. But until Dallas had asked her to study up on herbs, that had been it. No one relied on her, because all of her jobs were things anyone else could pick up at a moment's notice.

Even the herb garden. Once it was set up and established, it could be cared for like all the rest of the fruits and vegetables. And when the time came to make the tinctures and medicines from those herbs, anyone else could be taught how to do it.

But not this. This was a task that could help them out immensely—that could save their fucking lives in a way salves and balms couldn't—and it was *hers*.

Noelle leaned forward to touch her hand. "Welcome to Dallas O'Kane's spy network, Jeni. Population three, including you."

She folded the tablet in her arms and had to swallow hard before she could trust her voice. "I'd better get started."

kora

Kora couldn't remember her parents.

She must have had them—everyone did, even the soldiers in the special programs on the Base, the ones who had been conceived in tubes, perfected under microscopes, and birthed by surrogates. It was an unavoidable biological fact.

When she was young, no more than ten or eleven, she'd gone looking for them. She'd just finished a module about the role of genetics and heredity in disease, and all she could think about was the fact that she had no idea where she'd come from. Who were her mother and father—soldiers? Scientists? Farmers that the Base doctors had taken in and tried to heal? All her adoptive father, Dr. Middleton, had ever told her was that they were dead.

She knew she was healthy. Her regular tests

tions that needed attention. But she'd been positively gripped by the notion that the past *was* the future, that without knowing her history, she would be adrift with no direction for tomorrow.

Her search started and ended in the same place—with her poring through computer files for any mention of them, any hint of where she might have begun to look. When she found nothing, she dove deeper, accessing secured databases and poking around in classified data.

Still nothing.

She didn't simply *not know* her history. She didn't have one.

Maybe that was why she liked Sector One so much. It was impossible to ignore the history here, and not a shred of it was hidden. The people here celebrated their dead, with art and songs and shrines and tattoos. They marked their bodies with their shared history and bore the ink even more proudly than their scars.

All Kora had were two bar codes on the inside of her wrist.

Sector One was beautiful, not just the scenery or the architecture, but the people, too. Kora could stay here—easily, *happily*—but not when she was needed elsewhere.

She turned toward Gideon Rios, the sector's leader, and prepared to plead her case again. "I delivered another baby yesterday."

"That's wonderful." Gideon looked flushed and tired, but pleased. He'd been pushing himself hard to recover from his brush with death, but every day brought strength back to his body. He refilled their tea glasses and gazed out over the garden. "It eases everyone's minds, knowing we have someone qualified here

"Yes, but—" Kora bit her lip. Demands didn't work on Gideon, but an appeal to his sense of logic might. "They don't *need* me, strictly speaking. Your midwives are very skilled. They would have plenty of time to send for me if—"

"Kora." Gideon had a gentle smile for a hard man, a smile befitting a prophet. "The midwives *are* skilled. More skilled every day, in fact. If you leave now when they're still learning so much, I'll have a riot on my hands."

Her gut twisted. She had come to One with no other thought than to help the women and children who had been wounded when the city bombed Sector Two. She could still remember the *rage*, the urge to scream at the heavens that anyone could do such a thing, could kill and maim and terrify an entire sector.

But it would be childish and dishonest to pretend she hadn't known the city leaders could do such a thing. After all, she'd seen their files. They'd tried very hard to keep her and the other doctors oblivious to the depths of their depravity, but she didn't just have Special Clearance. She'd *used* it.

The patients from Two were all gone now, for better or worse. And she was left attending births and patching up scrapes.

At first, she'd assumed that Gideon wanted her close because of his own injuries. It hadn't taken her long to set that thought aside—Gideon possessed a wealth of concern, but he seemed to lavish it on everyone but himself. So she'd moved on to thinking he wanted her here for his family, in case the city attacked his sector next. But something about that didn't sit quite right, either.

Nothing did, and it was starting to make her

She opened her mouth to question him further, but Avery Parrino came out into the garden, holding a carved wooden tray with another glass pitcher of tea.

She set it on the table between them and winced when a bit of tea and crushed mint sloshed over the rim of the pitcher. "Sorry," she breathed. "I thought you could use a fresh one."

Gideon straightened slightly in his chair. "That's very thoughtful, Avery. Thank you. Would you care to join us?"

She began shaking her head before he even finished speaking. "Oh, I couldn't."

"Of course you could. You have to help me convince Kora that we still need her here."

She watched him for a moment. Her usual fidgeting ceased as she gazed down at him like an equation she wasn't quite sure how to solve. Then she turned to Kora, a warm smile curving her lips. "If you left, we'd miss you terribly."

Kora hid her answering smile. "Thank you, Avery."

She bowed her head, the heavy fall of her dark hair almost obscuring her face as she glanced at Gideon again.

He smiled as well, but Kora could sense the emptiness behind it. "Yes, thank you. If you're going back in, would you mind taking the empty pitcher?"

Wordlessly, she bowed, more deeply this time, and removed the pitcher. Then she removed herself, practically fleeing back to the house.

Kora snorted. "*Why* did you do that?"

The smile vanished, and Gideon rubbed a hand over his face with a soft sigh. "You'd think I'd be used to it, wouldn't you? Every stray word being mistaken for a command. But I'm not used to it *here*, in my own

Turmoil rolled off of him in waves that turned Kora's stomach. "You're the most powerful man in this sector, and all Avery knows is that powerful men are to be obeyed."

"Well, she'll have to learn otherwise," Gideon said firmly. Then he arched an eyebrow at her. "You don't share that problem."

"If I'd been taught obedience, I wouldn't be here." She'd be back at home, and a sudden wave of emotion swelled in her throat. *Home.* The city was a pleasant place to live—*if* you had money and status. *If* you could ignore the dark undercurrents of violence and greed that lurked beneath its polished surface.

Kora didn't miss it. But she did miss the Base, and her patients, and being able to do her damn *job.*

She put down her glass, careful not to betray her agitation. "Why am I not allowed to leave?"

To his credit, Gideon didn't deny it. He sipped his tea, then set his glass gently on the table. "I've been given information indicating that you could be in danger if you leave Sector One. And you're the best trained regeneration technician on either side of the wall. I had hoped you'd be happy enough here that you didn't want to leave, but..." He shrugged. "If happiness won't keep you here, perhaps responsibility will."

So many layers in those words. Kora turned them over in her mind, dissecting them, teasing them apart. The stuff about responsibility she discarded immediately. They'd already established that she could move quickly if she needed to return, and her sense of responsibility was the reason she wanted to leave in the first place. But the rest of it...

She was in danger. Someone had told Gideon this, someone who would know.

feel like a lie, didn't have that slick, greasy quality that made her shudder in revulsion as it slid over her. So Gideon, at least, believed it to be truth.

There was only one person she knew who was this involved with sector politics, who might have the sway to convince a sector leader to keep her out of the city's clutches. Thinking about him *hurt*, like falling onto a flat surface so hard it ripped the breath right out of your lungs for long, agonizing seconds.

It hurt even more when she closed her eyes and saw his face. Ashwin Malhotra was a patient, a soldier, and she'd had no trouble shutting him out of her thoughts when she shed her lab coat at the end of the day.

Until, that is, the night he'd kidnapped her.

She wasn't supposed to know it was him. He'd taken every precaution—bindings, a blindfold, he'd even blocked her hearing. But he couldn't blot out all of her senses, and when he'd touched her—

She knew who he was. But not *why* he'd snatched her out of her bed, not until he'd left her in a room alone with a dying man. She'd saved the man's life, of course, and he told her *volumes* in return.

Not verbally. Not wittingly. But his tattoos had been impossible to ignore, especially the skulls and crossed guns on his wrists. Later, using one of the dummy logins she'd bought at the side-street market, she discovered the truth—she'd been in Sector Four, and she'd saved the life of an O'Kane. She even found his face, and along with it his name—Alexander Santana. Ace.

Who was he to Ashwin, and why? Kora had always planned to ask. The next time she saw him, she decided, she would make him explain—and tell him that all he

She'd never had the chance.

Gideon's hand touched hers. "You're safe here, you know. Deacon and I did a complete security review after the assassination attempt."

"What?" She shook herself. "No, I'm not worried about that. I was just thinking."

"It's a lot to think about." He pulled his head back and reclined in his chair. "Do you know what would have happened if you hadn't saved my life, Kora?"

She didn't ponder such things. If she did, the weight of it all would collapse on her, heavy and stifling. Paralyzing. Because no one could save every life.

She rose abruptly. "I'll stay. But, at some point, I want answers, Gideon. Real ones."

"I don't have them," he replied, again with no hint or trace of deception. "But when we reach that point, I'll help you find them."

"I won't need help." This time, she knew exactly where to look.

12

Jeni had always thought that the sight of Hawk in the rooftop gardens was a transcendent experience. But it didn't hold a candle to him building things.

He'd discarded his jacket not long after they'd arrived at the workshop on his sisters' little enclave on the edge of Four. His thin white T-shirt clung to his chest, stretched taut over muscles that flexed and bulged with every swing of the hammer.

He needed a haircut. And a shave. And he was the most perfect thing she'd ever seen.

He glanced up as he reached for another piece of wood. "You look like you're thinking hard."

"Nope." She propped her chin on her hand and grinned at him. "Just enjoying the view."

Sometimes Hawk still blushed. But he smiled, too, and shook his head as he fit the board into place.

in broad daylight."

"With your *sisters* outside?" They were just as sweet as the ones she'd already met, and they'd welcomed Jeni with open arms. But she wasn't sure they'd still approve of her if they knew how thoroughly she'd corrupted their big brother.

They looked at Hawk like he was a superhero, and Jeni didn't blame them. As far as she knew, this was his first visit to their little farm in a while, but he'd provided them with everything—space, equipment. He even built their homes and furniture with his own hands.

Most of all, he'd given them a *chance*.

Jeni slid off the worktable. "What are you making?"

"A crib." He set the piece he'd been working on up on its side, and she could see it now—one side of the frame, lined with evenly spaced wooden slats. "Remember Amy, from the farm? She's seven months along now, and she and Robbie want to come here."

Did they think it was safer? It could be—if the city's forces spilled into Sector Four, they'd be focused on the O'Kane compound and its surroundings. Out here, right at the edge of everything, a tiny cluster of farms could go unnoticed.

For a while.

Jeni ran her fingers over one corner of the half-finished crib. "I've never seen so many babies."

"Not many people in Four have." He laid it gently back down and reached for the nails. "That'll change in nine or ten months, I guess."

"Doc's been keeping an eye on the water." Not just to measure whether the city was still pumping drugs to control the birthrate into the water supply, but also to check for anything more damaging. Or deadly. "He

"Yeah? Guess they haven't run out yet."

"Or it's an automated system."

"Or that." He shrugged. "Ryder probably knows. I'm sure as hell not gonna ask him, though."

"He's not so bad." She touched Hawk's arm, and he covered her hand with his.

They'd settled into a comfortable pattern of days over the last week. It wasn't quite a routine, but it was close—they usually went their separate ways in the morning, completing the tasks that filled their busy days. On the evenings she danced at the Broken Circle, Hawk waited for her backstage.

They spent their nights together. Some passed in a blur of sweat and skin. Others, they simply talked—about important things, or about nothing—until they drifted to sleep. The one constant was Hawk's quiet, steady presence.

Already, she couldn't remember what it was like not to have him there.

He squeezed her hand and turned it over. Then he dropped the nails into her palm. "Since you haven't got your mystery tablet, why don't you help me build this thing?"

She ignored the playful jibe about her secretive reading and groaned. "I came with you to take a break, not do more work."

He grinned. "You can charge me for the nails. One kiss each."

"On the lips, or lady's choice?"

"Lady's choice, of course. But you might have to save some of those for later."

"Uh-huh." Guilt scraped at her, and she sighed. It wasn't that she didn't want to tell him about the assignment Noelle had given her. It was just that, sometimes,

white. Right or wrong.

Safe versus *in danger.*

And that was the problem, wasn't it? There was nothing immediately dangerous about combing through Eden's communication logs, looking for the dirty secrets they'd tried to hide. It wasn't like picking up a gun and charging the electrified wall. But it carried a deeper risk, one that went beyond bullets in flesh. Knowledge always did.

And she knew—she *knew*—he wouldn't like it. Oh, he'd understand the necessity of it. He might even be proud of her. But it would be one more thing for him to worry about, another heavy layer of concern and responsibility weighing him down.

There was enough of that already, more than a dozen men should have to bear over a dozen lifetimes. He already worried about his family, their farms, the gang, the war. Sometimes it seemed like his only moments of peace were the ones he managed to steal in her arms.

She couldn't take that away from him. She wouldn't—especially when all her efforts with Eden's files might amount to nothing, anyway.

"Hey." Hawk rubbed his thumb between her brows. "You're thinking hard again."

"No." She hesitated. "You know that you can take a break too, right?"

"That's what I'm doing." Hawk tossed the hammer aside. "When I go out and check the roof gardens, that's work. I don't mind helping people and fixing things, because God knows everyone in this sector needs to see that—an O'Kane who's so confident we're going to win this war, he has time to fix their leaky sink. But this..."

His thumb passed between her eyebrows again,

get to spend time with you and build something that's not about war or raising morale or keeping us alive. It's just...the future. A cute little baby who gets to live in a cute little farmhouse, in a better world than we had."

His words twisted in Jeni's chest, curling around her heart until it ached. Silently, she handed him one of the nails, then dragged his mouth down to hers.

He smiled into the kiss, his lips curving against hers. Then he tilted his head and kissed her deeper. Slow, lazy, like they had forever with nowhere to go and nothing to do but this.

Jeni broke away and nipped at his chin. "Don't tempt me," she whispered, echoing his teasing warning.

"Later," he murmured, with a stern, steely edge that marked it as both a command and a promise.

She could live with that.

Hawk spun the nail between his fingers and turned back to the crib. "Do you ever think about it? How things will change when we win."

When, not *if*. "Honestly? As little as possible. I just..." Her voice failed her. "It doesn't seem fair, I guess, to the people who won't be around to enjoy it."

"What wouldn't be fair is giving up on living when people have laid down their lives to give you the chance." He set the nail in place and tapped a few times, settling it, then drove it halfway in with one firm swing. "I'll have to build one of these for Rachel. Might as well get a jump on that kid being the most spoiled baby within a thousand-mile radius."

"Hawk." She had to tug at his shoulder to turn him toward her. "I'm not giving up on anything. If I'm still around—"

He pressed his thumb to her mouth, silencing her words. "When I came to Four, all I could think about

211

for battle. No matter what I wanted for myself..." His thumb drifted back and forth, stroking her lower lip. "I can't get back all that wasted time, but I'm not wasting any more. I'm dreaming big, Jeni. I got enough dreams for everyone."

The vise around her heart twisted tight, then eased a little. So she slid her hands into his back pockets. "Share them with me."

"Jas wants babies." Hawk threaded his fingers through her hair. "He's not gonna say it, not while things are this dangerous, but he wants to make a family with Noelle. One with all the love neither of them ever got." When his fingers reached the end of her hair, he started at the top again, dragging his fingernails teasingly over her scalp. "Six and Bren are gonna make a family, too. With every goddamn orphan in Sector Three."

"Yes." It sounded better than good. It sounded *right*. "Don't forget Flash and Amira. Hana needs a baby brother."

"If they're not working on one already, I'd be surprised. And Jared can have his club back if he wants, and he and Lili won't even have to spy. Just fleece fools of their money and buy all their poor friends great presents."

"Lex and Dallas can finally get some *sleep*."

Hawk laughed. "Ford and Mia won't. Not until she's turned Sector Eight upside-down and organized it down to the paperclips. And I'm going to get Shipp to drag that car we found for Finn over here and help him fix it up. You and Trix can cheer us on while we race."

Her pulse stuttered. "We can?"

"Sure, unless you wanna learn how instead." His fingers traced seductive patterns on her scalp as his

want. I bet you'd look real good driving fast."

She closed her eyes, but even then she could barely see it. It shimmered in her mind's eye like a mirage, hazy and off balance. Too bright to be real. She wanted it desperately, this future Hawk seemed to visualize so easily, but she just couldn't seem to put herself in it.

Jeni knew it had to be about self-preservation, her mind shielding her from the worst-case scenario. If she never truly grasped the concept of this future, it wouldn't shred her to bits when—*if*—it never happened. But, staring up into Hawk's eyes, it felt more like a premonition, and she shivered despite the lazy heat of the day.

Hawk tilted her head back, his body so close that she could feel his solid warmth all through her. "You'd look good doing anything you wanted. Dancing. Working the bar. Racing. Settling down in a little place like this, so I could build you whatever the hell furniture struck your fancy that day."

She gripped his wrists and smiled. "You *do* dream big."

"Someone's got to." All traces of teasing vanished from his voice, and his dark eyes were serious. Earnest. "Maybe that's the worst thing Eden did to us. They taught us not to dream outside of these tiny boxes they shoved us in."

It was what Eden did to everyone, on both sides of the wall. Because people with hopes and aspirations were unpredictable, and nothing could disrupt their carefully ordered society quite like that. The sector leaders, even Dallas O'Kane himself—they didn't pose the biggest danger to the city.

No, Eden's real enemy was *possibility*.

It was hers right now, too, just in an entirely

this moment go. "I need to say this, Hawk," she whispered. "I need for you to *let me* say it."

"All right," he said softly.

Jeni took a deep breath. Her thoughts were racing, tumbling around in her head, and if she didn't get this just right, he'd misunderstand. "If this is all we get— us, here, like this—" His hands tightened, and he went tense, so she slid her arms around him. "It's enough. More than I ever thought I'd have."

His throat worked as he swallowed. "You're more than I ever thought I'd have, too. But this is *not* enough." He tilted her head back, the fingers tangled in her hair suddenly firm and demanding. "There's no such thing as *enough* of you. Not unless it's forever."

Her heart stuttered again, this time resuming in a thudding beat. "Hawk."

"You don't have to feel the same way." His lips feathered warm and soft across her forehead. Her cheek. The corner of her mouth. "But don't fool yourself, Jeni. I want all of you. And I'll fight for my big dreams as long as I'm breathing."

Simple, black and white. Struggling towards the future or resigning yourself to nothing. "I'm not trying to convince you to stop. I'm going to fight, too. As hard as I can, I swear, for us and for everyone else. But if we die—"

His mouth crashed into hers, swallowing her words. His tongue swept over her lips, driving them apart, demanding a response. Jeni gave in, letting the sheer, primal vitality of it spill through her.

And then she realized how selfish she was being. Hawk had always lived in the moment because it was all he ever had. Tomorrow had never been a certainty for him. And now, he was finally at a point where he

a time past the war—and she was dragging him right back down.

She broke the kiss with a shudder and leaned her forehead against his jaw. "What will we grow?"

"How about strawberries?" One strong arm slid around her, pulling her tight to his chest. "Alya can teach us how to make jam, and Lex will keep us in business all by herself."

"I know how to make jam." Jeni smiled against his shoulder. "In theory, anyway."

"Yeah?" His fingers smoothed circles between her shoulder blades. "Then we'll get goats, too. Tatiana's already been after me about goat milk. She wants to make soap with it."

He wove the rest of the O'Kanes into this fantasy future of his so easily, and the solid thread of connection to their present helped ease the anxious knot in her belly. She tipped her head back and looked up at him. "Are you sure you want a city girl?"

His smile warmed her to the tips of her toes. "As long as she's you."

13

Owen Turner's place was a dump.

The building Zan led them to was on the southeast side of Four, in the no man's land of utter hell. If you kept driving toward the edge of the sector, you'd hit the new buildings, nice and clean, constructed by people who could afford to buy themselves a little space. Past that were the places like Hawk's sisters' farm.

But here—right on what used to be the edge of Four—everything was grimy and rundown and desperate as fuck. Hawk couldn't imagine anyone with the money to bribe their way through Gia's front doors living in a shithole like this.

As if the outside wasn't bad enough, Cruz stopped when they reached the claustrophobic little third-floor landing. He tilted his head, frowned, and eased his pistol from its holster. "Someone beat us here."

walls, but unmistakable. The clomp of boots. The crack and crash of wood. Hollow thuds.

Jasper held up one hand, his brow furrowing. Then all but two fingers folded down as he glanced at Cruz and arched one eyebrow in question.

After a moment, Cruz shook his head and held up three fingers.

Four against three. Pretty safe odds for an O'Kane, especially with a guy like Cruz at your back. Not so long ago, Hawk would have wished for something riskier, the promise of a knock-down, drag-out brawl. But it seemed like a million damn years had passed since those nights Hawk had spent stalking the sectors after dark, spoiling for a fight, desperate to take out his frustration with his fists.

No anticipation filled him as he pulled his own gun and checked it. He didn't have tension and frustration anymore. He had Jeni, and he had dreams.

All he wanted was to get the damn job done and go home to her in one piece.

Jasper waited a moment longer, then nodded firmly. Zan kicked in the door, sending splinters of cheap wood and particleboard flying, and Jas swung into the room. Shouts greeted him, and Hawk stepped through the door just in time for a wiry, unwashed body to slam right into his chest.

Jasper already had one in a headlock when the second intruder—the one who wasn't trying to flee—rushed him. Hawk shoved the terrified man at Zan and hurried across the room.

Jas took a punch to the jaw and shook it off with a growl. *"Don't* make me wish I'd shot you."

Hawk grabbed the guy by the back of the shirt and jerked him back, dragging him up onto his toes to cut

Hawk's face, so Hawk shoved him up against the wall hard enough to knock the wind out of him.

"Where's Turner?" Jas demanded.

"Aw, shit, they're not gonna know. These three? They're about the small-time smash-and-grab. Isn't that right?" Zan shook the guy in his grip. "Weren't just dropping in to visit a pal, were you?"

The man was small, but he was fast. He aimed a punch at Zan along with a knee to the balls. Zan caught the swing, but the knee connected solidly, and the guy howled as Zan squeezed his hand until bone crunched.

"Mother*fucker*," Zan gasped.

Jasper growled again. "What did you take?"

"Nothing." The guy locked under Jas's arm was turning red. "The place had been tossed already."

Cruz nudged one of the pried-up floorboards with his boot. "Maybe it had, but you were still looking."

The man in Hawk's grip wasn't struggling anymore. He'd gone the kind of still Hawk recognized all too well—prey, trying not to draw the attention of a predator. Hawk stepped back, keeping the bastard crushed against the wall with one hand, and caught a flash of shiny silver in the man's back pocket.

A second later, Hawk had a brand-fucking-new tablet in one hand. No scratches, no dings, none of the evidence of a piece of tech that had changed hands enough times to end up in a dump like this—or in the hands of thieves desperate enough to rob it. "I think I got something."

Jasper whistled. "That's nice. I know you boys didn't bring that in here with you."

Cruz crossed the room and reached out. The thief in Hawk's grip started squirming, no doubt seeing the biggest score of his life slipping through his fingers as

He flipped it over and studied the tiny serial numbers etched into the back. "This is two models newer than the run they were on when I left Eden. It might even be the last batch the city got out of Eight before they turned on the wall."

Jasper's jaw clenched, and Hawk realized that he'd been hoping it was all a bunch of bullshit, that'd they'd come here and find Owen Turner with his thumb up his ass, drinking cheap booze and watching half-scrambled porn. That he wasn't a *spy*, just a lonely asshole who talked big when it didn't count.

Instead, they had a missing spy and a brand-new piece of Eden tech.

The man Jasper had been holding panted for air as he shoved him away, toward the door. "Get out. If I catch you stealing again—if you so much as *look* at someone funny—I won't be so cordial."

The guy nodded, already stumbling past Cruz, clearly ready to make a break for it. But the man who'd been holding the tablet was stupider, or greedier, or just plain desperate. "You can't just take that—"

Hawk dragged him up on his toes again, cutting off his words. After trading a look with Zan, Hawk gave the sorry bastard one good heave. He slammed into the dirty floor hard enough to skid several feet.

He came to a stop just short of Zan, who stepped down on his shoulder with one solid boot. "You heard the man. Now get the fuck out of here before I break your fingers too, you thieving little shit."

The three of them bolted for the door so fast they got stuck all trying to go through at the same time. One of them jabbed the other with an elbow and tumbled out into the hallway, and Hawk fought back a laugh.

Then his gaze dropped to the tablet in Cruz's hand,

As the would-be thieves' stampeding footsteps receded down the stairs, Cruz swiped his thumb over the tablet's face. "It's password protected. Five characters."

"Five?" Jasper turned to Hawk. "The girl over at Gia's place that Turner's stuck on—what did Jeni say her name was?"

Zan snorted. "No one's that stupid, man. Especially not a fucking spy."

A guy who ran his mouth about shit the way Turner had was exactly that stupid. "Paige. With an *i*."

Jasper tipped his head at the tablet. "Try it, Cruz."

Cruz tapped it in, and both his eyebrows rose as the screen sprang to life. Hawk had rarely put his hands on a piece of tech this shiny before joining the O'Kanes, so he couldn't follow what Cruz did next. His fingers danced across the screen, pulling up windows and entering text.

After another moment, he smiled. "He has decrypted data on here. Noah can compare it to the encrypted version, maybe get a jump on cracking their code."

"How long would something like that take?"

"A couple weeks?" Cruz shrugged and tucked the tablet into his pocket. "Maybe less, knowing Noah. I'll have him dump everything on here, too. See if we can get an idea of who Turner's been talking to."

"All right." Jasper cracked his neck and stretched his shoulders. "Let's move. I'll report to Dallas. Cruz, you take that thing straight to Noah. Zan, Hawk—hit the streets. Dallas still wants Owen Turner, and he wants him alive. Find him."

Hawk suspected Owen Turner was halfway to the ocean by now, but it didn't matter. "Yes, sir."

night," he reminded them. "Mad's been waiting a long time to take marks, so he deserves a good one. So do Dylan, Jyoti, and Scarlet."

Zan murmured in agreement, and Hawk shoved down the surge of envy.

Marks. Ink. *Forever*. The collar he'd given Jeni was reckless enough. Even if every day he spent with her made him more and more certain that he'd been right, that *they* were right...

Jeni couldn't see past the war. She couldn't bring herself to envision a future where the two of them got to spend forever together. And maybe it was cruel to keep trying, to build up her dreams, to bind her to him as tight as he fucking could. If he died, it would hurt her.

But if he stopped trying...

Sometimes, she stared up at him with a wonder she couldn't hide. As if she couldn't quite believe that the fantasies he wove around her extended beyond his bed and all the things she was willing to do there. That she was more than a pleasant interlude, or a diversion.

Whether he lived or died, that was one thing he could do. He could show Jeni how she deserved to be loved.

Completely.

14

The O'Kanes loved to party. And since that was part of their image—hard-drinking, hard-fucking hedonists in search of nothing more than a goddamn good time—they usually didn't mind if people showed up to watch. But not when they were celebrating new members or new marks.

Tonight, they had both.

Jeni accepted another beer from Trix and held the cool glass up to her cheek. Even if this hadn't been an occasion for O'Kanes alone, she suspected that no one without cuffs would have been invited. It seemed like everyone was pulling inward, and it was no wonder. They'd been scouring the sector for city *spies*, for fuck's sake. If there was ever a time to stick close to the other O'Kanes, this was it.

Jyoti pulled one side of her deeply cut gown aside,

her heart. It was shaped like an intricate knot, and Jeni had to lean closer to make out the lines in the dim light.

They weren't just lines. They were words, the names of her lovers wound through the knot in Ace's inimitable style.

She straightened and shook her head. "It's beautiful. Just gorgeous."

"It is." Jyoti slid her dress back into place with a gentle smile. "Mad swore he was willing to wait, but I wasn't."

"Neither was I." Scarlet's almost identical tattoo peeked above the low neckline of her tank top, and she touched it lightly before arching one eyebrow. "And if we'd tried to make Dylan wait..."

It was a familiar refrain, one that had suffused the sector for weeks and throbbed beneath the music tonight. It was impossible to exist in Four right now and not feel the sharp sting of desperation. "I'm happy for you, all of you."

Jyoti brushed a finger over Jeni's collar. "I'm happy for you, too. Hawk is a good man. One of the best."

"He is." Jeni looked across the room, spotting him instantly where he stood with Jas and Finn, all three clustered close with the intent expressions that usually meant engines were being discussed. He glanced her way, and the corner of his mouth tilted up.

A tiny smile, but it blazed in his eyes, transforming his face. Her blood thrummed a little hotter, and she pressed her beer to her flushed cheek again.

Noelle slid up behind Jyoti and wrapped her in a fierce hug. "Congratulations."

"Thank you, Noelle."

"I'm so glad we have something to celebrate." She

tonight?"

"Oh, I don't think so." Her cheeks turned pink. "I don't have my band, and it's not really that kind of night, you know?"

Jyoti stroked her fingers through Scarlet's hair, a slow caress full of as much promise as her words. "I'll see if I can talk her around."

Scarlet's blush deepened, and Noelle laughed.

"Only if you want to. It's *your* party." Noelle hooked her arm through Jeni's. "But I'm stealing her away. I'm in the mood to dance."

Jeni set down her bottle and followed Noelle out onto the floor, but there was clearly more than dancing on her mind. "What's up?"

"I think Noah's getting close." Noelle swayed with her, her voice a low whisper. "I couldn't even convince him to come up for the party."

"The decryption?"

"Yeah. That tablet the boys found gave him what he needed. He's thinking he'll have it cracked by lunch tomorrow."

It had been weeks since Eden had gone into lockdown, weeks since they'd started encrypting all their transmissions. If Noah managed to decipher their code, Jeni would have hundreds of thousands of pages of messages to go through. "Oh."

"Oh," Noelle agreed in a sympathetic voice. "Hey, Emma and I will be right there with you. Even if it's just to get coffee or look up anything that seems weird."

"No, it's not the workload." How could she explain without sounding irrational—or, worse, superstitious? "It's just that it means we'll be that much closer, right? There *has* to be information in those messages that we can use. That we'll have to use." She met Noelle's gaze.

"I know." For a moment, worry lined Noelle's features, then it twisted into resolve. "But we're ready. We have the supplies, and we have the hospital. We have a life worth fighting for."

Jeni had to smile. If sheer fucking force of will could pull you through a war unscathed, then they'd all be fine. No one was more stubborn, more relentlessly *alive*, than an O'Kane.

Before she could respond, someone banged on the makeshift bar. The music cut out, and Lex climbed onto the bar, where Rachel had already set up sixteen shot glasses in a neat row. She filled them two at a time, from the finest whiskey Nessa had ever bottled right on down to the roughest rotgut, as Lex shaded her eyes and scanned the room. "All right, where's he hiding?"

Whoops and cheers rose as Dylan began to make his way to the front of the room, a broad smile on his face. It was so different from the rare ones he'd always worn, sardonic and vague, that it was a little hard to recognize him. Being with Mad and Jyoti and Scarlet had changed him, and tonight was evidence of that.

Lex cleared her throat, then ruined her solemn air by reaching down to ruffle Dylan's hair. "Dr. Jordan. I guess there's only one thing to say."

"Yeah," Zan called out from the crowd. "Took you long enough!"

Lex hopped down as laughter rippled through the room. "Close, but not quite." She patted Dylan's cheek fondly and grinned. "Welcome home."

Rachel lifted the first shot glass and held it out, but before Dylan could take it, Mad appeared at his side. His brown eyes sparked with irrepressible joy as he plucked the shot from Rachel's fingers and held it up. "Might be a little redundant to stake my claim...

He tipped back the shot, drove his fingers into Dylan's hair, and dragged him into a liquor-soaked kiss that went on and on, long after the whiskey was gone. Dylan was breathless when it ended, his face alight with desire and satisfaction.

He reached for the next shot, but Dallas picked it up instead. Lex followed suit, and so did Jasper. One by one, the people closest to the bar stepped forward to claim the remaining shots.

It made sense. When Jeni had gone through the O'Kanes' version of an initiation, she'd passed the night in a giddy blur that had ended with her slung over Flash's shoulder and carried away to sleep it off. From a practical standpoint, they couldn't afford to have their only doctor get that trashed, not when Eden's MPs could beat down their door at any moment.

But this went beyond the practical. An almost reverent hush fell over the room as they raised their glasses—Dallas and Lex, Jasper and Bren. Jyoti and Scarlet, of course. Six, Lili, Ace. Their faces blurred together as tears burned Jeni's eyes.

Hawk picked up the last shot, the rotgut at the end of the bar. His gaze locked with hers, he smiled slow and warm, and lifted his glass in the air. He didn't look away, not even when he knocked back the shot without so much as a flinch.

The noise broke the spell, yelling and laughter that rebounded through the room in a chorus of revelry. Dylan began to make the rounds, spinning from one embrace to another.

By the time he reached Jeni, he looked a little dazed. She folded her arms around his neck, hugged him tight, and whispered, "It's okay. I know the feeling."

Someone else whisked him away, and Jeni stood

outside these walls could ever understand. O'Kanes didn't bend, didn't break. They were stronger than steel because they held one another up. If one of them needed help, their brothers and sisters would step in and shoulder some of the load.

It was unspoken, understood. Whether they were at war with other sectors or the city or no one at all, they stood together.

Jeni retreated back to the edge of the room and picked up her beer. It had gone warm already, the amber glass slick with condensation, but she finished it anyway, then leaned against the wall and looked around. If she stared at them all long enough, tried *hard* enough, she could fix this moment in her memory forever.

"I'll trade you," Cruz rumbled.

He was holding out a fresh beer, one Jeni accepted gratefully. "Thanks."

"No problem." He leaned against the wall next to her and watched the crowd of people jostling to congratulate Dylan. The stern lines of his face softened as Ace's laughter drifted over the din, and he lifted his beer. "I want to do something nice for Hawk."

It wasn't quite the last thing she expected him to say, but it was close. "Why?" she asked curiously.

His lips quirked. "The ginger tea he showed me how to make for Rachel has almost gotten rid of her morning sickness completely."

"Oh." That explained why the petite blonde wasn't in a corner with her head in a bucket—and why Cruz wasn't gnashing his teeth in helpless frustration. "Good. I'm glad she's feeling better."

"Me too," he murmured. "So if I can do anything for him—or for you—then you tell me, okay?"

Cruz. Not so you would owe him one."

"It's not about owing." Cruz braced one shoulder against the brick and stared down at her. "If we were keeping track of debts, I've already got such a mountain of debt to you, I couldn't repay it in a lifetime."

She did a double take. "To *me*? What for?"

"For helping me get here." His gaze was so, so serious. So solemn. "I've jumped off twenty-story buildings and been less scared than I was the first time I kissed Ace."

She remembered the moment—the hesitation, the challenge. How the tension had stretched out between him and Ace like a chasm in the earth, only instead of widening with every heartbeat, it had grown smaller and smaller. How Cruz had finally broken with a flash of guilt eclipsed only by his longing.

She hadn't seen it at the time, but here, in retrospect, she recognized his fear. "Of course you were afraid. You weren't falling off a building, but you were still falling."

"Yeah, I was." His gaze drifted back out to the dancing, going inevitably to where Ace and Rachel swayed with the music. "Still am. It doesn't stop, you know. It gets less scary sometimes...but it doesn't stop."

Jeni glanced over to where Hawk was finally getting a chance to congratulate Dylan. His smile was brilliant, so open that it almost hurt. Then he looked up, directly at her, and the bottle almost slipped from between her fingers.

She was starting to suspect Cruz was right.

#

If Hawk thought Ace talked a lot when he was

ing was damn near impossible.

"—so we had just rolled out our second real batch of the good stuff. The first one, most of those credits went to buying better supplies. But the second?" Ace grinned widely. "Oh, we were dick-deep in credits for the first time in our *lives*."

"And..." Lex stretched forward in her chair to grab another one of the tiny sandwiches Lili liked to make for parties. "What do a bunch of hale, healthy, dumbassed little boys like to do when they have that much money?"

Rachel stifled a giggle. "They get dick-deep in something else?"

Jasper leaned forward with a groan, pinching the bridge of his nose. "Please, *please* do not tell this story."

"Sorry, brother. Some tales are just too legendary to let slip into myth." Ace propped his elbows on his knees, deep into the story now. "So it's me and Jas and Zan's big brother. And that charming motherfucker didn't even have to open his wallet, because he was way better looking than Zan—"

"Fuck *you*," Zan enunciated slowly over the rim of his glass. From her perch in his lap, Tatiana mock-glared at Ace, but he only winked at her.

Noelle nudged Ace with her foot. "Come on, I want to hear the rest of it."

"Fine, so Jas and I bring a couple of pretty ladies back to the compound." Ace waved one hand around. "Which was basically just this building at that point, nothing else. We had bedrooms up where the storage is now, and we were all making *very* good use of them—"

"Too good," Dallas rumbled. "Since I was the only one who noticed when a handful of punk-ass thieves kicked in our damn door."

matic, Hawk choked on his beer. "I can't help that I'm focused," Ace drawled. "I don't hear Rachel and Cruz complaining."

"Right, you're a sex god," Jasper interjected. "The end."

"C'mon, Jas, this next part makes you look *heroic.*" Ace's grin widened. "I might have been distracted, but Jas wasn't fucking around. He comes roaring down the stairs, a gun in one hand, and with his other, he's still trying to pull up his pants. By the time I made it out here, he was in a goddamn shoot-out with his jeans around his ankles and his dick waving in the wind, just *begging* to get shot off."

Jeni turned her face into Hawk's neck, her shoulders shaking with silent mirth, but the others weren't as subtle. Warm laughter rose around them as Jas glowered.

Noelle bit back a giggle and stroked Jas's arm. "I'm glad nothing got...shot off."

"I bet you are, princess." Ace slapped Jas on the arm. "Gotta say, it wasn't the worst strategy. The punks were distracted by Jas in all his glory, and it only took so long to finish them off because I couldn't stop fucking laughing."

"You've had your moments, Santana," Jasper grumbled.

"Not like that." Ace sprawled back in the chair and threw his arms wide. "If it had been *my* magnificent dick, they all would have swooned on the fucking spot."

Dallas snorted. "If that was true, I'd kick your ass for not saving us all that work."

"My man's wise, as always." Lex flashed Dallas a wicked grin as she rose and reached for his hand. Without a word, she tugged him from his seat, toward the

The music had been turned down, relegated to the background as they drank and talked, but it still throbbed softly through the room. Together with the lowered lights, it created the illusion of a sheltered place out of time, a calm in the middle of the storm.

As Ace started in on another story, Hawk laid his hand over Jeni's and twined their fingers together. "Dance with me."

She slipped into his arms like falling into bed at the end of a long day, with a quiet, relieved sigh that warmed his skin. "I wasn't sure if you'd want to."

On any other night, he would have wanted something more. Something filthy and raw, the realization of all his fantasies of Jeni, shattering at his touch while the whole damn gang watched.

He pulled her more tightly against him and let one hand drift up her back. Her hair slipped over his fingers, soft and silky, and his thumb found the leather collar at her throat. He didn't need to stake his claim in a public declaration. Jeni had been his from the moment she said *yes*, and he was the only one who hadn't believed it.

Maybe he never would, entirely. Because having her like this, snuggled trustingly against his chest as they swayed with the music... It was too damn good to be true. "I'll always want to dance with you."

She laughed. "Not the *me* part. The dancing part. Some people don't like it."

"I suppose I didn't let you get much dancing done at the rally." He caught her hand and spun her around before dragging her back to his chest. "It's just about the only thing to do at those parties, since they're not quite as adventurous as us O'Kanes."

"Liar." She rubbed her thumbs over the ink around

232

rendezvous."

"Well, sure. Clandestine being the key word." He grinned and leaned close. "C'mon, Jeni. Admit it. Sneaking away can be fun, too."

Her amusement faded into a glowing smile. "With the right person."

With *him*. His heart dove toward his stomach before flipping up into his throat, and the emotion swelling through him was too big to contain and too new to share.

He twirled her toward the door as laughter rose behind them again, another round of affectionate ribbing as Ace finished a second outrageous story. They were reliving old memories and making new ones, fixing each one in place in their hearts because, this time, they really were standing on the edge of oblivion.

And there was one memory Hawk needed to make.

They slipped through the warehouse door, but when Jeni turned for the barracks, Hawk shook his head and steered her toward the garage instead. His car was inside, chrome gleaming in the flickering overhead light, the new paint job flawless.

He ran his fingers up the hood. "If we weren't on the brink of war, I'd take you out into the desert. Drive fast, and then ride you nice and slow."

Jeni walked around to the other side of the car, skimming her hand over the surface of one headlight as she moved. "We don't *have* to go anywhere."

The car had been an extension of him for so many years that he damn near felt the trailing of her fingertips, like she was stroking him, too. "You gonna make out with me in the back seat, Jeni?"

"Or the front seat." She tilted her head, considering. "We'd probably dent the hood."

his imagination. Her hair wild, her short red skirt up around her hips, ankles braced on his shoulders while he took his time working deep. "I might be willing to risk it," he rumbled, circling the front of the car.

"You wouldn't." Smiling, she leaned over the trunk, gliding her body across the cool metal as she slipped away. "This car is your *baby*."

That was an image to savor, too—Jeni, bent over the trunk. She'd like it like that, hard and rough, trapped between the unyielding metal and his unforgiving thrusts. He lengthened his strides, stalking her with a lazy smile that promised trouble when he finally got his hands on her. "Is that a challenge?"

"I don't know." She stopped and propped her hand on her hip, dragging that sinful skirt a few inches higher on her bare thigh. "Should it be?"

He took two more steps and lunged for her. Her squealed laughter echoed off the huge bay doors as she ran, threading softer warmth through the sharp edges of his arousal. His heart was pounding when he caught her with an arm around her waist and dragged her to him.

Her ass rubbed against his cock, and her hair flew wildly into his face as he bent to her ear. "I can't resist a challenge."

The only answer was the click of the handle as she opened the back door.

He caught the top of the door, hauled it wide, and nudged her inside. Her skirt fluttered up as she slipped onto the seat, flashing her thighs and the sweet, naked curve of her ass.

Hawk damn near dove in after her.

She squealed again when he caught her and pulled her into his lap. His boot slammed into the seat and her

the leather with Jeni astride him, her skirt hitched up to her hips and her bare ass filling his hands. He found the ribbon around her waist, some barely there scrap of nothing masquerading as underwear, and he dragged her closer and groaned as she ground down against his erection.

Jeni traced the corner of his mouth with her tongue. "You said nice and slow, right?"

"You're the impatient one," he teased, stroking up her back. The top of her strapless dress barely clung to her breasts, and it was so easy to coax it down as he kissed her throat. "I could make out with you like this all night long."

"Now *that* sounded like a challenge."

He licked the spot that made her squirm before teasing her with a soft bite. "I don't know," he echoed her words back to her. "Should it be?"

She closed her teeth on his earlobe—hard.

He *could* tease her all night, but fuck if he wanted to. He caught her mouth, groaning in approval when her lips parted for him. He fell into the kiss as he tugged at her dress. Her breasts spilled into his hands, warm and soft, with hard nipples begging to be pinched. He rolled his thumb around one, and she hissed in a shocked breath.

He did it again and murmured against her lips. "Open my pants."

Jeni smiled and tugged at his belt. They were pressed together so tightly that every movement was also a caress, the backs of her hands stroking his stomach through his shirt.

She left his belt hanging open and danced her fingers lightly over the top button on his jeans. Teasing. *Tempting.*

nipple. One hard suck, and she popped open the button with a throaty moan. He teased her with a hint of teeth but pulled back when she arched into him, switching instead to her other breast.

Another suck. Another button. Jeni squirmed in his grasp, and he cupped her breasts again, catching the wet peaks between his thumbs and fingers. When her dazed gaze locked with his, he pinched both of her nipples at the same time.

The last button yielded, and she rocked against him with a shudder.

"Now take my cock in your hand."

She didn't look away, and she was barely breathing as she freed his erection and wrapped her fingers around the shaft in a firm, possessive grip.

He dropped one hand to the leather seat, grasping the edge of it as his self-control faltered. For one heartbeat, all he wanted to do was thrust up into the sweet circle of her fingers, but he held himself back. Everything but the words.

"We're gonna fuck just like this." He slid his other hand up her thigh. He found the ribbon and traced it to the tiny scrap of silk covering her pussy, and a brush of his thumb rubbed the wet fabric against her clit. "I'm not even going to take these off, just push them aside and shove my cock deep, because that's what you want. You want me to lose control and *take*."

"Sort of." She shifted closer, until their bodies were pressed together, their hands trapped between them. "I want *you*. All of you."

Maybe he wasn't the only one who couldn't quite believe, who touched the collar around her throat and thought *too good to be true*. "You've had all of me, Jeni. From the first fucking time I put my hands on you.

He moved his thumb in a tight circle and inhaled her jagged sigh. "The words that come out of my mouth when I'm touching you... I can't even talk to anyone else, but with you, I can't fucking shut up. Every dirty thought, every fantasy I've ever had—I can't control it when you have your hands on me. I can't stop *wanting*."

Her gaze dropped to his mouth. She lifted her free hand, trembling as she traced his lower lip with her fingertips. "I'm the opposite," she confessed. "I'm good with words. I usually know what to say, just...not when it matters this much."

He kissed the tips of her fingers, his heart racing with more than just arousal. "You don't have to say anything. Show me instead."

Her hand fell away, and she kissed him, long and deep, every slick glide of her tongue reflecting the need that pulsed within him. She lifted her hips, and Hawk scrabbled for the control to think past her kiss, for the coordination to help her into place and nudge her panties aside.

It wasn't smooth. It wasn't easy. He knocked his knee against the front seat and almost put his elbow through the window, but he didn't care. He was more sure than ever that anyone who could hold themselves apart from Jeni didn't fucking deserve her.

And none of it mattered when she slid down his length, her slick pussy gripping him tight, the friction of fabric and the confines of the car making it all hotter, rawer. She bit his tongue and moaned into his mouth as she began to move—slow, so slow, but with an intensity that consumed them both, that narrowed the whole fucking universe to just them, here, in the back seat of his car.

He let himself pretend it *was* their universe, that

away. He gripped her hips, helped her rock, every slow withdrawal torture, every slide back like coming home. His life could be this—just Jeni, just the two of them, deep, drugging kisses and slow, sweet fucking and no pain but the kind she begged him for.

She was panting, gasping for breath, when she finally tore her mouth from his. Her head fell back, and the look on her face was beyond pleasure—a new expression that didn't exist in his careful catalog of all the ways she gave in to ecstasy.

It was more. It was *his*. "That's it, Jeni. Fucking show me."

She clutched at his shoulders, scratching him through his T-shirt. As sharp as the caress was, it paled next to the sensation of her nipples against his chest, rasping through the thin cotton. Different than skin on skin, but he liked this, too, how she would strip away all her protections for him, how she trusted him enough to be exposed even if he wasn't.

He couldn't work his hand between their bodies to touch her clit, but he could shift the angle of her hips. He dragged her close and tilted them until she was shuddering every time he met her thrusts. Her throat beckoned, and he couldn't stop himself. He bit the delicate skin just above her collar, and she turned her face to his.

Her lips brushed his ear. "You're the first," she whispered. "The only one I could ever give this much to."

The darkness inside him would have loved that, if there had been anything dark left. But Jeni had crawled under his skin and slipped through him, shining so fucking bright that nothing seemed wrong anymore, as long as she was right there with him.

her hair and urged her back, grinding out the words between each slow, endless thrust. "You're the only one who's ever made me dream."

Her breathing hitched on a noise that sounded like his name. Her mouth crashed into his again as she rode him faster, harder, fucking her way toward bliss. Using him for her pleasure, shameless and selfish—

It was the hottest fucking thing he'd ever seen.

She came with a rough cry, one that filled the confines of his car. Her teeth dug into his bottom lip, and she kept moving, even as she shook above him, clenched around him.

Control was a vague memory, and patience a joke. Hawk tightened his grip and drove up into her, gave her *all* of him. His hope and his future and then his pleasure, as the perfect grip of her pussy around his cock tipped him over the edge.

He kissed her as he came, traded her cries for his groans, and stopped himself from letting more words tumble out. Words that offered too much, too soon.

Words that would scare her away unless she was dreaming of the future, too.

She collapsed against his chest, her face nestled in the hollow of his shoulder. Hawk struggled to catch his breath, but pleasure lingered in lazy, tingling waves, set off all over again every time she exhaled against his skin.

He wrapped both arms around her and closed his eyes. "Would you believe this is the first time I've ever fucked a woman in my car?"

"It is *not*."

A smile tugged at his lips. "Yeah, it is. You weren't wrong. It's my baby."

She wiggled in his lap, in his arms. "All the more

There hadn't been anyone he wanted enough, anyone he could let become a part of this—the only thing that had been *his* during the hardest years of his life. "When you don't have a lot to offer, you save it for the people who matter."

Jeni went still for a moment, then snuggled closer. "Thank you, then. For sharing it with me."

He guided her hand down to the cool leather seat. "I rebuilt it, you know. Inside and out. Figuring out how to reupholster these seats, that was a pain in the ass. The guys kept razzing me, telling me to settle for the fabric we'd scavenged. But I wanted leather, so I saved for it."

Her hand flexed under his. Then she twisted her wrist, turning it so she could twine her fingers with his. "Tell me about it. I want to know."

"The car?" He wove his other fingers into her hair and smiled. "When I left the farm, I ran into Shipp not long after. I was pissy and mad at the world, and he wasn't *that* much older than me, but he had his shit together. Like Dallas, you know? You just look at him and you know that if you follow him, your life will be better, because he cares about making it better."

She made a soft, amused sound. "So you joined a gang of smugglers."

Hawk laughed. "No, I joined a gang of gearheads who smuggled so they could afford to fix up their cars."

Her laughter joined his. "An important nuance." She lifted her head. "Were you happy?"

Not an easy question to answer. "I thought I was," he said finally. "Not at first. But after about six months, Shipp dragged the bones of this car home and gave her to me. And he told me I could brood about what I'd lost, or I could make something new. Took me

240

do the seats, I was content."

She squeezed his hand. "And now?"

"Now I know what happy feels like."

"Mmm." Her eyes were shining. "Like this."

Exactly like this. But he still brushed his lips over hers and corrected her. "Like you."

15

Noah had spent the last three days in his work-room—and it showed.

He wasn't a slob, not by any stretch, but there were unmistakable, unavoidable signs of constant inhabitation. He'd slowly collected tablets and manuals and loose components and put them all into easy reach. Now, those items formed a clear semicircle around his chair where it was situated in front of his numerous, differently sized screens, like leaves shuffled to the side of a well-used wooded path.

Noah's eyes were red, his hair mussed. When he slept, it was only because Emma periodically dragged him away to bed. When he ate, it was because someone shoved a plate or a sandwich into his hands. He downed the food quickly, almost all of his attention still fixed on the lines of code scrolling across the screens.

know how much longer Noah could keep this up. She shot Noelle a pointed look from her chair near the door, where she sat with her own tablet, and the other woman furrowed her brow. "Noah—"

"No." He half-rose from his seat, his face intent on the screen to his left even as he reached out and tapped blindly on a tablet to his right.

Noelle exchanged a worried glance with Jeni and circled the table. "I know you said you were close, but that was five hours ago. You need—"

"Shh." He swept up the tablet they'd picked up from Owen Turner, leaning over so far that his chair rocked precariously. He thrust the tablet in Jeni's direction. "I think I've got it."

The last few times he'd uttered the words, adrenaline had surged through Jeni. But they'd turned out to be false alarms. "I think it's time to talk about diminishing returns, Noah. You're *exhausted*."

"One more," he shot back, waving the tablet insistently. "If this isn't it, I'll take a fucking nap."

"All right." She lifted both hands in surrender and rose. "Let's check it out."

She took the tablet from him and accessed the last message, some unsolicited offer for a free trial to the latest time-wasting, pay-to-play game on Eden's network. Noah jabbed his finger down on his keyboard one last time and collapsed back into his chair.

The cursor on his monitor blinked three times before spitting out several lines of text. Noah scrubbed his hands over his face and left them over his eyes. "I can't look. If it's not right..."

"I know." She leaned over to peer at the monitor, and all the shock and excitement that she'd shoved down before crashed through her. "...don't miss this

Noelle leaned over his other shoulder, her eyes wide. Her gaze skimmed to the end of the decrypted text, and she threw her arms around him. "You crazy bastard, I knew you could do it."

"That makes one of us," Noah said hoarsely. He dropped his hands and blinked blearily at the screen. "So that's it. We have an algorithm now. I can start the decryption process—"

"Or get some *sleep*," Noelle interrupted.

"Or get some sleep," he agreed with a rusty laugh. "I just need...wait a second."

He sat upright and snatched the tablet out of Jeni's hands. A swipe of one hand brought him back to the list of incoming messages, while his other hand flew over the keyboard. Another list appeared on the monitor—gibberish subject lines with only the dates and times visible.

Noah held the tablet up next to the screen. "There are messages missing. Incoming communications that we caught at the switch. Turner must have deleted them from the tablet."

"No wonder everything on it made for boring reading. Too boring for a spy." Jeni nodded to the screen. "Can we retrieve the deleted messages?"

"I already have them." Noah shoved two of the large tablets cluttering the table aside and came up with a third, smaller one. "Give me a second and I'll decrypt them."

Noelle watched him, her lower lip caught between her teeth. As soon as he'd transferred the decrypted messages onto the smaller tablet, she laid a hand on his shoulder. "I can oversee the decryption. I'll wake you up if I run into trouble. But you need food and a bed."

He rose slowly, passed Jeni the tablet, and started for the door with the too-careful steps of a man running on pride.

"He did good." And Dallas would reward him handsomely for it. "Now it's our turn."

Noelle flexed her fingers and slid into Noah's abandoned chair. "I'll have to decrypt this in chunks, *then* run the filter. We need some way to narrow down what we're looking for."

"May as well get started. Who knows what we'll find." Or if they'd find anything. Jeni dropped into her chair again and opened the cluster of restored messages on Owen Turner's tablet.

There were about two dozen missives to Paige, the girl who worked for Gia. They ranged from studiedly casual notes right on up to bad love poems. A few of the later ones had taken on an air of desperation, even of vague threat, and Jeni found herself wishing Hawk or Jas had found the motherfucker after all.

There were more, some of Turner trying to flex on some small-time hoods in *and* out of Eden, and others asking for jobs, loans, even transport out of the sectors to one of the nearest mountain colonies.

Then one message caught Jeni's eye—stark, terse, and nonsensical.

By the way, we're out of sugar.

And that was it. Not only was it phrased more formally than the rest of Turner's communications, but it seemed oddly domestic for a man whose apartment, by all accounts, didn't have a working kitchen. Beyond that...

Who the hell says *by the way* when they haven't said anything else?

She double-checked the time stamps, thinking

vious message, but there was nothing. Turner hadn't communicated with this address before or since.

By the way, we're out of sugar.

Something else about the message tugged at Jeni, prompting a flash of memory too brief and hazy to grasp. But she *knew* she'd seen these exact words before—in that massive pile of shit Noelle had given her to read through.

"Can we run a search on something?" she asked softly. "Doesn't have to be recent. Everything from before the wall went hot is fine."

"Sure." Noelle scooted her chair to one side and activated a second monitor. "What is it, a name? Phrase?"

Jeni propped the tablet in front of her. "What do you make of that?"

"Out of *sugar*?" Noelle made a face as she started typing. "Why would he even have sugar to...begin..." She trailed off with a frown, a deep furrow forming between her eyebrows. With a flick of her fingers across the monitor, the results of the search appeared on the wall in front of them. "Oh, my *God*."

Page after page filled the wall, pouring from the projector in a glaring, *damning* rush. All with those exact same words.

It had to be a code phrase. What it meant, Jeni had no idea—maybe it was an update, or a way to ask for a face-to-face meeting with a handler—but its purpose was clear. To be innocuous, so mundane that no computer program would ever catch it. So that you'd never even see it unless you were already looking for it.

Jeni walked toward the wall, everything numb and frozen but her galloping heart. She touched a page at the edge of the image, heedless of her body blocking

in the stuff you gave me. I didn't think twice about it because the lady owns a food stand in the market..."

Owned a stand. Another memory burned through her brain—Tatiana's face crumpling into tears when Jasper told her that Mila had died, had killed herself—

The numbness was nothing compared to the chill that swept through Jeni now. She almost stumbled back as she took in the names, trying to focus on them, to work them into some semblance of order while her mind whirled. "Anson, Ramirez, Schaffley—Noelle, do you see this?"

"They're all dead. Jesus *Christ*, Jeni." Noelle's face was pale as she rose. "I need to get Dallas and Lex."

She hurried out of the room, while Jeni kept staring at the wall until the names swam together. Those people weren't just dead—Hawk and the others had pried their corpses off the electrified wall.

For weeks, they'd all braced themselves against finding another body, another person who'd succumbed to the stress and pressure of an impending war. It had become a distillation of their larger worries, only instead of waiting to see when Eden would attack, they were waiting to see how far hopelessness had dug its claws into the people of Sector Four.

Suicide-by-Eden was sinister enough. This was something *monstrous*.

By the time Dallas and Lex appeared in the doorway, disheveled and a little out of breath, Jeni's numbness had given way to a strange kind of furious calm, a rage so deep she didn't even know how to express it.

Lex spoke first. "What do you have?"

"Your spies." Jeni barely recognized her own voice. "Do you want the good news or the bad news?"

"Give us the good."

trocuted on the wall."

Dallas's expression hardened as he stared at the projected data. "Who'd they send the messages to?"

"Throwaway IDs," Noelle answered. "You can buy them in Eden in the illegal market by the dozen. Usually they get shut down pretty fast by the automated checks, but if you know how to avoid those, or if Security has a vested interest in keeping them active..."

"Somehow I doubt they all got real guilty and marched out to off themselves in the exact same way," Dallas said.

"You know better, honey." Lex had gone pale. "Our spies were murdered."

Dallas clenched his fists. "Every fucking one of them died on the wall, but so did people who aren't on that list."

"Then we have two options," Jeni whispered. "Either people got wind of how they died and figured it was as good a way to go as any, or—"

"Or," Lex cut in, "they were killed along with the others as a cover. In case we started looking at things too closely."

"Shit." Dallas's hands curled into fists. "They're some fucking sadistic motherfucking murdering shitheads."

"Worse," Noelle said softly, her gaze locking with Jeni's. "They're Eden."

"They'd never pass up a chance to wage psychological warfare on the sectors," Jeni agreed. "But they wouldn't kill their own spies to do it unless they'd been compromised." Or outlived their usefulness.

"Loose ends," Lex whispered tightly. "The city's cleaning house."

"Which means they're about to move." Dallas

Figure out every other weird-ass email that's ever come and gone from those spies and see if anyone else was sending the same thing."

"Got it."

"Jeni?"

"Yeah?"

There was sympathy in Dallas's eyes. Pain. But also unbending, steely resolve. "Go find Hawk. It's time."

"I'll tell him." Alya wasn't going to like it. And *Hawk*— Jeni's peculiar calm shattered in an instant, replaced by pain, by a regret too deep for words or even tears.

Sector Four was his home now, but the farm in Six would always be a part of him. And now it was a part he had to destroy.

16

Hawk didn't argue when Jeni offered to come with him to Sector Six.

He should have. A stronger man would have. He could have left her at home, snug in the heart of Dallas's territory—

Except even that didn't feel safe anymore, not when they knew for sure there were Special Tasks soldiers outside the wall. Silent, invisible killers who'd been waging the cruelest, sickest kind of war on all of them. They'd sown desperation while cleaning up the city's messes, and some twisted part of Hawk couldn't help but admire their efficiency. They'd turned a handful of necessary, practical deaths into a spectacle of heartache and hopelessness.

So it felt wrong to leave Jeni behind. But it felt wrong to bring her into the most likely path of an army now that she'd confessed *how* they knew about the spies and their faked suicides.

The mystery tablet. She'd been nervous, admitting what she'd been doing with Noelle and Noah during all those long, secretive afternoons locked up in the tech room. No doubt she'd expected him to explode in a protective fury. But Hawk just nodded, because if there was one lesson he'd learned from watching Shipp with Alya all these years, it was to keep those explosions in check. Hawk couldn't protect Jeni if she didn't want to come to him with the truth.

And now that he knew the truth, letting Jeni accompany him to Six was the only choice he could live with. If she was with him, he could keep her safe.

He guided his car over the final rise and down the hill toward the farm. The moon and stars were obscured behind clouds, leaving endless darkness cut only by his headlights and the distant glow from a few of his family's windows.

The children were probably already in bed. The adults would be gathered around hearths and tables, resting weary bones and sipping Big John's godawful liquor as they prepared for another busy day of spring planting.

He was about to tear their placid little oasis to the ground and salt the earth beneath their feet.

Jeni reached across the car and touched his hand. "I'm sorry."

The soft caress helped. "She'll survive starting over. Most of us did, at least once."

"That doesn't—" Her voice broke. "That doesn't make it okay."

Tears roughened the words. The same tears he couldn't let himself shed, because when the children losing the only home they'd ever known, he had to be there. Solid and reassuring, confident enough to convince them everything was going to be all right.

Hawk twined their fingers together and pulled Jeni's hand to his lips for a kiss. "No, it's not okay. But I've got to go in there believing I can make it okay for them, or they won't believe me when I say they can do this."

"I know." She swiped at her cheeks with her free hand. "What can I do?"

"Help my sisters." They reached the bottom of the hill, and Hawk used one hand to steer, pulling the car to a stop close to Alya's porch. "They might have questions about Sector Four that they don't wanna ask their brother."

"I can handle that." Jeni squeezed his hand until he looked over at her. "Hawk, I'm here for them. But mostly...I'm here for you."

The kitchen light went on, proof Alya had heard his car and would be on the porch soon—probably with a shotgun. Hawk leaned in and caught Jeni's mouth in a quick, fierce kiss. Familiar sweetness washed over him—the way her lips parted so eagerly, the skill of her kiss. She could strip him raw with the honeyed glide of her tongue and the sharp scrape of her teeth, but she wasn't trying to tonight.

Tonight she was building him armor.

He broke away with a harsh sigh and pressed his forehead to hers. "This might get ugly."

She glanced at the kitchen window. "Do you need to talk to Alya alone?"

"No. Shipp'll be there anyway. And maybe you can help, if she has any questions about what you found." He pulled back with the best smile he could

thing from the O'Kanes, it was this. Laughing at the worst life could dish out. "If she grabs the shotgun, dive for cover."

But Jeni didn't laugh.

By the time they got out of the car, Alya was waiting for them on the porch, Shipp at her side. Hawk climbed the steps, the words he'd practiced for half the drive tumbling end over end in his head.

Before he had a chance to say anything, Shipp sighed roughly. "Either someone died, or your son's come to give us even worse news, Alya."

Hawk stopped on the next-to-last step, putting him at eye level with his mother. She was barefoot, dressed in worn jeans and a tank top that showed off her lean strength. The years usually rolled off Alya as if they couldn't touch her, but the eyes he'd inherited from her were ancient, the lines around them deeper than he remembered.

She knew. She'd kick and scratch and fight them down to the last minute, but Alya had seen too many bad days not to recognize one staring her in the face.

Hawk said it anyway. "It's time, Ma."

She flinched. Squeezed her eyes shut. "Why? What's changed?"

"We uncovered a network of spies in Four," Jeni said softly.

Shipp cursed. "Did O'Kane haul them in already?"

"No. They're all dead. Staged to look like suicides. I guess..." She looked away. "I guess they'd outlived their usefulness."

"So that's it." His voice was flat, but Shipp's hand was trembling when he touched Alya's shoulder. "Eden's getting ready to move."

"We don't know that," she insisted, her voice like

behind those eyes, begging him to reach out, to save her.

And he had to shove her under the water and let her drown. "Are you willing to take the chance? They could be on the move already. Do you want to wait until the army's *here*? Do you want to tear the babies out of their beds and try to get them past a bunch of MPs who won't give a shit about shooting them in the fucking head?"

Alya's hands curled into fists. "Do you want to burn their home down over a *maybe*?"

"Yeah," Hawk replied harshly. "Because we can rebuild a home, as long as they're alive to be in it."

"That doesn't have to happen." Jeni looked around, taking in the cabin, the fields and houses beyond it, then focused on Alya. "Do you have people who would be willing to stay behind? Just a few. Enough."

Alya hesitated, but some of the wildness faded from her gaze.

"They can wait out the *maybe*. But they should know—" Jeni stopped, then started over. "*You* should know they might not make it out."

Alya's mouth was still pressed into a tight line when she nodded. "We'll start the evacuation," she bit out, turning back to the door. "And no one lights so much as a damn match until I'm ready."

The door snapped shut with the force of her temper, and Hawk winced. "I fucked that up."

Shipp snorted. "There's no way to make something like that easy to hear."

No. Nothing about any of this would ever be easy. "Dallas wouldn't have sent us if he wasn't as close to positive as he could get. I trust his gut, Shipp."

"Settle down," he shot back. "She'll do it. She

chance. Even if they're ready and willing."

Hawk wasn't so sure—but he didn't need to be. He trusted Shipp's gut, too, and there was no doubt there, no hesitation. Just an understanding of Alya that went bone-deep, because they'd been together long enough to smooth away the sharp edges of uncertainty.

In a decade, maybe he and Jeni would be that easy, too. Hawk would have to add that to his dreams, to the promise that kept him moving forward while his past crumbled around him.

In spite of her objections, it was clear that Alya had been planning for this moment, maybe even for years.

Alya gathered everyone and quickly explained the situation. No one questioned her, even though she'd just told them to uproot their lives, to take only what they absolutely needed and leave everything else behind. They simply moved to obey as she went on to delegate more tasks and give instructions regarding the animals and machinery.

Jeni watched. She answered Shipp's terse questions as best she could, then soothed some of the younger children. She tried to keep them busy and out of the way, because it seemed like everyone knew what to do, had a job—

Everyone except for her.

She kept an eye on Hawk, too. He took charge as easily as his mother, directing the people who came to him for guidance. He focused on the equipment, getting whatever could be driven ready to move, and helping to load the rest onto flat trailers to be hauled away.

Outwardly, he looked calm. Collected. But Jeni

tighter, drawing him in on himself, as if the constant pressure was the only thing keeping him from flying apart.

It made her throat ache and her eyes burn. But she kept the tears at bay, kept *going*, because if he could do this, then she damn well better be able to help him.

The sky was just beginning to lighten along the eastern horizon when she seized the chance to pull him aside. Most of the vehicles were long gone, loaded down with possessions and people. Only Shipp's men and some of Hawk's family remained, finishing up what needed to be done.

Jeni urged Hawk into the barn. It was bare and cavernous now, stripped of everything they could haul away, a completely different place from the building where she'd accepted his collar—Christ, it seemed like a lifetime ago.

She gripped his shoulders and almost winced at how rigid his muscles were beneath her fingers. "Hawk, look at me."

He did, but there was nothing there. His usual guarded expression had hardened into something even more heartbreaking—a blank mask.

"*Hawk.*" She touched his cheek, right on the spot where a dimple would appear every time he smiled, and wondered if she'd ever see it again. "Are you going to make it through this?"

The muscles under her fingers tightened. "It's harder than I thought it would be."

Do you need to go? The words died on her tongue. Useless, a waste of breath, because he would never abandon his family. She would never ask him to. "I wish I could fix this for you."

He curled his hand around the side of her neck, his

"There's only one way to fix this."

It didn't sound like he was talking about winning the war. There was something too intimate, too desperate, in his voice. "I don't understand."

"By sunset tonight there'll be nothing left," he said softly. "My entire past, burned to ash. I need to keep dreaming, Jeni, but I can't do it by myself. I need to believe you see a future for us, too."

A tiny sliver of ice lodged in her gut. "You know how I feel about you. About us."

"I know." A feverish light filled his gaze. Instead of being hard and cold now, he was shaking with barely restrained emotion. "But today isn't enough. Now isn't enough. I want forever, Jeni. I want ink."

If he hadn't been holding her, she would have stumbled back. "What?"

"It shouldn't make a difference." He touched the collar again. "If you want me enough for this, then why not?"

Because his world was falling apart. Because he was spinning, feeling powerless about so many things that this could be nothing more than a way to center himself, to feel like he was in control of *something*, which meant it wasn't about her at all.

And, above all else, because he'd told her the same thing about the collar she was wearing—that it meant she was his, that it was more than enough. That it was everything.

"No," she whispered.

Pain twisted his expression, carving lines into his face before he forced the blank mask back into place. But it was imperfect, cracked, radiating his hurt and his desperation as his hand trembled on her skin. "Then maybe I don't know how you feel about me after all."

simply walking away. It *hurt* that he would ask her like this, with the earth shifting beneath them, when she couldn't be sure if he meant it or if he was just scrambling for purchase. But she couldn't do it. She *couldn't.*

She took a deep breath instead. "Hawk, you know this isn't the time—"

"When?" His harsh question cut deep. "When it's too fucking late? *There is no time.* Or am I just the guy you fuck when the world's ending, not after we save it?"

The ice was taking over now, everywhere but in her burning eyes. She clamped her lips together and bit her tongue, anything to keep the sob rising in her chest from escaping. Finally, she dragged herself under control enough to speak. "That's why not. Because you're upset. You're so upset you're saying things you don't mean."

"And you're *managing* me." Hawk's hand fell away, leaving them close but not touching. The empty space between them was a few insignificant inches— and an impassable chasm. "At least be real with me. Be honest."

"Why?" The word materialized without thought, without second-guessing, and Jeni plunged ahead. "You've been lying about everything. You're lying to me right now."

"*Lying*? About what?"

"All your dreams." It hurt to think, and even more to say aloud, with him looking at her like she was breaking his heart. "You paint pretty pictures, but you don't believe them. You think we're all going to die— that's why you need this now, now, *now*. Why you can't wait for both of us to have our heads on straight. And I don't even blame you. Sometimes I think we're all

act like it means I'm giving up or that I don't love you, and that's not fucking *fair*. It's not right."

Hawk reached for her, his hand hovering over her cheek, his face suddenly stricken. "Jeni—"

"Don't." Her cheeks were wet with tears, her vision blurred. "I gave you things that I shouldn't have, and I *knew* better."

He wiped away her tears with his thumb. "I'm sorry. I just— Fuck, Jeni. I just wanted one thing in my life—" He cut off as a wash of red light filled the barn through its open doors.

The sky outside blazed with exploding flares hanging high in the clouds. More were rising to the east—

In the direction of the city.

"Fuck." Hawk's hand closed around hers, tight and warm. "We need to get you to the car."

Jeni dug in her heels. "People are still here—"

"No arguments." His tension and uncertainty were gone, washed away. The man who dragged her out of the barn was a soldier who calmly and quickly assessed the chaos of the people spilling out of buildings and running toward cars before hauling her toward the main house.

Another flare shot into the sky to the northeast. Red smoke billowed from it, like blood spilling across the lightening sky. Hawk's jaw clenched as he hurried their steps. "Anderson's farm. We have to move."

A flurry of sharp pops somewhere off in the distance broke through Jeni's shock. "That's gunfire."

"No shit, that's gunfire." Shipp jumped off the porch, swung a rifle off his shoulder, and tossed it to Hawk. "They're headed this way."

Hawk checked the rifle. "Who's left to evacuate?"

Shipp hesitated. "Alya's freaking out. We can't

Jeni blanched. No one should have been running around alone on a night like this, a night when they were packing up their whole lives to flee. "One of the little ones was upset earlier. He couldn't find his stuffed toy—Luna promised him she'd bring it."

"Okay." Hawk prodded Jeni toward his car as Alya came out the front door. "Ma, Jeni and I are going to look for Luna. You guys need to—"

Something hot and wet splashed on Jeni's arm. She looked down, expecting to see water, rain, *anything* but the dark blotches that covered her skin and shirt.

Then Hawk slammed into her, driving her to the ground.

And Alya started screaming.

"Stay down," Hawk hissed before rolling away.

Wood shattered above Jeni's head. Everything seemed far away and in slow motion as she looked up. Fire, blazing in the distance. Big John reaching for Alya as she dove across the grass and clawed her way up Shipp's body—

Shipp's body. He stared into the night—fixed, unseeing. A dead man's eyes. The side of his head was gone, blown out all over the cool green grass.

All over *her.*

"Shipp!" Alya drove her elbow into Big John's face. He released her with a curse, and she crawled higher, her hands framing Shipp's face as if she couldn't see the hopelessness, the blood, the *death.* "Shipp, baby, you can't—you *can't*—"

Her fingers slipped on his bloody cheek. Found the edge of his wound.

She threw her head back and screamed.

Big John hauled her up, blood streaming from his nose, painting his face dark in the predawn light. "Go,"

261

Hawk froze on his knees, his gaze swinging from his dead friend to his sobbing mother. But John was already running into the darkness, shoving Alya's face against his shoulder to quiet her cries.

Hawk grabbed Jeni's hand hard, but she barely felt it. She barely felt anything as he tugged her to her feet and herded her toward the side of the house, hunched over her, his body forming a solid wall between her and the direction of the shots.

When they made it around the side of the wall, he crouched and tugged her down with him. "Which kid was it? Who was talking to Luna?"

Every time Jeni tried to remember the child's face, all she could see was Shipp. "Curly b-blond hair, about four years old. Reese?"

"Royce." Hawk tightened his grip on her hand and pulled her close. "He likes to play in the old chicken coop. It's back behind the garden."

Jeni had seen the old coop during her tour of the farm. They used it as a potting shed now, because of its proximity to the garden. But that was on the far side of the house, close to—

She clutched at Hawk's shirt. "The fields on that side are already burning fast. We'll need your car."

"I know." He still held the rifle in his other hand. "You remember where we parked it? Go as fast as you can and stay low. I'll be right behind you, Jeni."

She nodded and took off. It wasn't far to the shed Hawk used as a makeshift garage, but it seemed like she ran forever. Her lungs burned, and her heart thumped painfully. For one brief, terrifying moment, she imagined arriving at the car only to find herself alone, with Hawk nowhere to be found.

She didn't dare look back. Instead, she ran faster.

the unmistakable sound of a gun being cocked.

Hawk lunged in front of her, both hands up, his rifle pointed toward the ceiling. "Luna, it's us. It's Hawk."

The girl stepped out of the darkness with a sob. Her hair was a mess, her face streaked with soot and tears. She relinquished the huge revolver to Hawk, but she refused to let go of the grimy stuffed bear she clutched in her other hand. "I heard screaming."

"The soldiers are close." Hawk dragged Luna toward his car, and she scrambled into the back seat. Then he pulled open the passenger-side door for Jeni and pressed the pistol into her hands. "Can you use this?"

"Yes." Gia made sure all her girls could defend themselves.

He squeezed her hand once before clambering into the car, sliding all the way over to the driver's seat. Jeni followed, groping for the door as the engine rumbled loudly in the tiny shed.

She clawed the door shut, and Hawk shifted gears. "Hold on."

The car surged forward and crashed through the wall. Wood splintered, flying in every direction as they drove straight into hell. All around them, the grass and fields burned in patches that were quickly spreading.

Too quickly. How could it happen that *fast?* Jeni twisted in the seat to look back at the main house. The blaze was licking at the porch already, and she watched as a column of hot orange traveled straight up to the roof.

"Oh, my God. Oh, God." Luna whispered the words hoarsely, barely audible over the rumble of the engine, and Jeni realized the girl was staring at the blood that

Hawk shifted gears again, and they shot over the last patch of grass and out onto the dirt road. Gravel plinked against the car as the tires threw it up in all directions, and Hawk's hand clenched on the gearshift. "Shipp," he said finally, his voice flat and empty.

Luna shook her head. "No."

The glow from the fires growing behind them cast the interior of the car with eerie shadows. Hawk seemed carved from stone, any hint of emotion hidden beneath smooth efficiency. He checked the mirrors and flicked off the headlights, plunging the road ahead of them into darkness. "I'm going to try to outrun anyone who might be following us. Luna, take my rifle."

She reached over the seat for the weapon. "Did—?" Her voice failed. "Did Alya...?"

"Big John is with her." Jeni squeezed Luna's arm, but her words were as much for Hawk as for his sister. "She's fine. She'll be fine."

A muscle jumped in his jaw. "We only have to make it to Five. Ryder will have people watching for this. They'll have our backs."

Luna choked on another sob, this one more heartache than terror. "Does it matter? It's all gone, Hawk, everything is *gone*."

He shifted gears again. Jeni couldn't see the way ahead of him, but Hawk seemed to know it. Even as the bright glow behind them faded, the car stayed steady, following the curves of the road.

They climbed a hill, and for a moment Jeni could see the whole of the farm behind them, flames reaching for the sky, the entire house ablaze now. Then they reached the top and slipped down the other side, and everything plunged into pure darkness.

"The house is gone," he said softly. "But the people

264

Shipp would have cared about. Getting everyone out, and not giving up."

"And look where it got him," she shot back.

Jeni twisted in her seat again. "Luna..." The words died when something caught her eye off the side of the road—the dull glint of scarce moonlight off metal.

The moment hovered, drawn out by terror and disbelief. The sound of a second engine swelled, and blinding light filled the car. It took forever, an eternity, and it all happened so fast that Jeni didn't even have time to draw a breath.

The truck hit them hard. The impact jolted her against the window, and pain seared a single thought into her brain—*this is it, this is the end.* Someone screamed, though it might have been her. There was no way to tell, not with the whole world spinning, awash with agony and confusion and fear and the most unholy screeching she'd ever heard.

Then it was over. Everything was still, quiet.

Too quiet.

She opened her eyes. Hawk was slumped over the steering column, and all the fear she'd ever felt in her entire life paled next to this. She was mumbling something, something, but she couldn't even listen to herself because she needed to touch him, she needed to know—

Her fingers found the base of his neck and the pulse pounding there, too fast but strong, and she could breathe again.

She could breathe, and she sobbed her relief in hot tears that poured down her cheeks. "Hawk, wake up. We have to fight—"

"Jeni." Luna lay slumped over in the back seat. She didn't move, even when Jeni reached to help her sit up. "This isn't...exactly what I imagined."

of metal protruding from her side.

"It doesn't hurt," Luna whispered. "Something like this should hurt."

Then she died. There was nothing cinematic about it, no last rattling breath or profound words. The light didn't slowly fade from her eyes. She was there and then she wasn't, as quick and as horrible as the truck slamming into the car all over again.

Jeni screamed. She was still screaming when rough hands dragged her from the car and across the gravel.

She didn't know if she could stop.

ryder

He'd never watched a sector burn.

When Eden bombed Three, he only saw the after-math, the plumes of smoke that had risen from behind the city's shining towers for days. When they blew up Two, his view had been obscured by Sector Four.

But Six? Six was right in his fucking backyard—and it was in flames.

The wind shifted, blowing acrid smoke across the large balcony that ran the length of his private quarters. Mac Fleming had used this penthouse as a play-ground, a place to bring women, snort whatever, and survey everything he commanded. Mac's successor, Logan Beckett, hadn't used it at all. He never had the chance.

Ryder used it as his home, but not because he liked it. No, its overstated opulence served as a

He lifted the receiver beside him and waited. The internal line rang through directly to his second-in-command, a man he'd handpicked from a factory in Eight. The job would have gone to Finn, if he hadn't up and joined O'Kane's merry band of brothers. But he had, so Ryder had been left to look elsewhere.

It wasn't that he didn't trust any of the men he'd worked with in Five to get shit done, he just didn't trust them to get *his* shit done. Every one of them had an agenda, mostly involving money or drugs or fucking over the guys ahead of them in the hierarchy of power. They were selfish, and that was one thing Ryder couldn't stand.

Hector answered, his voice heavy with sleep. "Sir?"

"The city has taken Six." He gave the man a moment to process that before continuing. "They'll be headed this way next. Get as many men as possible on the western border. And tell the factory supervisors that it's time to switch to full wartime production."

"You got it."

War. The word should have filled him with terror, but there was no room in his heart for fear. It was too full of anger, loss. Vengeance.

He wasn't Dallas O'Kane, a man sitting at the top of a pretty little empire filled with people he was desperate to protect. Ryder had always been a soldier with a mission—take down the Eden-sympathetic leaders of Sector Five. Controlling the manufacture and supply of essential medications was the first step in Jim's eventual plan to bring down the city itself.

A plan that had almost died with him.

Ryder walked inside, secured the sliding door behind him, and reached for the tablet on his desk. With a few swipes, he sent a brusque message to the

them what they needed to know.

Because their sectors weren't in immediate danger. No, his was the one sitting between Eden's forces and their target—Dallas O'Kane. And it was just as well. He belonged on the front lines of this conflict. It was part of his destiny, his legacy.

Ryder hesitated, then pulled up a photo on the tablet. It was decades old, older than him, from a time before the Flares. It had been copied from device to device more times than he could count. One bad transfer had corrupted the image, left the upper right corner a mess of gray blocks instead of the vivid hues in the rest of the picture.

But he could still see the faces of the three people featured in the photo, and that was what mattered. Two young men, beaming and regal in their crisp blue uniforms and white gloves, flanked a smiling woman in a simple, flowered dress. His father. His mother. And Jim.

His father stood on the left, his dark skin a sharp contrast to his white shirt and the golden braids decorating the shoulders of his uniform jacket. He looked so damn happy, proud to be wearing that badge. Ryder's mother had tried to explain it to him, how there was a time before the Flares when the military and the police had been separate entities, but he could barely wrap his head around the idea.

How would they have reacted if someone had tried to tell them, on that pleasant spring day, that the world would end in less than two years? Laughter, maybe. Disbelief, certainly. Anger, that anyone would dare suggest their reality was so fragile that it could be ripped away at any moment.

Over the years, Ryder had tried to see pieces of

with his father—he'd only ever known him secondhand, through stories and fond reminiscence. His mother, that was easy. She never lost that spark, her belief that good would always prevail. She even looked the same—the smooth, unlined cheeks were the ones he'd kissed as a child, the ones he'd watched grow sunken and hollow as she neared the end of her life.

Jim was the opposite. The carefree glint in this young man's eyes was foreign to Ryder. His earliest memories of Jim were of a harsh man—not unkind, exactly, but hard, like tempered steel. Surviving the power shift after the Flares—and the death of his best friend—had cost him the contented ease that shone from this photograph. He became a man ruthless enough to survive, and broken enough not to bother.

Except he had. Ryder asked him why once. Why did he fight so hard, work so much, when he didn't *really* care if he lived or died?

It had taken him a long time to answer. When he did, it was in a gravelly voice thick with memories. "Because I made a promise. And I plan to keep it."

A promise to Ryder's mother, or to the father he resembled but never knew? And was it a promise to see this uprising through to the end, or to prepare Ryder to do it? Whatever those answers were, Jim had taken them to his grave.

Ryder locked the tablet screen and tossed it aside. His men would be gathering soon, and he needed to be there to explain the situation, and to fight alongside them.

Because he'd made a few promises of his own—and he planned to keep them.

17

Pain dragged Hawk out of the darkness, kicking and screaming.

Everything hurt. His arms. His back. His ribs— *damn* his ribs. The last time they'd ached this badly was the summer he'd slipped while reshingling the barn roof and fallen twenty feet to the ground. His head throbbed with the beat of his heart, and when he parted his lips, he tasted salt and metal.

He'd swallowed enough of his own blood after a few rounds in the cage to know that taste.

But this wasn't the soreness that came after a good fight or even a sound ass-kicking. And Hawk knew, he *knew* he wanted to linger here in the physical pain, caressing every twinge like a lover, savoring it. Because if he kept going, if he remembered—

Something vast and terrifying waited for him

Fire.

No, it was better here, where idly trying to squeeze his hands into fists shot off bright flashes of color behind his eyes. Like fireworks, like—

Flares against the night sky.

His breath rasped loud in his own ears. Faster. Panicked. Because it was coming for him, whether he wanted it or not. Consciousness. Memory. The truth, speeding toward him at a hundred miles an hour—

Metal crunching. Jeni's scream.

The denial rose in his throat, caught on terror. Came out as a name. "Jeni."

"I'm here."

Joy exploded, better than fireworks. For a few seconds, the pressure on his chest eased. Even the pain wasn't so unmanageable.

She was *alive.*

But her voice was hoarse. Not the warm, husky rasp that followed a long night in bed, but ragged, shredded. Hawk tried to force his eyes open and hissed as the agony returned, stabbing into his skull.

He tried to lift a hand to rub at his head, but his hand jerked to a stop a foot from the floor. Cold metal dug into his wrist, accompanied by the soft clink of chain.

All of the joy fizzled, but something more useful rose in its place—resolve. Fighting through the pain, he cracked his eyes open and blinked until the soft blur across the room turned into Jeni.

Blood splattered her torn clothes. Her hair was tangled around her face, matted with blood and darkened by soot. Her eyes were so red—as if she'd been crying forever. And wide metal cuffs circled her delicate wrists, each attached to a chain fastened to the

272

Hawk's chains jerked tight again, setting off a screaming pain in his shoulders, and that's when he realized he'd tried to move. Tried to get to her, to touch her and reassure himself she wasn't harmed.

Only ten damn feet separated them, and she might as well have been on the other side of the world.

But she knew what he needed. "I'm okay. I'm not hurt."

He slumped back against the wall and winced as the rough brick dug into the bruises on his shoulders. "What happened?"

"Someone hit us." She smiled, but it was a forced thing, tight and painful to look at. "They must have known they couldn't outrun you."

Us.

The cell wasn't that big. Fifteen by fifteen at most, and bare except for the hooks on the walls and the chains holding them.

Holding the two of them.

Dread contracted into a tight knot. There was no direction to turn that didn't end in pain. The farm, in flames. Shipp on the ground, his dead eyes staring blankly past Alya's screaming face.

Only two of them in the damn room. "Luna?"

Jeni's face crumpled. "I'm sorry, Hawk."

He clenched his teeth until the room swam and Jeni blurred again. He squeezed his eyes shut and regretted it when the memory formed. Luna, only four or five years old. Fearless, even though the other younger kids had been skittish around the older brother who'd roared back into their lives to turn their world upside down.

Not Luna. She'd fixed those eyes on him, big and brown and full of mischief, and he'd known that coming

curiosity out of her, bury her under harsh words about her own worthlessness until that sweet little face with the pointed chin turned pinched and hard and empty of hope.

Hawk had been twenty-five years old. So damn young to feel so fucking old—but Luna's smile had healed him a little. Made him feel like he'd done something right, maybe for the first time.

"How?" he asked, not recognizing his own voice. Not really wanting to know. "Was it—?"

"It was quick." Jeni breathed out a ragged sigh. "She didn't suffer."

Maybe not, but she'd died scared and hopeless, all because Hawk hadn't taken two fucking seconds to hug her and tell her she'd be okay. The guilt of that hurt worse than his ribs, but not as much as knowing he had to lock it down. Forget Shipp, forget Luna.

If he didn't pull himself together and think like a damn soldier, Jeni would be next.

He forced himself to breathe. Deep and even, three slow inhalations and exhalations. Then he opened his eyes and focused on Jeni. "Where are we?"

"You're in the dungeon," a man answered. "Civic Building. City Center."

Hawk turned his head as much as he could without setting off a cascade of stabbing pain. Bars made up the left side of the wall, like something out of a pre-Flare movie—not just ancient rusting metal instead of shining steel, but *theatrical*. Menacing and raw, all naked threat. The room they were in was like those spies fried on the wall and left as a message—psychological torture.

The hallway was dark, but he could make out a vague shape through the bars on the other side. Shaggy slacks that disappeared into the shadows. Bare feet and ankles wrapped in chains.

"Hawk, meet Nikolas Markovic." Jeni could have been making polite introductions at a party if she hadn't sounded so goddamn *scared*. "Dallas's missing councilman."

The one Lili had sworn she had a *feeling* about. Hawk didn't know if he wanted to laugh or break down in fucking tears. Because if whoever had seized control of Eden had the power to throw a councilman in a goddamn *dungeon*—

We're all fucked.

He wouldn't say it out loud, not with Jeni listening and already terrified. "Good. A councilman can tell us how to get the fuck out of here."

"Right." Markovic laughed, harsh and loud. "I'm still here because I like the view."

Hawk clenched his fists and tested the strength of the chains. "Maybe we have different skill sets."

"Aren't you the optimist?" A door clanged down the hallway, and Markovic leaned into the dim light, his hollow face changed, alight with fury and intensity. "String them along. If they think they'll get nothing, if you *have nothing*, they'll kill you."

For one blissful second, the advice didn't make sense. Then Hawk remembered the hooks high on the wall. The perfect height for some good, old-fashioned torture. And as the footsteps drew closer, Hawk whispered a silent prayer that they were some good, old-fashioned torturers, too. The kind who would look at Jeni and assume a woman couldn't know anything worth telling.

Because if they laid a hand on Jeni, Hawk might tell them everything.

275

lex

The message from Ryder was terse. *It's begun*, with no explanations or details. Nothing but their own imaginations, fueled by the thick smoke rising in the west.

Dallas paced the conference room, his gaze constantly swinging back to the display on the wall that showed a tactical view of Eden and the sectors. "We'll have to send Bren and Cruz to Five," he said finally. "That's where they'll hit next. The reservoir keeps them from going straight for Eight, but it keeps us from coming in behind them easily, too."

Lex placed both hands flat on the table to keep from clenching them into fists. "Ryder was anticipating a full assault on his sector. Maybe even looking forward to it."

"That's what I'm worried about." Dallas stopped

should send Finn, too. He's the only person who knows Ryder well enough to notice if he's starting to crack under the strain of all that revenge he's after."

"Agreed. I have my theories, but it would be nice to know for sure." Acid burned in her gut. "This isn't defense, Declan. It's war. Whoever we send out might not come back."

"I know." He shoved off the table again, pacing out his worry. "We need to get Dylan and Jyoti over here to arrange the first squads of medics. And make sure we have transport ready for the serious injuries. We can—"

Footsteps pounded in the hall outside, and Lex reached for the pistol strapped to her thigh. But it was only Jasper who pushed through the door, his face set in a concerned mask. "Alya's here."

Lex rose. "Is Shipp with her?"

He shook his head slowly.

Fuck. "Show her in."

Alya walked in. Her body told the silent story of Shipp's death in dedicated detail, from the blood dried on her hands and arms, on her jeans and her tank top, to her reddened eyes, flat and grim in an expression-less face.

She was a walking worst-case scenario, and Lex was ashamed of herself for wanting to look away. Alya deserved better. If it was ever, Christ forbid, Dallas's blood on her hands—Dallas *gone*—she'd want her unthinkable loss acknowledged. She'd want people to face her down—horrified but unflinching—and see what she'd given for the cause.

Lex stepped forward and held out her hand. "I'm sorry, Alya."

Her grip was hard, maybe even desperate. She

her pain recognized.

Then the moment passed, and she let go. "We stopped at the girls' farm at the edge of the sector. Everyone arrived there safely, but they said Hawk and Jeni must have come straight here."

The churning in Lex's stomach worsened. "We haven't seen them."

The man who'd come in with Alya stepped forward and curled one huge hand around her shoulder. "I took a long route. They should have beat us here."

Dallas exchanged a look with Lex, the helpless fury in his eyes eclipsing her own. The best possibility was two of their people trapped behind enemy lines. The worst wasn't even death, but capture—Jeni and her perfect recall in Eden's hands, at Eden's nonexistent mercies.

And there was nothing they could do about it. Nothing. "If they were cut off, could Hawk have gone to ground somewhere?"

"Maybe," Alya said. "He knows those roads better than anyone."

It wasn't enough. There were too many variables, too many possibilities where the bad outweighed the good, and Lex's hands wouldn't stop shaking. "Jas."

He stepped into the room, his hands folded behind his back. A soldier awaiting his orders.

And she and Dallas had to be the ones to give them. "Tell Noah to drop whatever he's doing. I want him monitoring Eden's traffic for troop movements. Tell him I want to hear about *any* mention of captures. Sector prisoners."

"Yes, ma'am." He turned to go.

Dallas stepped forward. "We can find you a bunk here, but we've already set up secure communications

be kept in the loop."

The fear of a mother and the demands of leadership fought a brief, painful battle across Alya's face. Lex wasn't surprised when the leader won. "They need us. And we can organize volunteers. When you need them, you'll have drivers."

"Good. We can use them."

They turned to go, every step Alya took stiff and careful. The big man followed her out, hovering protectively, but there was nothing anyone could do to ease Alya's pain.

Lex took a deep breath. "If they're not hiding somewhere—"

"I know." Dallas closed the door and leaned against it, sagging as if the strength had gone out of him. "Goddammit, Lex. I shouldn't have let her leave the compound."

"She wouldn't have stayed, not if Hawk was going."

"She would have if I'd locked her ass up," he snarled, exploding away from the door. Pacing turned to prowling as he crossed the room. "She's loyal, Lex. She's fucking *loyal*. You know what that means."

It meant that no matter what her captors did to her, no matter what threats or torment they dished out, she wouldn't betray the O'Kanes. She'd die first— or she'd want to. "She and Hawk are smart, Declan, and they're strong. Don't give up on them yet."

"It feels like I already have." He shoved a hand through his hair. "I hate this. I fucking hate this. It's why I avoided this fight for so long. We're the fucking O'Kanes, Alexa. Nothing was ever supposed to be more important than having each other's backs."

"That goes both ways." She slipped her arms around him and rested her cheek on his shoulder. "You

fighting for you anymore. They're in it for each other, for themselves. This whole thing is so much bigger than us now."

"It is." He covered her hands with his. "I guess there's one benefit to outright war."

"What's that?"

"We don't have to hold back anymore." He turned in her arms, his helpless expression gone. Instead, plans were forming behind his eyes. "We still have a few friends on the other side of that wall."

18

Jeni thought she'd seen awful things—the wanton destruction of Sector Two, Hawk's family having to burn down their own homes. Shipp's blank eyes. Luna's dying moments.

Nothing was worse than watching two MPs try to beat Hawk to death.

The interrogator stood to one side, watching stone-faced as they carried out their work. He hadn't asked a question in minutes, minutes that seemed like hours as Jeni bit her lower lip until she tasted nothing but blood, willing herself not to scream.

Finally, the interrogator lifted one finger. The men stopped immediately, leaving Hawk swaying from the chains that stretched his arms above his head.

He caught his balance and spit blood from his mouth, then grinned when his gaze locked with hers.

Flash when he's had a bad day."

She wanted to laugh or say something light-hearted, reassuring. She wanted to play his game, but if she unclenched her jaw long enough to reply, she'd start screaming.

Without altering his expression, the interrogator pointed to Hawk's feet. One of the MPs kicked them out from under him. His body dropped fast and jerked hard when the chains drew taut. Jeni's shoulders ached in sympathy, but Hawk just sucked in a breath and hung there.

"You won't be able to enrage us into killing you, you know." The interrogator circled Hawk and studied the blood slicking his skin and the rising bruises. "Even if I wanted to vent my temper on you, I could call someone to repair the damage and start fresh. But regeneration technology isn't magic. Your body will still hold on to every bit of the pain." He paused. "I can make you feel like you've died a dozen deaths."

Hawk got his feet under him slowly. As soon as he straightened, the MP kicked them out again. He flinched this time, but his smile didn't falter. "Only a dozen?"

"Defiance won't deter me, either." The interrogator crossed his arms over his chest. "The ones who bluster always break the hardest. So I'll give you one more chance, and then I'll let my men crush as many of your bones as they can without killing you. Who do the communes answer to now?"

Hawk was breathing raggedly. His smile faded, and his head dropped forward. Slowly, as if every movement hurt, as if he was anticipating the next blow, he shifted his weight and planted his feet, taking the pressure off his arms and shoulders.

to make it stop.

As if he heard her, Hawk mumbled something.

"Speak up." The interrogator stepped closer and grabbed a fistful of Hawk's hair. "Answer the—"

Hawk lunged to the end of the chain and slammed his forehead into the man's nose.

The interrogator wheeled back with a shout, clutching his nose. Blood ran over his fingers, and his eyes blazed with rage as one of the MPs drew his side-arm and smashed the butt into Hawk's face.

"No!" Jeni surged forward, straining against her chains. "Leave him alone! You leave him the *fuck* alone!"

The interrogator flung his hand toward her, splashing drops of blood on the painted wall. "Shut her up!"

The larger MP took a step toward Jeni, and the room exploded into chaos.

One second, Hawk was hanging from the chains. In the next, he had the slack wrapped around his fists. He shoved off the wall behind him with a roar, and cement cracked as the bolts securing his chains broke free. The MP who'd struck him fumbled with his gun, and Hawk took him down with a hard right straight to the temple.

The other MP took another step toward Jeni. Hawk surged after him, pushing the interrogator out of the way, and slammed into his back. He looped the length of one chain around the soldier's throat, drove a knee into his spine, and they both went tumbling to the floor, inches from where Jeni sat.

Hawk wasn't out for mercy, he was out for *blood*. The chain bit into the big man's neck, raising angry welts. His face had already turned red by the time he

Jeni kicked out, every thought centered on keeping the barrel of that gun away from Hawk. She caught the man's hand with one smash of her heel. Bone cracked, and the pistol went sliding across the floor.

The interrogator dove for the gun. He came up with one bloody finger on the trigger, the barrel pointed straight at Hawk.

This was it. Jeni reached for the distance and calm that had brought her this far, but she couldn't find it. Instead, what gripped her was a bone-deep rage that burned away her fear. This wasn't how they were supposed to end. Even in her worst nightmares, Hawk was alive, safe to carry on without her. But this—this was the unimaginable. The worst thing she could think of in the world.

She couldn't watch. She wrapped her hand around Hawk's, squeezed, and closed her eyes.

At least they would go out fighting.

"Briggs, what is the meaning of this?"

Jeni's eyes flew open. The man standing in the open doorway of the cell was painfully familiar, but it took her panicky mind a moment to place him—Edwin Cunningham, longstanding member of Eden's Council.

Noelle's father.

The interrogator straightened and wiped his bloody nose with his sleeve. "It's under control, sir. Just taking care of a few last things."

"Get out."

"But—"

Edwin glanced at the two MPs lying on the floor and then back at the man's bleeding face. "Your incompetence has been noted. You can leave and await a disciplinary hearing, or I can have my guard carry out a summary sentence right now."

tor straightened and stalked to the door with as much pride as he could muster with one hand still pressed to his face. When he drew even with Edwin, the councilman extended his hand in quiet command. After a brief hesitation, the man relinquished the gun and stalked from the room.

Edwin turned the pistol over in his hands and spoke to the guard behind him. "Follow him. Find him a nice cell to occupy while he thinks about what he's done. Somewhere out of the way."

"Sir?"

"I'll be fine."

With obvious reluctance, the guard inclined his head, then disappeared down the hallway. Edwin turned back to them, his gaze sliding over Hawk's injuries before landing on Jeni. "You're Ashley's daughter. Jeneva."

"Jeni," she corrected. "Why did you stop him?"

Edwin slipped a hand into his pocket, pulled out a key, and tossed it to Hawk. Hawk reached for Jeni's wrists, fitting the key into place and sighing with relief when the first cuff fell away from her chafed skin.

"I abhor everything Dallas O'Kane is," Edwin said quietly. "I loathe the fact that he's dragged my only child into sin with him. But I prefer the devil who owns his perversions to a liar who cloaks his sin in righteousness."

Jeni didn't have time to argue right or wrong with a true believer—and she didn't care to. Only one thing mattered to her as she climbed to her feet. "How do we get out of the city?"

"I've arranged—"

The shot was so loud, it was like thunder in the room. Hawk covered her body with his, but she could

all over again, but worse, because Edwin Cunningham was standing there without most of his face. Just *standing there*, as if time had frozen in the new worst moment of her life.

Then he fell, and she caught sight of the man behind him. The man with the smoking gun.

When Jared had opened his bar in town, Smith Peterson had made his life a living hell. He'd even gone as far as to have him picked up by MP thugs and beaten. Jared had chalked it up to a small man with a very personal vendetta—Peterson's wife was a long-standing client of his—but looking at him now, over Edwin Cunningham's corpse...

Hatred blazed in his eyes as he stared at them, but so did something else. Hunger, anticipation. Interest, but not in anything as base and simple as sex or even revenge.

Smith Peterson was after *power*.

He stepped over Cunningham, the barrel of his pistol trained on Hawk's forehead. "My best interrogator couldn't break you, so I won't try. But I think it's only fair to give you one more chance to talk."

Hawk met Jeni's gaze. The chains still attached to the cuffs on his wrists clinked softly as he lifted a hand to cup her cheek. "Remind me again what we're going to grow on our farm."

She knew what he was doing, what he was saying. Even if this had to be how they went, it could still be on their terms, not Peterson's. Fighting tooth and nail to your last gasping breath wasn't the only way to die with grace.

Jeni was so fried she didn't try to hold back her tears. All the back and forth, the ups and downs. They were going to die, they were going to live—she couldn't

it snatched away. Here she was, facing the unimaginable again—the worst thing she could think of in the world—

She couldn't do it. She *couldn't do it.*

"Strawberry," she whispered. Not an answer to his question, but the safe word she'd chosen by candlelight, a lifetime ago. Hawk stared down at her, the soft confusion in his eyes melting into realization too late.

She turned to Peterson. "Wait."

cruz

After so many weeks of tense waiting, there was a kind of sick relief to being at war.

Cruz walked the line of Five's growing fortifications, a row of trucks usually used for the sector's product deliveries. Men were busy at work on both sides, digging trenches and putting up barbed wire.

The same quick-expanding cement they'd used to block the tunnel exits was being used farther down, creating staggered barricades that would provide cover in a firefight and make it harder to move an army into Five.

Of course, there were downsides to ever-expanding sectors. Dallas and Ryder would have to pick a border for their southern defense—and warn everyone beyond that line to move closer or run for the damn hills.

Not everyone could. The communes would be

effectively, and too reluctant to work together. Jyoti had badgered and cajoled, had bribed and outright threatened. Some had refused to ally themselves with the sectors, foolishly thinking that neutrality was an option.

When Eden sacked the first farm and stripped them bare, with nothing but the empty promise of a payment they'd never see...

Well, by then it might be too late. But Cruz suspected the stragglers would fall in line quick enough.

Cruz stopped next to a truck and lifted a hand to activate his earpiece. "How are we looking from up there?"

Bren's voice crackled over the speaker. "I'm in position. Just waiting for a shot."

"Good." Resisting the urge to glance over his shoulder and seek out Bren's vantage point, Cruz continued to the cluster of men gathered around Ryder's makeshift command point. Ryder himself was there, looking calm and collected on the surface, but with an eager edge that was all too familiar.

Cruz wasn't the only one relieved that the waiting was over.

Ryder was directing his men. "These aren't punks out to roll you for your money or your stash. They're out to kill. That's what they're trained to do. You have to fight harder, and you have to fight smarter. Because this is just the beginning."

The men nodded, scattering in an almost-disciplined wave to take up their positions. Cruz fell into place at Ryder's side and watched the flames sweep across Sector Six. Some still raged toward the sky, but there were darker places now. Places where Eden had contained the blaze.

the farmers made it out?"

"We know jack shit."

"We know they're coming." If they were smart, they'd make a run against Ryder's defenses at least once before falling back. Five would never be less prepared to meet Eden than at this moment—and if the farms hadn't sent up a warning, Five wouldn't have been prepared at all.

"Yes," Ryder agreed. "With some luck—and if you're as good as they say you are—we can take out the first wave completely."

"He's better," said a voice behind them, a familiar voice that had Cruz reaching for his gun as he spun around.

Fear tightened in his gut.

Ashwin looked the same. Tall, with brown skin and black hair buzzed so short, Cruz knew he'd been to the Base recently. He was dressed in standard-issue night gear, a black-clad shadow decked out with knives, guns, and grenades. A one-man army, the same as always, but his eyes—

Something seethed in their brown depths, something Cruz hadn't seen since his training days. A Makhai soldier on the edge.

He eased his finger onto the trigger.

Ashwin's gaze flicked to his hand, and his lips curled up into a mockery of a smile. "Not today, Lorenzo. I have work to do, and so do you. They're here."

A shot sounded overhead, followed by another, and Bren's voice blazed in Cruz's ear. "You have infantry incoming."

Ashwin took off, reaching a run in the five steps it took to draw even with Cruz. He planted one hand on the hood of a truck, vaulted over it as if he wasn't

darkness.

On the other side of the street, gunfire erupted. Men screamed—in fear, and then in pain.

"Shit." Cruz spun and took his place, raising his voice. "Dig in! Hold the line!"

Ryder's men fell into ragged formation. They were green, uncertain. Five minutes ago, Cruz might have been worried.

Five minutes ago, he hadn't seen the look in Ashwin's eyes.

Cruz almost felt sorry for the soldiers from Eden.

Almost.

19

Hawk had held strong through a beating that should have put him on his knees.

Jeni got him there with one word. "Wait."

She faced the other man, resolve radiating from her bruised, dirty face. "He's not the one you want, Peterson."

"Oh, is that so?" A sneer twisted his mouth as his gaze raked over Jeni with a disdain that had Hawk shifting his weight. But the minute the chains clinked, Peterson swung the gun away from Hawk.

To point at Jeni.

"I was listening," he continued, every word dripping with condescension. "You're the sector-tainted brat of that social-climbing whore. Do you share her delusions of grandeur?"

The words rolled off of her with no visible impact.

put together. I mean, was he ever going to figure out he was beating on the wrong O'Kane?"

Hawk's heart thumped wildly. He could protest, beg her to stop talking, but that would only confirm to Peterson that she had something of value to tell. Or he could bluster and swear she knew nothing—and confirm to Peterson that she was of value to *him*.

"The wrong O'Kane?" Peterson pointed the gun toward the ink on her wrists with a rough laugh. "Oh, I get it now. You *do* have delusions. You think a man like O'Kane put that ink on you because he gives a shit about anything other than having you around to keep his men happy?"

"Men talk in bed," she shot back. "So do women. But you already knew that, didn't you? How many of your secrets did your wife spill?"

Peterson turned red. "You mouthy little—"

"I don't forget." Jeni clenched her hands into fists. "Ever. Your people brought us up in a service elevator, but we passed a directory—fourth floor, Legal Department and Planning Commission. Suite 400, Sebastian Bell, Senior Legal Counsel. 404, Lydia Laterza, Executive Assistant. 405, Cameron Feldt and Iona Simon—"

"Stop." Peterson frowned, his rage bleeding into thoughtfulness. "Describe the men who brought you in."

"There were three. One your height—white, bald, with a brown beard and a scar on his left cheek. The second one was taller, by maybe four or five inches, black, clean-shaven. Also bald. The third guy was wearing a dark cap and had stubble. Only he used names— he called the others Banks and Sullivan—and he was left-handed." She paused. "He groped my ass when he was dragging me out of the truck."

barrel of Peterson's gun, but it didn't waver from Jeni's face. Any movement, any *word* could end with her bleeding out on the floor.

Hawk had never been so fucking helpless in his life.

"All right." Peterson gestured with one hand, ordering Jeni to take a step closer to him. "Do you know who's calling the shots in the communes?"

"No one." She took that step—slowly, deliberately. "They just don't like any of you."

He made a rude noise. "Assume that I believe you're telling the truth. What's your price? I could make you and your grasping excuse for a mother very comfortable in exchange for actionable intelligence."

"There's only one thing I want." She glanced at Hawk, but she kept her eyes averted—as if she couldn't bear to meet his gaze. "You get him back to Sector Four, *alive*, and I'll tell you everything you need to know."

"Jeni, *no*—" Hawk bit off the protest. This had to be a ploy, a way to buy them both some time, because she wasn't stupid. She wasn't a traitor.

And she wasn't serious. She couldn't be fucking serious.

But his outburst had already drawn Peterson's attention. A smug, mean little smile twisted his lips as he surveyed Hawk. "Not so different from your mother after all, hmm? Always looking for a better meal ticket."

Jeni stared at him. "Sure."

"I'll consider it." He backed out the door and gestured to a guard in the hallway. "Clean this mess up."

"Peterson?"

Men swarmed the cell, dragging the unconscious guard back while someone covered them. Peterson stood on the other side of the bars, one eyebrow raised.

"Ask yourself if it's worth fucking me over," she said softly. "Everything I've seen, everything I know. All you have to do is let him live."

The guards dragged the bodies free of the cell. Peterson slid the door into place, and the *click* of the lock was a spike through Hawk's heart. "Believe me, young lady. You have my attention."

Jeni stood there, motionless, until the sound of solid steel clanging shut rang through the hall. She flinched, then dropped her face into her hands.

Hawk surged to his feet and wrapped his arms around her, dragging her against him. She was stiff in his arms—scared, as scared as he was, but he buried his face in her hair and steadied himself with the familiar scent of her shampoo, still there under the blood and soot. "It's okay. You did good, Jeni. You bought us time. We can make a plan—"

"Hawk." Her voice was flat and steady. "This *is* the plan."

His heart stopped beating. Just fucking stopped. "Bullshit. Bullfucking*shit*."

She pulled free of his embrace. "It's one or both of us. I'll take that deal, and don't try and tell me you wouldn't."

It would be a lie, and she knew it. Worse, he knew the chance of getting both of them out was slim. He stalked past her and grabbed the bars on the door, testing their strength. "It doesn't matter. It *can't* be you. You've seen too damn much, Jeni. You know too much."

"I know what I'm doing."

Maybe she did. This was her world, after all—Eden and all its sick games. "You think you can fool them with false info? Maybe the first time or the second..." He reached through the bars and groped for the lock, metal, probably controlled electronically. "I won't let you do it."

"*Hawk.*"

He spun around and stopped dead. Jeni stood three feet in front of him, her eyes sad and her throat bare.

Her fingers curled around his collar.

"Jeni—" Her name came out broken. The pit of loss inside him opened so wide it swallowed his heart, his voice, his *hope.* "Put it back on."

"I'm sorry," she rasped. "About everything, about Shipp and—and Luna. I'm sorry that I have to leave you. But I can't be sorry that you have a chance to live."

Laughter shredded his throat. It came out rough and mean, and he didn't care. He didn't fucking *care.* Maybe if it hurt her enough, she'd change her mind about throwing away her fucking life over a future he didn't even want anymore. "You really think that, don't you? Did you ever know me at *all?*"

She looked down.

He clenched his fists against the temptation to advance on her. To press her back against the wall and kiss her until she melted, because he knew *her.* He'd learned her, studied her, memorized everything he could about her so that she'd be safe trusting him. So he wouldn't hurt her.

Either she didn't know this would destroy him, or she didn't care. He didn't know which hurt more. "Look at me."

Trembling, Jeni met his gaze. She was breathing too fast, shallow and almost panicked.

Instinct clashed within him. The need to soothe her, to hold her. The need to rage because she'd taken away any chance he might have had to *save* her.

break you?"

Her breathing slowed, almost stopped, and a tear slipped down her cheek. "You can't break someone who's already broken."

They were both shattered. All his precious control lay in shreds, and his tongue was running away from him again. Not with dreams though, not this time. *Nightmares.* "You think you can send me back out there, with my home burned down and Shipp's blood— *Luna's blood*—still on my hands and…what? You think I'll want to live, knowing that I failed you like I failed them? That any time I touch someone, I wreck their lives. That no one trusts me to save them and *they're fucking right not to.*"

She pressed one hand to the center of her chest. "What's the alternative? This is all I can do, Hawk."

"All you can do *now.*" He closed his eyes to block out her big, sad eyes, because he couldn't do it. Helplessness could give way to fury, but her pain stirred something worse. "You took away my choice, Jeni, without even fucking *asking.*"

"I know I did."

Nothing he could say or do mattered now that she'd proven her worth. He could offer himself up, and they might keep him, too. But they wouldn't let her go. Not unless he offered them something they wanted more.

Like the sectors on a silver platter.

He considered it. For a few seconds, he actually fucking considered it. Striking a deal for Jeni's safety, betraying the O'Kanes and his family and everyone in their fucking world. Because they wouldn't give her up for information, not when she could convince them she had all they needed. No, they'd want something

knife into Dallas's damn heart.

And, because she'd backed him into a corner, he had to wonder if he'd do it.

Maybe.

His stomach churned with loathing. For himself. For her, for finally dragging him all the way down to the very darkest part of his soul. To the possessive monster who'd do anything, kill anyone, destroy *everything* if it meant keeping her.

"You ruined us," he rasped. "You killed us both."

It was too much, too far. The emotion drained from Jeni's face, and she held out the collar. "You should take this. They won't let me keep it."

He couldn't touch her. He couldn't take the damn chance. The brush of her fingers against his might be enough to tip the balance, and the monster would slip free. He'd betray himself and everyone he knew, and it wouldn't matter.

Even if he saved her, she wouldn't be his. Not if he hurt the people she loved to do it.

"It's yours," he said, turning away. "I'm not taking it back."

He heard her moving, but she didn't say anything for a long time. Then, finally, she sighed. "I didn't expect you to make this easy. I wouldn't ask for that. I don't have a right to. But I thought..." She sighed again. "It doesn't matter."

He couldn't touch her, but he couldn't do this, either. Let her spend her last hours standing here, alone and small and scared and bleeding from verbal wounds. He should fill up the rest of the time they had with each other. Try to live the life they'd never have, try to make her feel the love he'd waited too long to offer.

sies—and this was what he'd built for her. The choice between a slow, painful death, or watching him burn down her family to keep her safe.

Almost as shitty as what he'd built for himself. Live knowing that he'd let her die, or die knowing he'd ruined what was left of her life.

"Jeni—"

The click of the door cut him off. It started to slide open, and Hawk stumbled back, instinctively shielding Jeni.

A plump blonde woman in white coveralls ducked inside, her ponytail swinging. "Got to go. Not much time."

Suspicion clashed with razor-sharp hope. "Go where?"

One eyebrow rose in an *are you kidding me?* arch. "Anyplace is better than here, sweetheart. Is that a key?"

It was on the floor next to Jeni, where he'd dropped it on Peterson's arrival. Without taking his eyes from the woman, Hawk swept it up and started unlocking the cuffs still clasped around his wrists.

Jeni didn't move. She just stared blankly, a reaction that seemed to elicit more sympathy than his questions. The blonde touched Jeni's shoulder gently. "Come on. Just a little bit longer, and you'll be back home. Coop is fetching Councilman Markovic—"

"Coop." The name snapped Jeni to attention. "Bren's friend."

"That's right, Bren's friend."

Jeni's eyes focused on the woman's face. "You're Tammy."

Tammy smiled. "Yeah, see? You're all right. Now let's get out of here."

302

door. Markovic's cell was open, too, and the councilman was on his feet—kind of. An older man with snowy white hair and a face carved with deep lines stood under one of Markovic's arms, bearing his weight as the councilman tried to take a step.

Coop, the former MP who'd scooped Bren off the streets as a surly orphan and trained him into a soldier. He was stooped with age, but his eyes were sharp as he appraised Hawk. "You look like you went a few rounds, but you're still on your feet. Can you help Markovic?"

If it meant getting Jeni out of here sooner, Hawk would have crawled on busted limbs over broken glass. The ache in his side bloomed into throbbing pain when he bent to get his shoulder under Markovic's other arm, but he ignored it and braced the councilman's weight. "Where are we going?"

"Out," Coop replied. "Tammy?"

Tammy hustled Jeni out of the cell and past Hawk. He tried to meet Jeni's eyes, but she looked away, and somehow the pain stabbing through his heart made all the rest of it worse.

It was better this way. Both of them alive, no one betrayed. He wouldn't have the dream or the nightmare, just the brutal, miserable grayness of life that always existed somewhere in between.

With every miserable step, Hawk told himself it was fine. He told himself over and over, until Coop ushered them out into a loading dock, and he saw the reason Coop had been so vague about the plan.

Dead bodies filled the back of the truck. Noelle's father lay sprawled across the top—part of his face gone, his remaining eye staring up at the night sky. Jeni balked, but Tammy wrapped an arm around her and whispered, soothing and reassuring in a way Hawk

It was still better than death.

But once Jeni was in the bed of the truck, Hawk slid into place over her. She stiffened beneath him, and he knew he deserved it, but it was his turn to take this choice away from her. He sprawled over her, struggling not to wince with every rock and sway of the truck, and when they stopped at the gate, he listened to Coop's laughing claim that he had a message for Dallas O'Kane and tried not to puke.

The tarp above him rustled as someone jerked it back, and Hawk lay as still as possible. His blood and bruises would paint him a plenty convincing corpse, but the guards might sink a few bullets into his back anyway, just for the fun of it. But Jeni would be safe, Jeni would *survive*—

The tarp settled over him again, and the vehicle lurched forward.

Under him, Jeni choked on an almost-silent sob.

Broken inside and out, surrounded by death and listening to her cry, Hawk groped for some reason—any reason—to be relieved they hadn't just shot him.

20

Jeni didn't know what day it was.

It was dark when Coop pulled onto the O'Kane compound, dark when Dylan whisked Hawk and Markovic both off to his underground hospital in Sector Three. She started to follow before remembering that she'd used her safe word. Her collar was in the pocket of her filthy jeans, and she'd smashed Hawk's heart.

She stayed put. People surrounded her, faces she knew, faces she *loved*—a tearful Lex, a concerned Ace, Dallas wearing his best stern-but-worried expression. But none of it seemed real. It was all far away, happening to someone else. Because she'd given up on this, on ever seeing home or these people again. It was the price she'd been willing to pay for Hawk's life, something she'd already accepted as fact.

And yet.

tions, and she understood. It would have been irresponsible of them not to debrief her. She didn't flinch, even when Lex dropped her head to the table and sobbed. Even when Dallas's voice broke. Jeni answered his questions, and watched the window behind him slowly lighten with the growing dawn.

And she still didn't know what day it was.

By the time Ace took her by the arm and led her across the courtyard, the sun was peeking up over the eastern horizon. As if nothing had changed, and this was any other day.

"Jeni." Gia was waiting for them, her eyes shining with unshed tears. Her arms trembled as she wrapped them around Jeni and held her tight.

Jeni stood there, breathing in the familiar scent of Gia's perfume. Underneath it, the scents of blood and death lingered. "I need a shower."

"I know." Gia drew her deeper into Ace's bedroom. Ace followed, another familiar presence at her back. "Rachel's on her way back with food and a med kit. Are you hurt anywhere?"

Everywhere. She didn't realize she'd said it aloud until Ace and Gia traded a serious look. "No, I'm not hurt."

"We'll check anyway," Ace said soothingly, gathering her tangled hair back from her face. "We're gonna get these clothes off, okay? And maybe light them on fire."

She kicked off her shoes as they tried to tug her shirt over her head. Her shoulder ached where she'd smashed it against the frame of Hawk's car, but she lifted her arms anyway.

Gia pulled at her jeans, then stilled. Her gaze flew to Jeni's naked throat as she drew the collar out of her

"I don't—" Thinking about it threatened to splinter Jeni's apathy. "Can you just put it somewhere?"

"I got it." Ace took it and tossed it onto the table. The metal medallion *clinked* on the wood, and the tiny sound echoed in Jeni's head as Gia and Ace helped her step out of her jeans and led her toward the open shower.

Steam already poured from it. Ace coaxed her in and climbed in after her, still fully clothed, ignoring the water that soaked through his T-shirt and jeans. "Baby girl, you are all-over bruises. Do you need some painkillers?"

For a moment, she thought about it. If they drugged her up, she wouldn't have to worry about anything. She wouldn't have to *think*. But she'd never used that particular escape, and doing it now seemed...treacherous. Like a narrow path with no place to turn around. "No."

"All right." He tapped her shoulder gently. "Turn around, honey."

When her hair was wet, he started to wash it. The shampoo was the stuff Rachel always used, thick and coconut-scented, and Ace worked it through Jeni's hair carefully, avoiding the sore spot on her temple.

She must have hit her head, too, but she couldn't remember when or how.

"What day is it?" she asked as he steered her under the hot spray again.

"What day?" Ace frowned as he drew his fingers through her hair. "Tuesday."

Noah had cracked the city's encryption on Sunday. She and Hawk had left for the farm in Six that evening. It had only been one day—one long, interminable fucking day—

It didn't seem possible that so many things could

destroyed, the future she thought she held in the palm of her hand, in her *heart*, gone.

In one fucking day.

The first sob wrenched free of her aching throat like a bullet. She couldn't hold it back, even when Ace gathered her close with a look of alarm. She slumped against him as the dam broke, sob after sob, coming faster and faster until her knees gave way.

Hawk woke up in a hospital bed.

A machine beside him beeped softly. A bag hung from the side of it, with a tube leading to an IV attached to his arm. His clothes were gone, replaced by thick bandages around his waist and ribs and another around his arm. He drew his other arm out from beneath the pristine white sheet and stared at the bruises, scrapes, and the tape wrapped around two of his fingers.

"We almost lost you," a hoarse voice said next to him.

Hawk turned his head, and Alya's face swam into focus. She looked tired, her eyes red-rimmed and bloodshot, her hair scraped back from her sorrow-lined face in a tight knot. She gripped his hand and guided it back to the bed. "You stay still until Dylan comes back around to check on you."

It was so bossy, so *motherly*, he couldn't stop a tired smile. "Yes, ma'am."

"Don't you *yes ma'am* me," she retorted, her sharp tone in contrast to the gentle hand she laid against his cheek. "You came in here with your brain bleeding and three of your ribs broken. The doctor said it's a miracle you don't have a punctured lung."

He didn't? Funny, considering how hard it was to

Alya's expression softened. "Yes. I haven't seen her, but Lex has been keeping me updated. She has some bumps and bruises from the crash, but otherwise—"

"The crash." Hawk swallowed and squeezed his eyes shut. "God, I'm sorry. You trusted me with Luna—"

"Shh." His mother stroked his hair, and a memory stirred. An early one, blurry around the edges—the summer a fever had swept across the farms. He'd been four or five years old, and so sick, but his father had reserved the medication for the men and boys strong enough to work the crops. Alya had held Hawk in her arms, rocking him through the tremors, her fingers soft and cool on his forehead as she sang under her breath.

She'd barely been Luna's age.

"Big John sent out a search party the first morning," she said softly. "They found your car and hauled it back. And...her."

"Jeni said it was fast. That she wasn't in pain."

Alya stroked his hair again, her fingers trembling. "We're planning a memorial for her and Shipp next week at the new farm. He'd want to feel like he was there with us, starting our new lives."

Hawk swallowed another lump. "Next week?"

"So you and Jeni are recovered enough to come."

Oh God, she didn't know. Of course she didn't fucking know. Alya could stare at the bruises and the lacerations, number his broken bones, know about his *bleeding brain*, but the worst injury, the one that might never heal...

Dylan wouldn't have found his broken heart on any of the scans.

"Hawk?"

He had to look at her. He opened his eyes, and the worry creasing her brow broke his heart all over

in front of her, had held his bleeding body in her arms.

Jeni was still alive. Even if Hawk never got to touch her, even if he never got to hold her, she was safe. Whole.

And Alya's sympathy would kill him.

"It's nothing," he choked out. "We just—we had a fight."

"What, baby?"

Maybe it would be easier to admit it because Alya had always been more like a fond, easily exasperated older sister than a mother. Someone not so much older than him, who knew what it was like to grow up hard and not understand all the rules about love. "We broke each other. There was a moment..."

The horror of it came rushing back. The sick helplessness. Alya squeezed his hand tight and forced him to look at her. "What moment?"

She traded her life for mine. He couldn't get the words out. Every time he tried, he saw Shipp on the ground, heard Alya's scream.

He couldn't do this to her.

"Hawk." Her voice was as steady and unwavering as her grip. "I don't know what happened between you, but I know about regret."

"Alya—"

"Listen to me." She leaned closer, her eyes bright. "Shipp tried to love me for *years*. I beat him back with everything inside me because I was scared of letting anyone close. And those are years I'll never get back, baby. Years I wasted, because I didn't know how few we'd have."

His eyes stung. "Ma—"

"Don't interrupt me." Her grip tightened until his hand ached. "You take everything on yourself, Hawk.

Luna's choice to run off after Royce's toy. Even all the goddamn mistakes I made with you. You carry our mistakes like *you* made them happen."

The pain in his chest wasn't from the beating. It was a torrent of tears, lodged deep and fighting its way up. "I wanted to protect you. All of you."

"That's not a compliment, baby." She touched his cheek, her eyes swimming. "A little bit is fine. But when you take it too far—it's just another way to make us less than human."

He swallowed around the knife in his throat. "I'm not trying to do that."

"We know," she whispered. "It's why we keep letting you do it. But it's not good for us, and it's not good for you. And, Hawk—" Her tears spilled over. "You were a *child*. You couldn't have protected me. You shouldn't have had to. It was my job to get you the hell out of that nightmare."

Hawk wiped the tears from her cheek. "You were a kid, too."

"Goddammit, Hawk, stop *forgiving* me," she growled, sounding so exasperated that Hawk laughed, and then she was laughing, too, laughing through the tears as he pulled her into a hug that dislodged the sensor on his finger and set the machine behind him off into alarmed screeching.

The confused nurse found them like that—Hawk's laughter edged with hysteria, Alya's with tears...but laughing.

It didn't heal his heart. That was still shredded in his chest, and would be until he saw Jeni.

But it was a start.

21

The Broken Circle was shut down until further notice, and no amount of arguing that she was fine would convince Dallas—or Noah and Noelle, for that matter—to let Jeni back into the workroom to help with monitoring Eden's current transmissions.

Which meant she was stuck, with nothing to do, and not a damn thing to occupy her thoughts in place of her regrets. So she retreated to the rooftop garden and threw herself into chores there. She watered, she babied the herbs, she thinned plantings, she weeded beds that didn't need weeding.

And she laughed at herself, because she was working so hard so she wouldn't have to think about Hawk, and yet, here she was, in the one place that reminded her of him more than any other.

"Jeni."

out of nothing—or that Dylan's gentle warnings about post-traumatic stress were coming to bear. But when she looked up from the spinach planter and brushed her damp hair back from her forehead, Hawk was there.

His hair was shorter, and his beard had been trimmed. The vicious bruise on his cheek was slowly fading from purple to green. Otherwise, he looked the same—jeans, boots, a black T-shirt. If she let herself, she could almost think this was any other day. That she'd never come along and destroyed his life.

She swallowed hard. "Hi."

"Hi." He shifted his weight awkwardly. "I hope this is okay, me coming up here."

"Yeah. I mean, this is more your thing than mine." She stepped back from the planter and tugged off her gloves. "I didn't know you were out of the hospital."

He shrugged. "Dylan wasn't thrilled. But I needed to see you."

Guilt stabbed at her. "I thought about coming by, but I wasn't sure..." No, she couldn't put that on him. "Dallas and Lex haven't been crazy about the idea of me going anywhere."

"Good." He took a few steps forward but stopped just out of arm's reach. He shoved his hands into his pockets and stood there, his gaze roaming over her face, the silence building. "I don't know what to say," he admitted finally. "I thought the right words would just happen if I saw you, but I still don't know what to say."

That would be too easy, the kind of thing you'd see in a romantic pre-Flare movie, right before the heartfelt declarations of love and the swelling music. A few lines in those always seemed to fix the characters' problems.

314

she said. "I never meant to."

"I know." He swallowed and looked away. "I wanted to hold you so bad, Jeni. Before Coop and Tammy came? You were so hurt and so scared, and I was making it worse instead of better. But I was afraid to touch you."

"You were upset—"

"No," he interrupted. "I was terrified. You still don't get it. How far I'd go for you. I didn't even get it until we were standing there. If I'd touched you..." He closed his eyes. "You think I couldn't have made a deal with Peterson to get you out? If he'd asked me to come back here and betray Dallas and Lex..."

Goose bumps prickled over her flesh, and she rubbed her bare arms. "You wouldn't have, Hawk. Never. There's too much at stake."

"I wouldn't have," he agreed softly. "But that's how crazy I get when I think about you hurting or dying. I wouldn't have done it...but I would have been tempted."

It was all a tangled mess of recriminations, one that Jeni couldn't even begin to unravel. She'd made a split-second decision in a moment of weakness, out of broken-hearted desperation—but that didn't mean she thought it was a mistake.

"I would do it again," she confessed. "The hardest part of all of this has been trying to figure out how to tell you that I was wrong. And I guess it's because I don't think I was. I made the only decision that I could live with, and if I regret anything, it's that it turned out to be for nothing. I hurt you for *nothing*."

"We hurt each other," he corrected. "For nothing."

"Yeah." And if that was all it was, harsh words in a moment of unimaginable stress, then it would have been easy to get past it. To work through it. "I think we

His mouth flattened into a hard line, and his eyes went bleak. "Me. I'm the problem."

"It's not about blame." She sank to the low bench along one wall of the greenhouse and patted the spot beside her. "I wanted to give you what you needed. I wanted it so much that I did some not-smart things."

After a moment, he lowered himself carefully to sit next to her. "Like what?"

One thing loomed larger than all the others, the very beginning of her bad decisions—the collar. She pulled it out of her pocket and held it out to him. "I shouldn't have accepted it. We weren't ready."

She half-expected him to surge off the bench and refuse it. He stared at her hand forever, his expression impossible to read.

Then he reached out and closed his fist around the leather. "No. We weren't."

Relief warred with a completely unfair disappointment. It wasn't like she wanted him to argue with her, but something about seeing the collar clutched in his hand was so *final*. "I knew it was too much, but I took it anyway. Not my finest moment."

He smiled sadly. "And I offered you ink for all the wrong reasons."

Hearing that shouldn't have made her feel better. And it didn't, not exactly, but it did make her doubt herself a little less. "We were reckless."

"War makes a good excuse for recklessness." He pressed a hand to his ribs and winced as he shifted. "Doesn't keep it from hurting when it blows up, though, does it?"

"No." Sitting here with him could have felt like a beginning or an end, reflecting on the past or looking toward the future. But all Jeni could focus on was the

knowing whether you really wanted *me*."

"That's the one thing you never have to wonder. I wanted you, Jeni. I just..." He trailed off, his expression stormy.

She nudged him with her knee. "You just what?"

He flexed his hand. "When I'm scared, I hold on too tight."

"Maybe we all do." Jeni leaned her head on his shoulder. He felt the same as always, solid and strong, *steady*, but there was a stiffness there too, a distance she hadn't felt since before their first kiss. "I don't know where to go from here. I don't know if we can. But I don't regret it. Even with all the things we fucked up."

"I don't regret it, either." Hawk slid his hand over hers and twined their fingers together. "Lex and Dallas won't let me near Five until my ribs are healed, so I'm picking up the slack for Cruz while he oversees the defense. If you need anything, I'll be here most of the time."

"I'll remember that."

"Can I ask you for a favor?"

She squeezed his hand.

"They're having a memorial for Shipp and Luna in a few days." He cleared his throat. "Will you come with me?"

Closing her eyes painted a picture of Luna, gasping with mock outrage as Hawk teased her. Jeni rubbed her fingers over her eyes to banish the image and nodded. "Absolutely."

He turned and brushed a kiss to the top of her head. "Thank you."

"It's the very least I can do. For you and for them."

They lapsed into silence. It wasn't comfortable, exactly, but it *was* comforting. Jeni hadn't realized

not to hate her. Even if they didn't stand a chance of being together, they could still mean something to one another. She wouldn't lose him for good.

She couldn't lose him for good.

"Well." Big John propped both hands on his hips. "This car *was* cherry. Damn crying shame, for a host of reasons." He cursed as he crossed himself.

Hawk stared at the wreckage of his car and tried to let it be just a car, not a symbol for the mess he'd made out of his life. Someone had already ripped out the ruined back seat, but Hawk could reconstruct the crash well enough in his head. The driver's side of the car was bent inward, the metal twisted and split, gaping open. The truck from the city must have slammed into them fast and hard.

It was a miracle they'd pulled him out of there with any of his ribs—or the left side of his body—still intact.

He didn't want to be here, staring at the twisted metal and shredded upholstery. He didn't want to remember dragging Jeni's fingers down to stroke the leather as he told her how building the car had given him hope.

His car had never been just a car. Every moment that mattered had pivoted around it—bringing Shipp back to the farm. Helping Finn and Trix get to Sector Four and earning a place in the O'Kanes in exchange. Bringing Jeni home to meet his family.

All of it, slipped away in the sick crunch of metal.

"I suppose I have to rebuild her," he said with no real enthusiasm.

Big John snorted. "This isn't a rebuild, it's a

frame's bent to hell and back, and there's almost as much body damage. It's a mess."

That sounded about right, for the car *and* him. "So it's a lost cause?"

"I don't know if I'd go that far." John rubbed his chin. "Plenty of good parts left, you just have dig 'em out."

Maybe John could see the good parts. Hawk couldn't stop staring at the caved-in side. "It feels morbid."

"Maybe it is. But throwing it away just because it's gonna take some work is a dumbass move."

Jesus *Christ* that struck home, too.

A little *too* well.

The bittersweet ache that had replaced the Jeni-shaped hole in his heart flared into longing. He wanted to believe there was a future there for them. But the frame of their relationship was twisted beyond repair. The collar, all the rules that went with it—

They'd sat so calmly and listed everything they'd done wrong, and it was all he could see. Just like the crumpled side of his car.

John was a fucking meddlesome old asshole. Hawk squeezed his eyes shut. "If you're gonna call me a dumbass, at least do it for the right reason."

"Sure you want to open that door, kid?"

No. He wasn't sure of anything anymore, except for the fact that Jeni's collar was burning a hole in his pocket and he couldn't seem to put it aside, even knowing it had done them as much harm as good. "Lay it on me, Big John."

John leaned on the busted car and eyed Hawk over the top of it. "I've known you for a lot of years. How many is it now?"

"Right." His eyes went a little vague, like he was looking at something far away. "I'd never seen you happy before. Not just with someone—that shit can come and go, believe me. I'm talking about with yourself. Like you finally kinda liked who you were."

He had. He *did*, and that wasn't just on Jeni. He loved his family, but for all the affection he got in return, he could never forget how firmly their lives rested on his shoulders. How completely responsible he was for their collective future and happiness.

The O'Kanes had been a different kind of family, one he hadn't known how to join at first because he wasn't used to having the responsibility go both ways. The crushing weight of his family's lives wasn't so crushing with Dallas willing to give him land, and Finn ready to help build them houses, and Zan eager to shake down his black market contacts and find whatever was necessary.

Surrounded by O'Kanes who could pick up the slack, he'd finally had room to breathe, to want something for himself. To find someone who could turn his contentment into joy.

And then his pride and fear had fucked everything up.

He reached into his pocket and curled his fist around the collar. The jewels dug into his fingers, but the medallion was cool against his palm. "Jeni and I hurt each other bad inside Eden. She offered to—" He swallowed queasiness at the memory and forced out the words. "She made a deal. Her life for mine. If Coop hadn't rescued us, I'd be here, and they'd be torturing her to death."

Big John's gaze sharpened. "That's rough."

Having it acknowledged—having him agree

320

traded places with her in a heartbeat. That means I shouldn't be so upset about it, doesn't it?"

"I don't know. Hell, I don't think *not* getting upset about that is an option, no matter how you're coming at it. It's making me want to puke right now, and I wasn't even there."

That hysterical, desperate laughter from the hospital bubbled up again. "That's saying something, considering you actually *like* that rotgut you brew up."

"It ain't the best, but it's what I got." John dipped his head, then pinned Hawk with another assessing look. "Finding someone who means that much, and who feels the same way about you? It's like running across a Holley four-barrel, mint in the box. You're lucky to have it happen just once."

"And if your frame's bent to hell and back, and there's too much damage?"

John shrugged. "Fuck it. Start over. Put that Holley carb in something new and make it work."

Hawk studied the car again. He looked past the damage and saw an intact front fender. The engine was probably fine, and the radiator looked good. He ran his thumb over the medallion in his pocket, then stopped trying to imagine him and Jeni fitting into the framework of collars and ink and things with complicated rules and unspoken expectations.

They'd done so many things wrong, but they'd *cared*, and Big John was right. Only a dumbass would throw that away.

22

Coming back to her room after dinner with Jared and Lili, Jeni had two things on her mind—an early bedtime and a good, long cry.

Being surrounded by people in love sucked. She'd always known that, but only in the vaguest sense. She knew she was missing out, but the details had been hazy, unformed. Now, she knew exactly what lay behind all those secret looks, the soft glances and casual caresses.

And it hurt. She missed Hawk. Not just the things she'd expected to miss, either—his smile, or having him hold her, or the way his voice went rough when he whispered her name. She missed knowing he was *there*, that he was happy, and that she'd played a role in making that happen.

She climbed the last landing and stopped short.

door, along with an envelope bearing her name. Nothing else, just four little block letters in handwriting she didn't recognize.

But she had her suspicions. She snatched up the package and the letter and hit the stairs again, this time heading up to the third floor—and Hawk's door.

She had to bang on it five times before it opened. Hawk stood there, his wariness melting into confusion when he glanced from her face to her hands and back. His brow furrowed. "You didn't open it."

"Not yet." The paper crumpled a little under her shaking fingers. "Can I come in?"

Silently, he stepped back and pulled the door wide.

Jeni walked in, but she didn't know what to do with the package. Set it on the table? Hand it to him? Go ahead and open it? "What is this?"

Oddly, the question seemed to relax him. His lips twitched, almost forming that warm smile she loved so much. "That's what the letter's for."

If she looked at it, she'd never forget the words scrawled on the page. They'd be burned into her memory, whether she wanted them there or not, and not even the passage of years would dull them.

She held it out. "If it's that important, I want to hear it straight from you."

"All right." Hawk took the envelope and pulled out his pocketknife. He edged the blade under the flap before glancing up at her. "Don't get your hopes up, thinking this'll be all fancy. I'm still not good at words."

Sometimes the simplest things held the greatest truths. "I don't like fancy words. I like yours."

"I hope so." He flipped his knife shut and unfolded the letter. "I'm still going to read it. Just don't laugh at me."

offended. "I wouldn't."

"Okay." He gripped the paper until it crinkled in his fingers and cleared his throat. "We made a list of all the things we did wrong, and there were a lot of them. But while we were listing all our mistakes, we forgot to list the things we did right. And there were a lot of those, too."

The box rattled in her hands, and his face blurred.

He went on. "The first one was just being able to talk to each other like that. Honest, without getting mad. I can't find words like that with anyone else, but with you it's easy. We did other things right, too. We laughed with each other, and we helped each other. We wanted each other." His voice went hoarse. "But mostly we loved each other, even if we weren't saying the words."

She couldn't see him at all now through the haze of tears.

"When you tried to save my life, all I could hear was you saying that I'd be fine without you. But you were also saying that you loved me too much to let me die. And if we love each other that much, so much we'd die for it, then it seems pretty stupid not to try to live for it, too."

"Hawk—"

He shook his head and took a deep breath. "Sometimes a car's so wrecked there's no putting it back together. But that doesn't mean you can't take the parts that are good and bring them with you when you make something new." He cleared his throat again and looked up at her, his eyes red. "I'm not asking for collars and ink. I don't need any promise or proof. Just don't give up on loving me, and maybe we can build something good."

might *think* he wasn't good with words, but that those were the most beautiful ones she'd ever heard. She set the box on the table instead and crossed the room.

His cheeks were warm under her hands as she cupped his face. "Yes."

"Yes?" His hands covered hers. His whole body seemed poised, tense—as if he was barely holding back from pouncing on her.

"Yes." She licked the tears from her lips. "If you love me, that's all that matters."

"I do," he said without hesitation. His gaze dropped to her mouth, and he smoothed another tear from the corner. "I love you, Jeni, with everything in me. All the bad parts and especially the good ones."

It hurt to breathe again, but this time, it was because she was so full of *hope*. "Do you love me enough to kiss me?"

He smiled. "Close your eyes."

She complied, and he stroked his thumbs over her cheeks and kissed her forehead. Then her eyelids, the tip of her nose. He took a step that brought their bodies close together, and another that pushed her back toward his bed. "I'm so sorry I made you cry."

"Shh." She tipped her head back. "Don't be sorry. Be mine."

He wrapped his arms around her and hauled her up against him, and the world swooped dizzily. She clung to his shoulders, even when he dropped on the bed with her straddling his lap. And then the world kept spinning, because he thrust his hands into her hair and kissed her.

It was the first thing that had felt right in *days*. When Jeni parted her lips, he deepened the kiss, his tongue sweeping her mouth with the desperate edge of

He kissed her until she was squirming in his arms. Until she was gasping for breath every time their lips parted only to lose it when he claimed her mouth again. His hands began to move—slipping over the skin bared by her silky halter top, tracing up and down her spine. His fingers found the tie at the back of her neck and deftly tugged.

The fabric slid over her like a caress. She broke away, running her lips over his cheek to his temple. "I remember the first time I saw you. I had just finished a set, and you were sitting at the bar with Zan and Noelle. You wouldn't even look at me."

He chuckled, but his cheeks heated under her fingers. "Maybe that first night. After that I couldn't *stop* looking at you."

"I noticed," she confessed. "I couldn't stop looking at you, either."

He turned to kiss his way down her jaw and over her throat. His lips smoothed over the bare skin of her throat—over her pulse, which had always been protected by his collar before. "I never saw it."

She remembered every time their gazes had clashed and held, that indescribable but undeniable connection. "You saw it." She stripped her shirt over her head and dropped the peach-colored silk to the floor. "You just didn't believe."

His teeth closed on her neck, sharp enough to jolt pleasure through her and arch her back. "I believe now."

"Good." She tugged his shirt up, carefully maneuvering over the bandages at his side. "Because it was always you, Hawk. Even Lex saw it. I just couldn't look away. Like part of me already knew."

He waited for her to toss his shirt aside, then

his chest teasing her nipples. "There's no collar now, Jeni. No rules except the ones we make. Tell me what you want."

If they'd gone wrong before by trying to confine their budding relationship, then maybe what they needed was to set it free. "Everything we've done—the pain, the control. That wasn't about the collar for me. I need that, Hawk. To belong to you and know that you'll take care of me."

"Okay." That simple, like it was all he needed. He claimed her mouth again, licking her lips until she moaned. His fingers curled around her throat, lethally gentle, and he lifted his mouth from hers, just enough to make her strain against his grip to reclaim his kiss. "I want to go back to that first night. I want to watch you dance, watch you fuck yourself with your fingers until you come screaming. And then I want to fix the biggest mistake of my life."

His hands were steady, but hers were trembling. "What mistake?"

"Every day before the day I kissed you."

The hope bubbled over into joy, and Jeni slid off the bed to stand in front of him. "There's no stage," she pointed out as she plucked open the clasp of her belt. "Guess it'll have to be a lap dance."

Hawk dropped his hands to grip the blankets. His gaze never left her face as he smiled slowly. "The kind where I'm supposed to keep my hands to myself?"

"Oh, absolutely." She slipped out of her flats and shimmied her pants and panties down her legs. "Can you?"

His arms flexed as his fists tightened, and his voice turned rough. "I guess we'll find out."

Dancing without music was out of the

over him again, her knees on either side of his hips, and stopped with her breasts only inches from his face.

He inhaled sharply. Exhaled slowly. His tongue dragged across his lower lip, demanding she remember how *good* it felt when he did the same thing to her nipple. "Touch yourself, Jeni."

She braced one hand on his shoulder, then lifted the other to his mouth. Just two fingers, and she snatched them away before he could part his lips, trailing them down the center of her body instead.

Slowly, so slowly. He watched, riveted, as she slipped them between her open thighs. When she touched her clit, her whole body jerked, and Hawk echoed the movement with a tortured groan.

He swayed forward. Not touching her, but close enough that his breath feathered over her tightened nipple. "Faster. If those were my fingers, I wouldn't be patient. Not the first time. I'd do whatever it took to feel your pussy squeezing them tight while you came screaming."

She tried to swallow a moan, but it escaped as a whimper. "And you say you're not good with words."

"You inspire me." He straightened, his body coiled with tension, his eyes so dangerous. "Or maybe it's all those months I spent dreaming of all the things I should have done to you."

"We can do them now." She shifted her hips, riding her hand the same way she would ride his. "Every night."

"We'll have to," he rumbled. "Or we'll never get through them."

Jeni's laugh dissolved into a groan as a bolt of pleasure weakened her knees. She swayed, almost falling back—and Hawk wrapped his arms around her,

"I got you." His hand splayed across her lower back, holding her in place. Her hand was trapped between them, her fingers still buried deep, and all she could do was squirm helplessly when he urged her hips in a slow rock. "I'll never let you fall again."

"I know." She buried her face against the crook of his neck and inhaled his scent. "You'll always catch me."

"So let go." Hawk pulled her hair, tight enough to sting tears into her eyes. "It feels good, doesn't it? Your fingers so deep, but you can't move even though you want to."

Every word twisted the delicious tension a little higher. "I love it."

"Because you know you're mine." His lips brushed her ear. His whisper was so soft, so warm, but his words were deadly. "Give me your body. Tell me it's mine. Promise you'll take everything I give you."

"I promise." He moved her hips faster, and a shudder wracked her as the heat centered low in her body began to unfurl. "Hawk—"

"Take it, Jeni," he ordered. "Take your pleasure."

The orgasm hit her hard. The initial shock of it stole her breath, but it was what came after that made her close her teeth on the soft skin at the base of his neck—wave after wave of ecstasy. Of *release*.

He groaned, holding her mouth against his throat. She was still coming when he flipped her onto her back, driving her down to the bed with his hips. His cock strained at his jeans, a heavy weight grinding against the back of her hand, pushing her fingers even deeper. "I could do this forever. Just this. Fucking you with your fingers, because they might as well be mine. Every part of you is."

shaking, still shuddering. "Please..."

His hips lifted, but before she could pull her hand away from her sensitive flesh, his was there. He ground the heel of her hand down against her clit and curved two fingers over hers, working them in alongside hers with slow, relentless little rocks. "I'm the only one who can do this to you. I don't need a whip. I don't need pain. You'll open right up for me, won't you? Just because I want it."

"Yes." Everything was *Hawk*. He surrounded her, filled her, his body putting his words into action. He owned her—completely, utterly—and he knew it. He loved it.

He loved *her*.

She came again, this time with a choked scream. Hawk groaned against her ear, his fingers pumping into her, dragging out her orgasm, twisting it to unbearable heights. "Just like this, every night. You'll take the pain and you'll take the pleasure..."

"Everything," she gasped.

"And then *me*." He closed his hands around her hips and turned her over onto her stomach. His zipper rasped. "Then you'll take me."

She pushed up on her knees, past ready to have him inside her, to hear the relief in his voice when he finally thrust home. Instead, she got the stinging slap of his open palm against her ass.

The growl caught in her throat, then tumbled free as a laugh. "Tease."

"Never." He soothed the spot with a scrape of his fingernails. "I thought about making you choose between this..." His hand fell again, on the opposite side, the sound of the blow sending a shiver up her spine even before the pain reached her. "And this..."

pressed against her pussy. He drove deep, all the way in with one long thrust, and her knees almost slipped from under her again.

He hauled her back into place. "You never have to choose. Say it."

"I never—" She shivered again, and even that slight movement generated enough friction to drive a cry from her throat. "Never have to choose just one."

His hand fell again, brutal and sure, lighting up every nerve ending with sensation so intense, it was past pain, past ecstasy. He'd spanked her before, every bit as hard, but he'd been different then. Uncertain, hesitant, desire and doubt all tangled together.

Stripping away the collar had freed him. Now, every deliberate touch screamed confidence. She cried his name when he plunged into her again, and he picked up the rhythm, alternating swats with driving thrusts.

Her skin heated, not just where he was spanking her, but all over. The mounting pleasure swirled together with the afterglow and the pain-fueled rush until it coalesced into an anticipation, a *hunger*, sharper than anything she'd ever known.

His hand slammed against the bed, and he leaned over her until his mouth grazed her cheek. The heat of his chest burned against her back as he slipped a hand underneath her and stroked her clit. "You never have to do without. Not while I'm here."

The words vibrated through her, tipping her over the edge. She couldn't scream, couldn't even draw a breath as it crashed through her this time, because all she wanted to do was focus on this feeling—the two of them, tangled together, connected in a way that went beyond bodies and fucking. By a need deeper than desire.

with every pulse of her body around his, the sensation drawing him into harder and harder thrusts. Then he jerked, cursed, and came with a shudder that rocked through her body.

He lay there on top of her, panting, his breath hot on her cheek. She was trapped, and yet she'd never felt safer than when he threaded his fingers through hers and squeezed her hands. "Everything okay?"

It didn't hold a trace of the anxious concern that usually gripped him. This question was satisfied, almost smug. Jeni smiled. "Very."

"Good." He brushed a kiss to her temple and eased away to sprawl on his back with a soft groan. "Now I regret not going for the regen. If I had, I might still be—"

"Oh, my God." She sat up and reached for him, then stopped with her hands hovering over his bandages like an idiot. "Your *ribs*."

"Hey." He caught her hands and pulled her back to his side. "I may not be good as new, but Doc has some damn nice drugs over there. I'm all right. In another week or two, I'll be fucking you up against the door to prove it."

"Laugh at me if you want, but Lex said—" The memory of the panic that had gripped Jeni choked off her words. "She said you almost died."

"I know." He turned slowly, so they were face-to-face, with only a few inches between them. "I'm sorry I laughed. I know how scary it is."

The panic subsided as she placed her hand over his heart and felt its healthy, steady beat. "I know that what I did hurt you, and I'm sorry. And I'm not—" She shook her head to cut off his protest. "I'm not getting into that again, I swear. I just think we need to say it."

"Things are dangerous right now. Hell, they always have been, even before this standoff with the city." She took a deep breath. "I don't know how much time we have, whether it's thirty minutes or thirty years. However long it is, I want to *live* it. I don't want to be afraid all the time."

"Wait." He groaned again as he rolled from the bed and padded to the table. He kicked free of his jeans and swept up the box, returning to stretch out next to her with the little paper-wrapped package on the bed between them. "Open it."

Jeni tugged at the twine and snapped it when it snarled into a knot. Then she pulled the paper away to reveal a plain white box. Inside, nestled on a bed of black, was the medallion from her collar, remade as a pendant strung on a delicate silver chain.

"I figured you could wear it under your shirt." He brushed a finger between her breasts. "So it matches mine. It doesn't have to be about anyone else, just you and me. The best parts of us, in something new."

She stared down at the pendant, and the last piece of the puzzle slipped into place. He hadn't asked for proof—but that didn't mean she couldn't offer it. "I want the ink, too. It doesn't have to be anything like a collar. It can be whatever we decide." She met his gaze, and the barely leashed longing glittering there made her suck in a breath. "And I want to marry you."

He caught her hand and tangled their fingers together. "Really?"

It was a piece of his culture, part of the home he'd lost, and another way to show him that she would always be there for him. "Really."

He pulled her hand up to his mouth and kissed the back of her fingers, his eyes shining. "Will you marry

For a moment, she thought he was making a joke. Then she remembered. "You want to do it there?"

"If you're willing."

"I am." She cupped his cheek, then grinned when he turned his head to kiss her hand again. She'd been happy before, just being with him, but this was more. Joy, contentment. Looking forward to a future that only they could build.

And that was the real promise—that they'd been through hell, come out the other side, and, still, the only place they ever wanted to be was in each other's arms.

23

At the rate the night was going, everyone would be drunk before Hawk managed to get Jeni married to him. And somehow he couldn't bring himself to mind.

The memorials always involved drinking. Shipp's boys would circle the cars, headlights shining in, and the adults would gather to laugh and cry while they passed around bottles of Big John's stomach-melting moonshine.

Finn and Trix had arrived at the edge of Four in a car loaded down with the good stuff. Not just the top-shelf liquor, but a couple of bottles from Nessa with labels Hawk had never seen before—the small batch runs that had aged for years and went down so smooth, Big John was swigging it like water.

Nessa would probably be horrified. Hawk just hoped the man would still be steady enough to perform

They'd already performed the other one. Three small stone cairns stood in the middle of the circle, constructed from rocks gathered by the children, held together with mortar mixed from the dirt of their new home. Maybe someday they'd go back into Sector Six and gather up the other cairns to bring to their new home. Maybe they'd go back to the farm and take Shipp's and Luna's with them. Either way, the people they'd lost would be remembered, and loved.

The third cairn was for Noelle's father.

Hawk glanced across the fire at her. She still hadn't left the protective circle of Jas's arms, but some of the bleak uncertainty had faded from her eyes. Every last one of Hawk's brothers and sisters knew the miserable confusion of grieving a father who had caused you so much pain.

They'd help her find solace, and peace. They would understand if she cried and also if she didn't. Sometimes that was all it took, breaking free of everyone else's expectations.

"I'm so glad you decided to do this tonight."

Hawk turned to Alya, who had come up to lean against Big John's car beside him. "Are you sure?"

"Hell, yes." She slung an arm across his shoulders and pulled him into a half hug. Though her eyes were still rimmed with red, they were clear tonight. Alya was in leader mode, strong and resolute in the face of her people's grief and uncertainty. But there was joy there too—sincere pleasure—and Hawk had to wonder how much his solitary, determined existence had worried her over the years.

Probably more than he wanted to know.

"She's a good girl," Alya said softly, watching as Jeni and Trix hugged Bethany, all three of them

story Bethany was telling. "She'll take care of you. That's all I ever wanted."

"We'll take care of each other," he countered.

She smiled. "Even better."

"All right," John said as he stepped into the middle of their loosely gathered circle. "Let's do this before I get so liquored up I can't see straight." He peered down at the slim, leather-bound book in his hand, rubbed his eyes, then tossed the book over his shoulder. "Fuck it, I don't need it. Not for this."

Alya nudged Hawk with her elbow. "Go get your girl."

Hawk kissed his mother's cheek before pushing away from the car. Bethany nudged Jeni toward him, and for a second he felt as stunned as the first moment he'd laid eyes on her. The bright headlights lit her up from behind, just like the lights on the stage, but she wasn't dressed in her costumes and masks. She wasn't hiding.

She walked toward him, her simple sundress swaying in the night breeze. The necklace he'd given her circled her throat, the medallion resting over her clothes. Over her heart. His own heart pounded as hard as it had before his first race.

He caught her hand in his and turned to face John. "I've had about all I can stand of not being hers."

"I hear that." He straightened his shoulders. "Most things in this world don't last. They're made and eventually fall apart. Plants grow and wither. People are born, and then we—" His gravelly voice hitched. "Well, we die. It's just how things work. There's no start without a finish. No beginning without an end."

Jeni squeezed Hawk's hand.

"The only exception, the one thing that never has

are tough, what helps our people remember us when we're gone." He glanced at Alya, so quickly Hawk could have blinked and missed it. "Love can last forever."

Alya lifted her bottle in silent tribute. Around the circle, people echoed the gesture, raising flasks and tin cups and sometimes just their joined hands. Hawk's eyes burned as he clung to Jeni's hand...

And let go of the rest of his fear.

If he died next week, he'd want Jeni to go on. To hold him in her heart, to remember him with love, but to *keep living*. To do it for his sake, until eventually she wanted to live for herself again. Just like Shipp would be looking down from wherever he was, whispering to Alya to love him hard enough to love herself someday.

And if Alya had gone down fighting, she'd have wanted the same for Shipp. Just like Jeni would have wanted for Hawk.

That was all she'd meant that day in the workshop, the day he'd shut her down over and over again with his promises of the future. Not for him to say he'd had enough of her, but to promise she could be enough. That he'd love her every day like it was the only day that mattered, because they were fighting to fix a broken world. Putting his life on her shoulders, making his survival conditional to hers...

It was selfish. And they would both break under the strain of it.

He rubbed his thumb over hers and met her gaze. "I promise to love you. Wherever we go, whatever happens. In this life and anything that comes after it."

Jeni touched the pendant around her neck. "Me too."

John broke out in a huge grin. "Right on. Now go forth and multiply, or some shit."

did too, even as he hauled Jeni to him. She was smiling when he kissed her, her lips tilted up, and he realized he wanted to spend the rest of his life kissing her while she was smiling.

"Congratulations," she murmured against his mouth.

He pulled her closer. "That's right. Everyone should be congratulating me. I just married the best woman in the whole damn world."

"I know better than to argue with that."

Hawk kissed her again.

Alya's voice rose above the hoots of the crowd. "Enough, enough. You're scandalizing the babies."

"The babies went to bed hours ago," someone else shouted. "The rest of us are enjoying the show."

Hawk broke away from Jeni with a fake scowl. "Who said that?"

Half a dozen people called out different names, and Alya smiled as she walked toward Hawk. Then she slipped her hand out of her pocket and held it out, and Hawk's heart kicked in his chest.

He recognized the keys. A simple set, with a tiny metal flag hanging from the ring. Just three bars of color—green, white, and orange. It'd been banged up over the years, the colors fading, scratches and dings marring the surface, but Hawk had seen those keys in Shipp's fist a thousand times.

"Alya, I can't—"

"Hush." She jerked her head toward the far side of the circle. "Big John got her all cleaned up for you. Shipp would want it this way. I have too much damn work to do to go driving. She deserves to be with someone who'll love her like he did."

He saw the pain under her joy. Maybe someday,

car back. Maybe she'd want the memories of all the times they'd disappeared for an evening drive. All the times they'd vanished for even longer.

Until she was ready, Hawk could take care of this part of Shipp's legacy. Lord knew his mother would have her hands full with the rest. "I'll take care of her."

"I know you will." She dumped the keys in his hand and dragged Jeni into a rough hug. "And you take keep taking care of him."

Jeni smiled, but she didn't reply until she was back at Hawk's side, her arm around his waist. "It's what I live for."

dallas

After years of bitching and moaning, Dallas had finally developed an appreciation for technology.

The entire back wall of the meeting room had been converted into a constantly updating display of the battle lines they'd drawn around Sector Six. Without leaving the Broken Circle, he could watch the notations on the map shift when Cruz or Bren came up with fresh recon.

Eden was pulling back. Not into the city, but deeper into Sector Six. They'd established a buffer zone between Five and Six and were moving out now, no doubt trying to salvage anything left from the fires they'd finally gotten under control. From there, they'd go out and start picking off the communes.

They'd taken out the bridges on the west side of

the reservoir, meaning Dallas and Ryder would have to get an army across a river to attack from the other side. If they tried, Eden could open the dam and dump the entire fucking reservoir on top of them.

Their stalemate had broken, but it could reform awful fast. No doubt Eden wanted it that way. Every day they spent digging into Sector Six would make it harder for Dallas to dig them the fuck back out. They'd be able to resupply the city, and the war of attrition could go on for months. Hell, *years.*

All of the rebellion's advantages would vanish if they let Eden get comfortable.

They couldn't let Eden get comfortable.

"Dallas? You wanted me?"

Dallas didn't turn away from the wall as Noah slipped into the conference room. The display updated again, revealing another piece of Eden's fortifications. "They're settling in for a nice long war over in Six."

Noah came to stand next to him. "That wouldn't be good for us."

"No, it wouldn't." He glanced at the younger man and weighed what he was about to do. Noah had fallen into his lap so many months ago, a perfect weapon he'd had to hold patiently in reserve. With the hacker's access to Eden's network, Dallas could bring the city to its knees.

But he could only do it once. Thank fucking *God* he'd saved it for this. "We can't let them get comfortable."

Excitement lit Noah's eyes. He flexed his fingers. "Are you saying...?"

"You're off the leash, Noah." Dallas waved his hand over the tablet on the table. Five vanished, replaced with a rendering of the city. Tens of thousands of people lived crowded within those walls. Some of them were innocent. Some were pure, undiluted evil.

Dallas didn't have the luxury of keeping them all cozy anymore. "Shut them down. Start with the power grid. Let's see how those fancy motherfuckers like the dark."

about the author

Kit Rocha is the pseudonym for co-writing team Donna Herren and Bree Bridges. After penning dozens of par-anormal novels, novellas and stories as Moira Rogers, they branched out into gritty, sexy dystopian romance.

The Beyond series has appeared on the New York Times and USA Today bestseller lists, and was honored with 2013 and 2017 RT Reviewer's Choice awards.

acknowledgments

As always, our thanks have to start with the people who turn our manuscripts into books and keep us go-ing: our editor, Sasha Knight; our proofreader, Sharon Muha; Lillie Applegarth, queen of timelines and bibles; our assistant, Angie Ramey; Jay and Tracy, the tireless mods who reign over the chaos at the Broken Circle; and our friends and family and raptors, all the people who hug us, poke us, kick us, pick us back up, and love us. Thank you all so much.

A special shout-out to the girls in the Broken Circle VIP Lounge. Seeing the sisterhood of the O'Kane wom-en brought to life in a sisterhood of women who en-courage, celebrate, mourn, and conquer together is touching and humbling. And if you haven't visited yet and are ever feeling alone, stop on by. They'll pour you a drink. It's on us.

O'Kane for life.

the beyond series

Beyond Shame
Beyond Control
Beyond Pain
Beyond Temptation
Beyond Jealousy
Beyond Solitude
Beyond Addiction
Beyond Possession
Beyond Innocence
Beyond Ruin
Beyond Ecstasy
Beyond Surrender

gideon's riders

Ashwin
Deacon
Ivan
Hunter
Gabe

www.kitrocha.com

Printed in the USA
CPSIA information can be obtained
at www.ICGtesting.com
LVHW021143100923
757771LV00023B/598